MEMORIES OF NOW

MEMORIES OF NOW

TAJALLI KESHAVARZ

Copyright © 2019 Tajalli Keshavarz

The moral right of the author has been asserted.

Cover Painting: Neda Dana-Haeri
Cover Design: Simon Bunegar

Apart from any fair dealing for the purposes of research or private study, or criticism or review, as permitted under the Copyright, Designs and Patents Act 1988, this publication may only be reproduced, stored or transmitted, in any form or by any means, with the prior permission in writing of the publishers, or in the case of reprographic reproduction in accordance with the terms of licences issued by the Copyright Licensing Agency. Enquiries concerning reproduction outside those terms should be sent to the publishers.

This is a work of fiction. Names, characters, businesses, places, events and incidents are either the products of the author's imagination or used in a fictitious manner. Any resemblance to actual persons, living or dead, or actual events is purely coincidental.

Matador
9 Priory Business Park,
Wistow Road, Kibworth Beauchamp,
Leicestershire. LE8 0RX
Tel: 0116 279 2299
Email: books@troubador.co.uk
Web: www.troubador.co.uk/matador
Twitter: @matadorbooks

ISBN 978 1838590 444

British Library Cataloguing in Publication Data.
A catalogue record for this book is available from the British Library.

Printed and bound in the UK by T J International, Padstow, Cornwall
Typeset in 11.5 Aldine401 BT Bembo by Troubador Publishing Ltd, Leicester, UK

Matador is an imprint of Troubador Publishing Ltd

To Jila

-1-

'Do you want to tell me? Do you want to tell me all?'

She looks at me, with her hand under her chin, as if she is interested. As she smiles sitting on the sofa, the wrinkles show at the corners of her eyes and, slightly, at the corner of her lips; this reminds me of her skin some thirty years ago, or more. Good old Ana.

'Fancy seeing you here, in a hotel lobby. How long has it been?' Ana asks.

'Over thirty years I would say,' I say.

'That's for sure, but look, it's more, don't you remember…'

There is a loud voice from the restaurant. We both say, 'It's Colin.'

'I thought people wouldn't be here so early,' I say.

'I had a momentary loss of memory about it all,' says Ana.

We walk fast to the restaurant.

Colin's loud voice comes from the other side of a table at the centre of the restaurant.

'This is to us, those who are here and those who couldn't make it. Can I have silence for a minute? We are *not* in uni anymore. Behave yourselves, act your – dare I say – age!'

Yes, those who couldn't come and those who wouldn't come. Al had been dead now for five or six years. He, more than any of us, would have liked to be here to sit next to Ana where Frank is sitting with his persistent cough. I remember her small purse with shining fake stones looking awkward… impractical. I remember the way she used to open it while talking, taking the coins out.

'You'll have coffee too, won't you, Adam?'

Of course I would. I would have done anything she asked me back then. Looking at her, where she was sitting, the trees were growing behind her head. I could hear their buds opening, their young branches stretching out to catch some more of the sky.

Then she would press the lid of the purse to close it shut again. I would look at her thumb, delicate, pressing on the lid. I remember her nails with and without the varnish, I remember the chipped-off varnish, her hair glowing or tired, her face fresh and bright, pale and withdrawn.

'Here's the coffee, Adam.' She would put the cup on the long black table. 'Are you better? Are you better now?'

Her hair was soft and black then, long, shoulder-length. I liked summer, when her shoulders were happy under the sun.

'Adam! Where have you gone? Where are you? What are you looking at?' She would slide the cup closer to my hand resting on the long black table; her finger touching my skin with a breeze.

'Why do you call me Adam? I am—'

'Oh come on, what does it matter? It's easier. You are Adam, native of paradise! Coming from a mysterious land, always dreaming, you *are* Adam, let's face it.' She laughs together with Colin and the others, but Frank is deep in reading the paper.

'And Frank, Frank, what are you reading? The best part of it is the crossword, isn't it? Isn't it? Confess, you take it to bed with you,' Ana says.

That was the only time I saw Ana so forthcoming in those days.

And now she is sitting next to Frank. I liked him then with his tidy uniform complete with the tie from his school years… wearing them religiously in the university. Every day, over the winter days, he used to add to his gear a striped woollen scarf; I firmly thought it once belonged to his father. 'I like biography books,' he used to say with a low voice, and none of us took him seriously, apart from Ana, of course. I guess they exchanged notes on the books they read. I was curious to know, but then I was curious about Ana, and whatever she did. I remembered the breeze of heat from her hand, the smell of her hair; I carried it with me while washing the plates alone in my flat, while drying my hands, feeling my skin…

while passing by a bush, my hand touching the leaves accidentally.

Very few leaves are left in the garden of the hotel; those remaining are soggy, brownish-black, and slippery. No hard work for the gardeners; a week before the snow, a strong wind had blown what remained of the leaves on the deciduous trees, blown them to the corners. But conifers are standing tall and dark green on the grey background cloud, and ferns are wet with the melted snow.

What am I doing in that room, watching in a daze, mother raising her hand? 'Be careful when you go out! Don't trip, do something properly for a change; only God can help you the way you are. You are so careless, so clumsy. What do you look at when you walk? You and your dried leaves... are you in this world?'

I have waited a long time, but I am in that room again, and can say 'Look! I am in this world, living with voices of your world mixed up with the voices of mine.'

I look at the characters at the table, yes, we are each a character! I waited long to come here; waited as if I knew I would come over one day, but I didn't do anything for it to happen, it just happened. I just waited and waited.

-2-

'Are you going to do it or not?' Al would say, looking at me with his mocking eyes. The first time I saw him, and for some time after that, I thought he was making fun of me but no, it was the shape of his eyes, and everybody knew it. 'He says what he means sort of guy,' they would say, 'he is what he is.' And he liked rugby. I used to tell myself, 'What else? The man is a simpleton. I shouldn't expect refined manners from him.'

'You are hopeless, Adam,' Al would say. 'Stop flirting with the girl, she has just arrived at the damn place; let her settle in, you miserable sod.'

'I see she has already caught your small eyes, Al, but eyes off. She is spoken for.'

'This is a free country,' Al would say.

'Yeah, exactly, feel free to look around, give yourself a chance. Don't limit yourself to my quarters!' I would say.

'His quarters! What a presumptuous low-life, we shall see whose quarters she belongs to.'

And none of us asked her about it.

Wouldn't she love to know this? Wouldn't she have loved to know this then, some thirty-five years ago, when she held her books close to her chest, walking fast in those corridors?

'Good old Ana is a fast walker,' Al would say.

'You can't keep up with her, Al; choose someone you *can* catch up with,' and I would laugh.

'Don't you worry, Adamus, don't you worry, mate.'

Now I know he really meant it when he said "mate".

Then we would go to the bar. College bar was always busy, but you could hear Colin's loud voice before getting in.

'I don't care what you all might say, that bloody exam was unfair.'

And of course everybody agreed with him.

'What do *you* think, Ana?' Colin shouted.

And Ana? She was sitting in a corner, reading in the semi-dark. She was always reading, head down, her hair covering her face.

'I am talking to you, young lady, do you think the exam was fair?' Colin said from afar.

She looked up, with her eyes looking at no one. 'I am not in your class, Colin, how would I know?'

Colin wobbled on his feet with the half-full pint of bitter in his left hand.

'Doesn't matter, you can have an idea.' He wobbled again.

We laughed. Ana had already started reading her book again as if she were at a beach in a faraway island. Then people moved around and I couldn't see her face.

-3-

I liked the gravel grounds at the Student Centre, the tall green hedges and the round pond in the middle of the gravel surrounded by the geranium pots and the jasmine leaning against the wall. Almost Mediterranean, so at odds with an eroded imitation Roman statue facing the narrow gravel path. I suppose the whole design was a momentary whim of a vice-chancellor with a degree in history; and it had survived the winters, year after year. I liked the weak coffee there and the muffins… biting into them, feeling the softness of the cake and the occasional softness of the berries while listening to the music, often classical.

'They have done a good job here, Al,' I said.

'Stop talking like your grandfather.'

'Still, they have done a good job.'

Then the tiny girl with the pale face with spots would come out of the room. We had named it "the workshop", a few canvases on the stands, some with unfinished paintings, other ones leaning next to the walls.

'What else do you want, Al? You can do what you want here,' I said.

'You know what I want,' Al said.

And I would look at the girl. I wanted to call her "pale face", but I felt bad. I wasn't that sanctimonious, but I couldn't. It didn't stop me thinking she was in a constant state of bleeding though.

Ah… I do remember her name… Maria, now sitting next to Ana, across the table from Roy.

And the birds sang throughout the spring, and come to think of it, most seasons, at the Student Centre with the old walnut tree in the corner. I didn't look much at things then… I didn't look much. And one day I wasn't there anymore. I didn't even go there for a last farewell. I just passed the final year exams, and that was it.

'They cut down the walnut tree, did you know that?' Al asked me a couple of years later when I saw him by chance at a small do-it-yourself shop. I had a couple of 40-Watt bulbs in my hand busy paying.

'Hello Al, what are you doing here?' as if the shop was my territory.

'Not buying lamps!' he laughed. Fancy a pint?

I paused. 'Yeah… yeah… good idea, long time eh?'

'You could say that.' He said.

I thought he had aged drastically, and it was only a couple of years after I had graduated, he graduated a year after me.

I put the bulbs on the small black round table. He was already ordering the drinks. I went to the counter and stood next to him.

'So, tell me what you have been up to?' I said.

'Trying to find a decent job,' he said, 'not too late yet… been busy sorting things out.' He handed me a pint.

'Ta, but you've always been a busy body.'

'This time wasn't my choice, mother died.'

'Oh, sorry.'

'It was good for her… she was tired at the end.'

Then he said, 'They cut down the walnut tree, did you know that?'

'Walnut tree?'

'Yeah, you know that… come on… you remember the tree in the corner at the Student Centre?'

I remembered it all right, we had so many arguments under it.

'What happened?'

'Nothing much, apparently a smart-ass came up with the idea that there would be better use of the space.'

He drank half of the pint in one go.

'And then they decided to refurbish the whole place; the last thing it needed was a face-lift. They ruined it fast… was good you weren't there to witness all that. Some people are born lucky!' Al said.

'But you were the one who stayed a year longer… with good old Ana.'

'I knew it wouldn't work out from the start.' He drank the other half of the pint. 'You had ruined it for me.'

'Me? What rubbish; how could I? I didn't see her after I left.'

'Well too bad… too bloody bad.'

We remained silent for a while. Then he said, 'Listen, do you want to grab something here? I'm starving.'

'Sorry, I have to get back. I just popped out of the shop to get a couple of bulbs.'

'Wife and kids then?'

'No! It's just a couple of years… I'm not that fast, what do you think?'

'I don't know; people do all sorts of things. What do you do anyway?'

'I run a small bookshop,' I said.

He laughed. 'I should've guessed; you old romantic! One day Ana will come in through that door, dressed up neatly as always, and you will suggest a couple of books just released.'

I remained silent.

'Off you go then, Mr. Bookshop-man! I want to eat now.'

As I stood up he said, 'And do you know? They sold the place after they refurbished it; it is a small shopping centre now.'

'I'm sure we will meet again,' I said.

'Don't be sure, don't be sure about anything,' he said.

I smiled and came out. Walking to the bookshop remembered the round pond and the geranium pots sitting around it. When I arrived, Lucy at the counter asked, 'Is it a special day today? People seem to want to buy books!'

'Yes, it is.' I thought it was good not to be at university anymore; I had finished my Bachelor's, and could wrap up my memories and take them with me.

-4-

We did try, Al, we both did. OK, it didn't work for either of us, but we did try. Did it stay with you? The whole thing, I mean. I guess it wasn't difficult to let it go with that shrew of a wife you had. It wasn't difficult to forget everything. Never asked you how you ended up with that shrew, how could you continue? I guess that's what killed you. Easy to lose interest in life having to live with that thing, lie next to her every night, have breakfast, get back home sharp at 6.30 pm or else. You didn't have much choice, you had to get a divorce or die. And you weren't a divorce-type person. You believed in "till death do us part", and all that crap. So you had to go for the easy option. Well, that was you, Al, I should have persuaded you to get rid of that miserable situation. Meeting her a couple of times was enough for me to know. A couple of times was too much! Talking incessantly, nothing seemed to satisfy her. Beats me, Al, how did you continue with her? One hour was excessive! Hah, and what was in your mind all the time? Did you imagine stroking Ana's hair while you were taking flowers home for the wife? Was it the classic table set with glasses of champagne followed by red wine every night? I wonder what you were thinking in your last moments. But the way you went, you didn't have a chance to think about her, did you?

'Oh, you don't know?' your wife said on the phone with that shrieking voice of hers. Still can't remember her name… Alison? Miranda? 'Al died a month ago,' she said, as if she was a newscaster at a local radio.

'What? What happened?' I said. I wanted to say why didn't you let me know then, but I stopped myself.

'He died on his way home. He died on the Tube. It was such a palaver – he had to choose to die like that – typical him, nuisance! They were on my neck those officials. He had to die on the Tube.'

Did you have a bag of shopping for the night with you, Al? Did you forget to buy the bunch of flowers?

Never! Friday evenings, early home, bottle of wine and bunch of flowers. I never stopped wondering why. None of my business really, but what was she to you? You must be good in pretence; all for a charitable cause! Let's drink to it! And what did you drink to with that wife of yours? And all the time you were thinking of Ana! Good old Ana. She doesn't know a thing. After all, what's the use of her knowing? Knowing that Al was besotted, head over heels for her. What's the use of knowing now? She must have known in those years. But it's always nice, a good feeling to know someone loves you. Don't you think? Don't you think, Al? But don't ask *me* to tell her.

-5-

Ana looks for something in her bag. A mobile phone perhaps, I hope something intriguing; I have seen women taking out their lipstick in-between courses at the dinner table, applying it to their lips as if the sticky coloured paste can add taste to the next dish. Perhaps they want to, politely, change the bad taste set in their mouth from the previous plate. They have a special relationship with their make-up gear, and lipsticks are central.

She takes out a pen though, writes something on a tissue paper and puts it in her bag. Her hair has the shine, has kept the shine it had, all those years back. She looks at me, and smiles. Her smile is a breeze. It blows my image of her in front of me back to the time of long coffees at university, and superimposes it onto the fresh images of laughter and anger.

The breeze touches my skin; I feel it on my face, I touch my face gently, and the breeze passes over my fingers. I forget all those words that have been boiling in my head sitting alone in the bookshop gazing at the door; *I've had enough of you and your tricks; you think I've forgotten? You think I forget?* That smile, that mixture of "I know" and "I'm going to stay silent" fills me with a desire to express my feelings. But it coils into itself in despair, and disappears. My feeling of humiliation for my weakness in expressing what I had in my mind, something that was so naked to her inquisitive eyes, and a chaotic mind to intrigue, to kindle speculation.

The breeze takes my glance away, far away through flowing time, through the way the curves of her lips move, and touches the corners of her eyes. I adored the movements, the changes in her face as her skin stretched; the way the colour of her lipstick brushed her lips… and she would start saying something I was afraid to decipher then. And now it is happening again; this time, with all the wrinkles, the effect hasn't died off.

She turns to Frank and says something. Frank's face lightens up with a vague smile. I try to remember him, how he was in those days. Not much to say. He was always calm and quiet. He would sit there with the newspaper under his arm. He would open it to the crossword page, and, while listening to what we talked about, fill in the puzzle as if our chatter was necessary for him to move the pen on the paper.

'Is it difficult?' Ana would ask with a contained naughtiness.

'Not more than usual,' Frank would reply, without lifting his head to look at her.

Now, as I look at him, I can imagine him sitting alone in his home in front of a chess set, playing against himself, lighting a cigar, one of his hands on his lips as if trying to stop himself uttering a secret word; only moving the hand away to bring the cigar close to his mouth to inhale deeply. He would sit there playing for hours looking at the knight, contemplating the rook, sacrificing a pawn. I always wondered how one could lose playing against himself. I'm sure Frank has the answer.

-6-

And on Ana's right-hand side? The "paleface"! I always pretended not to remember her name. Maria, such a non-assuming name, one of those names that you attribute to a particular face with no or little make-up, long soft fair hair with slow movements conveying a sort of innocence.

'She loves you, Adam. Take her… she's yours. Look at her skin!' Al would say each time she was around.

'You think you can distract me? While I am around you have no chance with Ana. Just forget it. Wipe her out of your mind, Al,' I would say.

'Oh, you are a fool, you won't have Ana, and you know it. And you will not have this one either, a total loser.'

'Well, don't worry about me, that's my business; you bother about yourself, Al.'

And all that time, it was Ana walking under the old plane trees chatting away with Paul, the vulture!

The Persian! Everyone was fascinated by her, the mystery of the country, paradox that she was, mixing the ancient history and the latest fashion, the unknown and the tangible. I remember the first day, yes, I remember how I saw her, how she came in complete with her make-up, the perfume, the whole gear. Nothing excessive but enough to turn heads; perhaps we were easily impressed then. I thought, *yet another spoiled one. Rich father, prestigious family, little substance. They go together don't they?* And she didn't help it either; talking to Paul, girls' heart-throb. The way he walked about with his light blue jumper over his shoulders, and the designer belts... you would think he was Italian, not a boy from the Worthing suburbs! All was made for him to be a winner, the whole story was written, I could write it all. I could read it all too; read it for Al, all in one session! And who started first calling her Ana? Was it that rat? I hated them calling her with that name, Ana! Could anything be more artificial? What was wrong with her beautiful name, Anahita? But "Ana" stayed with her, she didn't mind either. Actually, I think she liked the nickname somewhat, so Ana... it stayed.

-7-

She takes the napkin and cleans the corners of her lips. The red lipstick is smeared on the thick beige cloth. There is a silence. It is unusual, unexpected, but I have confronted it again and again; a vacuum sucks all noises into an invisible silk scarf, and a breeze with no directions takes it away. She puts the napkin on her knees and looks at me. And then a fork drops. It's Colin's. A heavy designer fork, old style, simple but curvy. As Colin leans to take the fork, the waiter rushes to help him. Ana takes her hand to her hair falling free on her naked shoulders. Soft dark hair brushing the skin. *Aren't you cold?*

Do I have a headache? I put my hand in the pocket of my jacket. My fingers dip through pieces of napkin and touch the two pills in their thin cover. I move in my seat and try to listen to someone, anyone. At my left, Helen, with her light brown... blonde curly hair, has one foot bent under her as if she's still eighteen, sitting on the campus lawn talking excitedly about Led Zeppelin. Now she has two grown-up kids.

It's Colin with his loud voice. 'So... eventually, we are all here. I am sure you are feeling at home, just like the old times.' He moves his head as if he wants to convince someone. 'Only us, the magnificent seven! Hahaha! So... good that we all managed to come, and we still have a long night ahead of us.' He pauses. 'I don't want to make a speech, no! Not tonight! But don't hold your breath! Tomorrow is another day. Hahahah!'

He continues and I gaze at Ana's naked arms leaning on the table as she is talking to Frank. Her face in profile looks healthy. Her muscles have kept their tone. Really? I look at her arm more intensely. I should have been sitting next to her, not next to this fake blonde! It is all Colin's doing, the rascal. Why did he end up doing the seating plan? Well, who else? Thankfully Al is not here. He would have been furious sitting somewhere else than next to Ana.

Helen turns to me.

'So, Adam, what do you do these days?'

'I have a bookshop,' I say.

'That's interesting, would've never thought of that.'

'What did you think I do?'

'Don't know, an office job maybe.'

'I'm not that tame.'

'I hope not, but I judge you from your record.'

'What record?' I ask. 'You hardly knew me.'

'I knew enough,' she says. 'Remember the walnut tree? Anyway, tell me, have I changed a lot?'

'We all have changed,' I say.

And I want to say, 'all of us have changed, but some have lived through the changes, some others are fixated at a certain age!' I am sure she still buys her outfit from the Salvation Army shop; the whole gear for a fiver. The hippy girl, they used to call her. 'Have you scored, Adam? Everyone has. Go on. She doesn't mind, she's all for it.' And I do remember the walnut tree that night, the shade of the leaves on the gravel under the tall lamp, with a globe-shaped lampshade.

'You haven't gone back for the break,' she said. The Student Centre was quiet. Students had gone home for semester break.

'Neither have you,' I said.

'Yeah.' She wore a light flowery dress.

'Like it here?' I asked her.

'Lots, why do you think I am here? I would've gone home.'

'Why didn't you go home?'

'Are you crazy? Go home to do what? I escaped home. The uni is a legal refuge, don't you know that?'

I said nothing. She came closer.

'You are so innocent, Adam. This puts me in the mood.'

'Not as innocent as you think.'

'Yeah, more! But soon not anymore!' I watched her face closing in.

-8-

What did I like about her then? Nothing seems to have changed about her now, apart from her being over thirty years older, of course; she even wears the same clothes she used to wear then! I can imagine her taking the dress out of an old suitcase tucked away under her bed. She should be a romantic to have kept it, or a lonely one, or a possessive one. I suppose she could be all of these. Whatever the reason, she has kept her figure to be able to wear it again after so many years.

'Did you do it Adam? Come on, own up.' And I would keep silent. I kept silent when I saw Helen the next day and passed her by as if we had never met.

'Adam, you look pale, Adam,' she says. She thinks I am the same person to mother. I lift the glass of wine.
'If you ask me, you haven't changed a bit. OK, some wrinkles here and there, nothing more,' she says.
'I have to say, you don't seem to have changed either, Helen.'

'Only more experienced. Not wiser though.' And she smiles.

My headache is getting worse. I have another gulp of the wine.

Her skirt was so light in the dark and the night was unusually hot and humid. I had the taste of dust in my mouth. It was a hot summer, the park was more like a desert, all the green grass had gone, what was left was dust, and we had walked in the park most of the morning.

'We bet you she didn't wear anything under it. Come on, Adam. We all know it. You can't get away keeping your mouth shut,' one of the boys says.

'Oh, leave him alone, the miserable sod. He thinks he is in love with Ana,' Al says.

And I throw him a punch. Oh, I wanted to do that for a long time. I had clenched my fist a hundred times thinking about him and now it was the time. He took it in his face but it wasn't a hard blow.

'You are an idiot, Adam,' Al says, stroking his face. He sits on a short stool, looking at me, shaking his head.

'I remember those brutes, remember them all,' says Helen, 'but you were different.' She puts her hand on my thigh; it disappears under the beige tablecloth.

I didn't want to be different then; but I did keep silent about her. Some things better kept under wraps, I suppose.

Her hand moves. I pick up a boiled green pea on my plate.

'I see you are still innocent, Adam.' She strokes her hair but doesn't let go, pulls at it. I think, just like the way she was. She continues, 'And mind you, only once wasn't enough. I should have persisted. I shouldn't have ignored you the day… you know, the day after… when you passed me by.' She squeezes my thigh and smiles.

Ana is still talking to Frank.

'What are you looking at, Adam?' Helen says. 'That's the problem. It was your problem then, and it seems it is still the problem now.'

I stroke my forehead; the headache doesn't seem to want to go away.

'What do you want to happen? A miracle? Things don't just happen like that. You need to take them in your hand, feel them, act on them.'

I move in my seat. She is right, so right! I should have been more active, more decisive about Ana. More? What do I mean more? I didn't do a thing, not a single move. I just passed by Ana through the long corridors, again and again, saying nothing then. And I blamed Al for it! Good that he is not here, good that he is dead. He would have said, 'Easy boy, easy! You were incompetent. There was no need for me to stop you, you were already in mud up to your neck!'

-9-

'I am sorry, I will be back in a minute,' I tell Helen.

'I shall follow you then,' she smiles.

'Must forgive me with my unfortunate headache; I just need to get some fresh air.'

The garden shines under the neon lights. It is cold, but I want to stay out here with the conifers, the single old naked plane tree, the narrow line of thin snow which still remained after a week.

I take a couple of pills from my pocket and put them in my mouth.

'How do you do that?' asks Colin. He walks towards me, lighting a cigar. He thinks he is wiser when he smokes a cigar, lifting his face up. His looks change. He narrows his eyes as if he has found an eternal secret looking at the thick clouds.

'How do you manage to swallow those dry?' he says.

'Hi Colin, it's years of practice!'

'I thought you practised something else! Have you met Ana yet?'

'Yes, I had a short chat with her in the lobby earlier on.'

'Like the old days, ha?'

I don't say anything and Colin inhales heavily.

What got into me to come over? Come over all the way to stand out in the cold with a headache, Colin smoking his cigar next to me.

'So here is where you have escaped to!' says Roy. He is one of those who gives you the impression they never change. He has his thin oily hair, and the bow tie. I wouldn't miss a bet if I say he had had this tie since the second year of university. And he smelled. Boy he smelled! He looks at me. I smile, briefly.

'Adam!' He smiles and comes over. He stretches out his wet hand to me and his handshake reminds me of him thirty years ago, those sweaty hands, and I smell the wine as he breathes heavily, signs of his breath disappearing in the cold air.

'You are in good shape, Roy,' I say.

'You too, Adam; are we having a meeting here in the cold?' asks Roy.

'Just a bit of fresh air,' Colin says.

'Since when've you become so concerned about this sort of crap? Fresh air?' Roy asks.

'Since I started smoking!'

'This is Adam's effect on you! What a waste he was,' says Roy. 'Nothing personal, Adam, but face it, face it now for goodness sake.' He topples but controls himself. 'You've been such a waste. Wonder what did you do with all those girls? No, I don't wonder, I know! Fucking nothing. You are a waste of a prick, Adam.'

'Cool it off, Roy,' says Colin and moves towards him.

'No, but it's true, isn't it? Isn't it, Adam? What a shitty name he has too.'

I wonder what has got into him suddenly.

'What's bothering you, Roy?' I ask.

'Get real, if you don't know yet, get a life! Everyone knows. You live in cloud cuckoo land… even now. Get real, you are a grown-up man now! You are an old hard shit if you ask me.'

'Watch it, Roy,' I say, 'what's eating you?'

'What ate all of us! Poor Al told me you were a hopeless case. Wonder what you did with those girls? Nothing, eunuch! I am sure they were thinking the same, thinking they had wasted their time on you. What did you have to talk about with them? Aren't you still untouched, Adam? Hah! Virgin Adam!'

'Let's go in, Roy,' Colin says, and tries to walk him in. On his way back, he drops the cigar and kills it with his left foot. He had a good left foot, he even got a trophy of some sort – the footballer of the county – but then he stopped playing suddenly. I never asked him why.

I walk into the garden. I feel cold but I walk further out. I walk further in, into the dark, and stand under a cypress tree where the snow hasn't melted yet.

A cold, sharp breeze. I see Colin and Roy going back. I think of catching up with them but I stop on the pathway leading to the entrance; the winter lawn is wet and partly covered with a thin layer of snow.

'What do you want at this moment, right now?' Helen asked me, putting her hand on my shoulder.

We were standing under the walnut tree. I was silent next to her.

'I don't know,' I said. I knew what I wanted.

'I don't believe you,' Helen said. I paused.

'OK, I wish I had finished all this studying crap, I wish I was out of it.'

'You are kidding me. Is this *really* what you are thinking about now? I am disappointed.'

I remained silent.

I feel cold. I look at the snow on the ground and feel colder. I turn back and move fast to go in, back to the dining room. As I'm just getting in, Helen is coming out.

'I thought I could grab you alone out there,' she says.

'You have!'

'No, not like this. You know what I mean. Not under the nose of Colin and that idiot Roy.'

'Not fond of Roy?'

'Must be joking.'

I move towards the dining room. 'See you back at the table.'

'Yeah,' she is looking for something in her bag. 'You don't have matches, do you? Still don't smoke?'

'Sorry, no.'

'You must promise to go for a walk with me before we return, would you?'

'Yes, promise.'

'Good boy.'

It was an old walnut tree and she was casually leaning against it. She had a cigarette in her hand.

'Do you have matches?'

'I don't smoke.'

'My innocent little boy!' She looked agitated. She searched her bag and found a plastic lighter; a transparent plastic lighter, there was hardly any gas in it. She lit her cigarette, leaning against the tree.

'You don't like me, do you?' she asked, sending the smoke off to the branches.

'Why? What have I done? Why do you say this?'

'Don't evade my question, young man, and don't patronise me. You don't like me, right?'

I didn't like the way she was asking me the question; putting that "right" at the end of her sentence was too American for me.

'No, it's not the case.'

'But I feel it; I am not stupid, you know. And I'm not loose as some of you think, but I just do what I like to do.'

'Then you shouldn't bother about what other people think about you.'

'My innocent boy, some of them don't even talk with me afterwards… I need friends too, you know, someone to have a drink or two with.' She paused. 'Hah, mind you, some of them want to marry me. I guess they think I am good at it… more likely *they* don't know much about it, whatever I do would be good for them!'

'Do you want a cup of coffee?'

'Does it mean we are friends?'

'Of course we are.'

'Perhaps too soon to say, perhaps too easy to say. It's half-term now, and nobody's around. Let's see if we are still friends when people come back next term,' she said.

And the next term, I passed her by, pretending I was talking to someone. Other occasions? It was easy. You just ignore someone a couple of times and she ignores you after that; quite a workable scenario.

-10-

Back at the dining table Colin was talking loudly enough for Ana to hear at the other side of the table.

'I have to say, Frank has changed so much, I couldn't recognise him, I didn't recognise him at all.'

'Thanks, Colin,' said Frank with a low voice, 'I know I have changed.'

'Don't get me wrong, Frank, I mean it in a nice way. You've lost weight big time. I wish I could do that.'

'I am not sure, Colin,' said Frank. 'I'm not sure that's what you want.'

Ana looked my way, stressed, and turned her face away again.

'Frank had such a gift guessing the exam papers! I never believed him and always regretted it afterwards,' Colin continued.

I imagine my hand sliding on Ana's hair as it brushed her shoulder sitting next to Frank. Would she *ever* stop talking to him? What is there to talk about?

Where was Ana hiding? I had looked everywhere for her, but after all, she was sitting where I should've looked first, at that small black table in the university coffee shop, sipping a black coffee and reading a book.

'Hello Ana.'

She looked up.

'Hi,' and continued reading.

'Interesting book?'

'Don't know yet.' She didn't stop reading.

I know when I'm not wanted, I thought.

'Mind me joining you?' I said.

'No,' and continued reading.

'Want another coffee?'

'Hah?'

'Want another coffee?'

'No, no thanks.'

I sat in front of her with the coffee cup in my hand, the warmth of coffee penetrating through the cup onto my skin. I watched her reading, her hair masking part of her face. Her hair was longer then. I finished the cup and stood up.

'I know when I'm not wanted,' I said. She didn't lift her head.

I walked out to the small courtyard, thinking of the butterfly I had seen earlier that morning, so unusual. I forgot the small black table. I sat on the bench over the lawn facing the old silver birch tree with its leaves flickering under the breeze, like the butterfly wings.

Now, I don't like them, rarely look at them. They seem irrelevant. So what if they have colourful wings. Have you looked at their antennae and the minute hair on their body, millions of those short, seemingly innocent, hairs covering their body? Just put the beast under the microscope and have another look. You wouldn't like to go close to it; you know what I mean, a real and present danger! Well, OK, I grant you it is the same with everything; take sex! We consider it as a pleasurable act, but looking at it out of context it can be seen as an invasion, a fight. This is on a visual dimension. But at an emotional level, how does fascination give way to repulsion, and at best to indifference? Something clicks sooner or later, and things are not what they were before. The problem is, you don't want to admit it to yourself, let alone to the other side; a case of stability and morality! Do you insist that your fascination for the butterfly is everlasting? Why is it easier to admit accepting some changes, but not others?

The tablecloth hangs long and heavy; leaning on my knees, it irritates me.

Ana laughs, and Frank looks at her as if she has achieved a difficult task, solved a puzzle with great mental demand.

'Toilet seats were so cold,' Helen says as she sits. She has reapplied her lipstick, didn't use lipstick those days. I wonder why women use darker, more imposing lipsticks as they grow older? I can understand, with difficulty mind you, when they choose darker colours when they get a promotion. They wear austere clothes to say look, no jokes with me anymore! What a miserable state of affairs, more of a joke, I'd say. I am sure Helen agrees with me on this. I like to think that my perception of people is more refined now... after so many years. An old romantic sitting next to an old hippy! Ah, and what happens to the old romantics? They become husbands in pinstriped suits, sitting on the corner seats of trains going home late evenings, trying to finish that business article they couldn't finish in the morning. What is the content of a power-nap dream? Is the wife sitting in the car in the station waiting to take him to their semi-detached house?

And how does a hippy turned housewife behave with baskets of laundry to deal with, and tables and shelves to dust? For me it is the dust setting on the books. I take a book in my hand and the knife starts to cut deep into my flesh. The internal bleeding is slow; the sharp ends of the words, their hidden intentions reveal themselves as they unravel into my blood, forming thorns with a mission.

Colin has the napkin hanging from his collar and is biting into a chicken leg with eyes protruding. Helen looks at him, trying to say something.

'You remind me of a movie… when was it? Good old times… it should've been then, yes, it was… you remind me of this man who ate burgers all the time throughout the movie. He was knifed at the end. He had a half-eaten burger in his hand and—'

'OK, OK, you made your point,' Colin says. Roy sniggers. 'Do you still read comic books, Helen? Have you kept your Led Zeppelin poster?' Colin continues.

Helen makes a gesture with her fingers and lifts her wine glass.

'I drink to those who are not afraid to remain faithful to themselves,' she says.

-11-

Colin's e-mail came unexpectedly. I hadn't heard from him for some time. I was cataloguing the new batch of books that had arrived earlier in the morning.

'Don't you think it's about time we had a reunion?' The e-mail was sent to a list; I could recognise most of the names, some with immediate mental picture. But reunion? What reunion? There was no special relationship between us then to instigate a reunion now! If there was anything, I wasn't part of it. But you know how these things are, in a spare moment someone feels nostalgic about the past, it might be a piece played in a busy department store, a new fashion imitating the old one, the colour of sunset… and you think, ah, we had such a good time in those days. We should have a reunion… what reunion?

Well, now I'm here anyway, close to Ana after so many years. Did I quietly wish to see her here? Did I come over with that hope?

Something breaks. Breaking of a bowl is one thing but the splashing sound is another; like a whisper, and I can picture the liquid... white on dark orange. I see it happen again and again, the tomato soup spreading on the marble; a curved line of carefully painted cream gradually penetrating the thick orange liquid. The calm but surprised look on Frank's face... the orange colour drops on Ana's skirt.

She stands up with a handkerchief in her hand and tries to compose herself. She smiles at Frank, says a few quick words and goes out. Frank, sitting there, smiles at the plate in front of her while Colin looks at him and a waiter starts pouring soup into his plate while the other cleans the floor. Helen raises her glass again.

'I have this one to you, Adam,' she says and drinks all of it in one gulp. I think *the plonk*. 'Thanks, Helen, any occasion?' I ask her.

'Do you need to have reasons for everything? This is a good moment. That's all,' she says.

I raise my glass. 'And this is to you, Helen.'

'This is cheating, but thanks all the same, Adam, you are a nice boy.'

Colin hits his glass with a spoon.

'Can I have your attention, please? I have been told there is a special event tomorrow night. Apparently, people of the nearby village have a ceremony. It is a winter ceremony, nothing mythological, just a community custom, a whisky punch party. So don't expect a Viking fancy dress party! They have heard of our reunion, yes, the news goes fast here,' he is nearly shouting, 'and they have invited us to join them. What do we say?'

Ana comes back. She has combed her hair and renewed her lipstick. There is a wet spot on her skirt and the orange has gone. There is a silence.

'Don't mind me, continue,' Ana says, laughing.

Frank leans towards her as she sits and starts telling her something.

Colin says, 'What do we say then?'

'Why not? Like old times, Colin,' says Helen.

Colin goes red. 'I can see it so vividly.'

'Why not?' other voices say. Ana is still talking with Frank.

'Are you still interested?' Helen asks me, 'I mean in her.'

'What do you mean?' I say.

'So, you *are* interested; tell me, what does she have? Is it her face? Her body? I suppose you don't go for skinny ones at your age anymore, do you? Or is it that she is good in business?' she smiles, looking into my eyes. 'It isn't her brains you're after, I safely assume!'

'You are amazing, Helen,' I say.

'Am I? People used to say I am easy!'

'*I* didn't—'

'Don't worry, I am happy with what I am; and I know what I want. If people have a problem with that, then that's their problem.'

'You take it too seriously, Helen.' I sip at the wine.

'Contrary. I take it with enjoyment!' She laughs loudly.

What is Ana talking about? I wish I could hear it.

Frank stands up and slowly walks out.

'You didn't tell me,' Helen says, 'what's so special about her?'

'Sorry Helen, I just want to catch up about something.' I stand up and go to Ana. It seems to me it takes ages to get there, going around the long table, walking on the polished marble. I sit on Frank's chair.

'*I* should have been sitting here,' I say. She smiles.

'But you are not.'

'I am now.'

'Very briefly.'

'I suppose it depends on how long it takes him to…'

'You don't need to be too graphic.'

'But it is true.'

'Have you come here to talk about Frank's urinary activity? There is plenty of time for that,' Ana says.

'I just wanted to see when we could talk alone.'

Frank comes back.

'Hi Adam, long time, eh?'

'Indeed,' I say, looking at him standing by the table.

'I remember you with a book under your arm all the time. I envied you for that.' He coughs.

'I just wanted to show off, Frank,' I laugh. 'Anyway, what do you do these days apart from living extravagantly?'

'Nothing much! Busy dying!'

'Frank has been diagnosed with cancer of the colon,' Ana says.

I look at him standing there, smiling.

'It's not as bad as it sounds,' he says.

The room is warm, and around the table people are busy talking. Helen has moved next to Colin.

'Oh, I'm sorry,' I say. 'When did that happen?'

'Not very recently, Adam, long enough!' Frank says.

'He is remarkably well,' Ana says.

'Yes, I wouldn't have guessed.'

There is a silence between us. I try to remember Frank in those days but it is difficult. I have little memory of him; only some snapshots. He is standing behind Ana and me, and I suddenly notice I have taken his seat. All this time, Maria, sitting next to Ana, is looking at me with her hands under her chin.

'Oh, I'm sorry, Frank. I have taken your seat,' I tell Frank.

'Nobody can take my seat, Adam,' he smiles. 'You are welcome, do you want to sit here? I can move over to your seat.'

'No, no, I am just going back.'

'Do you want *me* to move?' Maria says.

'No, that's fine, I'm just going back now,' I say.

'I am Maria, in case you don't remember me, Adam.'

'Of course, Maria. I am old, but not so much that I forgot your name!'

'You never remembered my name.'

'You think so?'

'Yes,' she says in a low voice.

'I'd better be moving, sorry Frank.' And I stood up. I felt sticky in my shirt. The room was too hot for my liking.

'Boy, it is like a sauna here,' I say to myself.

Colin hears me.

'What are you complaining about this time, Adam?'

I ignored him. I was back at my seat with empty chairs both sides. I had forgotten about my headache, no pain any more. The waiters, both of them, started bringing desserts, serving from the two ends of the table. The tall, thin waiter with a narrow moustache came over with a plate of tarte tatin with a scoop of ice cream next to it. He put the plate in front of me. 'Tea or coffee, sir?'

A French waiter! What brought a Frenchman to this cold rainy place?

There was a taste of fish in my mouth.

'Double espresso, please,' I said.

He smiled as if I had given him a compliment.

I looked at him as he walked out of the room. With tidy suit and trimmed moustache I imagined him putting the key in the door to his flat; wife and a kid? I couldn't picture that. He would be alone. The type who reads books of etiquette, not because of his job; and friends? No, no friends. He is probably a difficult person to make friends with!

Ana smiles at me from the other side of the room. How would it be to be in the hotel room with Ana? Walking in, looking at her saying something. And I? I… thinking of something to say…the mini-bar would be useful.

-12-

Yes… I have changed. I could see it in the eyes of these people as I arrived. Thirty-five years. Hah, still, what *has* changed? I tell you what has changed! I am not talking about the nose, the earlobes, and the lines one sees in the mirror. Those are the mirror's momentary reminders. Mine is something I carry with me all the time, no need for a mirror to remind me.

The coffee comes with a smile. The waiter *is* polite. I guess he likes his job. I guess he had always wanted to be a waiter; watched intensely as a child at the way the waiters served in the movies, upright, letting heavy plates sit on their open hands, looking straight-on proudly as if they were victorious knights entering a surrendered city.

I look at him and smile back with appreciation. Yes, I know about your life, your flat, type of music you like being played as you lie on your bed listening, forgetting about the noise out there. Ah, that was the top floor neighbour's brat banging her feet on the floor, that was the sound of the neighbour's door across the short narrow corridor; she went in after a long kiss. You can imagine now the boyfriend is walking down the stairs. One, two, three steps. And why is he walking so slowly? You lie there, not thinking. You lie there, letting images go through your mind without being processed.

The coffee is strong and long, it's warm, exactly as I like it. I take another sip. I used to make strong coffee in the hostel; others used to come over to my room, we sat and talked about everything from Cuba and Vietnam to free love and Bob Dylan. I listened while making Turkish coffee on the small alcohol burner, putting the metallic pot over it and stirring the coffee to arrive at the correct consistency; small cups ready. They loved it.

'What are you doing with these girls?' Roy would ask, leaning back on one arm, combing his hair with the other hand, using his fingers as a comb.

'Nothing much if you ask me,' Al would say. 'Nothing, he just talks.'

'Give the man the opportunity to express himself,' Roy would say, always trying to use words older than his age.

Now, sitting next to Colin, he is old enough for words. He looks at least ten years older than his age. If you asked me, I would say he is easily seventy. OK, he had a bad time, the wife dying and all that, but so what? Should I feel sorry for him?

'Ask Adam. He knows these sorts of things.'

I hear Ana saying it loudly, leaning on the edge of table, masking Frank to reach Roy.

'Oh, he doesn't know,' Roy shouts back.

Ana says nothing, and I say nothing.

Aren't you interested to know what he wants to know?

Not really, I tell myself. As far as I am concerned, he can die in ignorance. After all, it has to be something mundane. Whatever comes out of him is nothing more than mundane or toxic gossip. I bet you his house is full of women's magazines. He had an excuse when his wife was alive, the poor woman. Now what? I can imagine him coming home, sitting in a corner reading garbage while his wife prepared dinner. Probably it was him who briefed her on the latest garbage gossip as detailed in those magazines.

'What's the dinner?' he would ask.

Sitting drunk on his chair, he is gulping away glasses of wine. Do you think he grieved his wife's death?

He would say, 'You talk like an old bitter man, you are a waste of space.'

Do you think I care? You can say whatever you want to say. I have lived enough to choose to be bitter if I want to. This is a free world.

Yeah it is. But you are trembling with anger. Let me listen to your heart beating so fast. That much for a free man! You don't want to die like this, do you? Dying with past events imprinted in you with grudge. Oh, look across the table, Ana is smiling!

Yes, I have experienced these smiles, powder and lotion-mixed smiles, trying to hide anger and hatred. The only thing is that some people can pretend better than others.

Stay the way you want. I just thought you might enjoy yourself in this reunion, that's all.

I take the napkin and clean my mouth. I look at Ana. She is not smiling. She is looking at her coffee cup. When I go back home, I will work on my smile.

-13-

'We will celebrate, we will celebrate, two of us. Don't laugh. You are transparent like a piece of…. turd, Adam. I can see you will be laughing listening to this message and then getting angry, saying I am filling up your phone-box. But I am serious. I know we didn't see things the same way but now… listen… yes, I have had one or two. And listen. I have put aside a bottle, a special one. It is old, red and… I had kept it since those times to have it… with the hope to have it with… you know whom… yes, that one. We both were head over heels for her. Now… none of us I guess… well, what the heck. I thought I'd keep it for us; after all, we had something in common. Listen, we must get together. Life is not worth it, you know. I know what you think but let's get together. Only two of us and have this bottle together. There is a lot to say. There's not enough time, I know, but perhaps it will be a start. There is little time left, you know… anyway. I hate talking to answerphones. Just let me know where. Let's celebrate somewhere exotic, somewhere… what the heck, somewhere to have this bottle. I have been keeping it for long enough, all the time thinking about her… about us. Let's do it soon.'

I was in a hurry. I listened to Al's voice breaking on the answer-machine and went out.

'Have you heard about Al?' Roy asked me on the phone. He was talking as if he was going to reprimand me for a hideous crime. I felt I was ambushed, was tempted to give him a piece of my mind, but I didn't. Just paused a minute.

'Who are you talking about? Al? What about him?'

'Well he died, didn't he?'

Roy, the poor sod, went AWOL enjoying himself somewhere when his wife died. Now he was sanctimonious, telling me off for my reaction at Al's death. How would I know he was dead?

'How would I know?' I said. And my mind wandered. So, good old Al had died. Who was going to be next?

'Why? When? What happened? Car accident?'

'No, you idiot. It was his heart. I thought you were friends. He gave me something for you,' Roy said.

'For me?'

'Yeah, in the hospital, dying, he made me promise I would contact you, he knew I wouldn't waste my money on a phone call to you.'

'Thanks, pal.'

'He made me promise to get the bottle to you. It's a bottle of red. I don't know what the whole fuss is about… anyway it's a waste of wine but as they say one must keep the promise to the dead.'

A bottle of red, hah! Bloody autumn, they say more people die in autumn than any other time of the year. What would I have to say to Al? *Listen I am in a hotel with Ana, but not alone, it's a reunion. She is fine! I wish you were here!*

'Do you have to be so intense? Cool off,' Helen says.

I look at her, can't respond; who else wonders about my mind? The old ego should be tickled a bit! But no, I smile and say nothing. She rearranges her red woolly hat and doesn't wait for an answer. She had asked me the question because she wanted me to ask *her* a question, giving her a cue to start telling me all about herself. She lives alone in a flat near the bookshop; quite well-off to have a flat in this neighbourhood.

'Oh, it is quite entertaining Adam… you know… I like the way Suzy treats her friends… you see, she is not a push-over, she knows what she wants and she goes for it,' Helen says.

Who's Suzy anyway? And do I care? A random character in the life of yet another lonely soul.

The waiters, both of them, are standing there by the top of the table with their uniforms. Dark green, golden buttons, wide golden stripes the sides of their trousers. I guess they are happy with us leaving the table eventually. We stand up.

'Drinks at the bar?' Colin says.

No one answers; we all walk to the bar. I talk with Ana. Helen walks between Frank and Roy.

'This is all very strange,' I say.

'What is?' says Ana.

'The frozen time, I say.

'For me, it has melted away, Adam.'

She smiles and holds my arm.

'Have you looked at yourself in the mirror?' she says.

'Oh, that,' I say, 'I make stories in my mind. The images… the images I build from people, from the past. I have an old mansion in the mirror full of ghosts; bottles of red colour it.'

'My problem is that I have to look at my face in the mirror every day,' Ana says.

'You should be pleased with it,' I say.

'I get bored with it,' she smiles, 'but you weren't a flirt then, what has changed?'

'I have looked in the mirror as well, you know.'

'And you've found the flirt in yourself!'

'You can say that, but I meant what I said. I should have said it years ago, Ana,' I said.

'There was no need.'

'Still… perhaps…'

'Perhaps,' she said, 'but let's touch base now, enough of that, OK?'

'Yes, yes.'

We arrived at the bar. There were some tables near the counter and more were spread to the open space in the lobby, with large comfortable chairs in crème colour.

'OK, I start the run, who wants what?' says Colin.

-14-

The drink went down well, didn't it? That warm feeling moving through the veins, the flesh, the skin; sitting next to her in a corner, others all there but away, away as you always wanted.

This is your move, Adam, your move, I am not there anymore, I have shed all my grudge, just make the move, just do it. I tell you… do it.

I hear Al talking as if he is pulling my sleeve, and I notice Ana tapping on my fingers resting on the table.

'Tell me, Adam, what was it all about between you and Al? You *were* friends, weren't you?'

'I guess so, in a funny way.'

'Funny?'

'Strange, you get to know things much later, much, much later.'

'You can't be cured, you are a romantic; through and through. And the thing is, even the passage of time hasn't helped it.'

'And this is a disease? Perhaps an ailment?'

Ana has a sip from her gin and then another.

Her fingers are slim, now slimmer, and the skin is dry. I see all this under the dim light.

And her hair? Has it lost its shine?

Come on Adam, you are trying to give a wrong picture of her. True, I cannot do anything about it now, but I can just say oi! Watch it! You don't need to be so bitter. So what? You couldn't have her those days, what about now? I'm not there to stop you! You have my blessing, honest. Better at least be one of us!

Ana puts her fingers in the glass and takes out an ice cube; a small partially-melted cube with edges eroded. It drips on the tablecloth. She puts it in her mouth. She bites into the ice, exaggerating the movement of her mouth, her lips more pronounced.

'You are silent,' she says.

'Contemplating the fate of a piece of ice,' I say.

'Lucky!'

'For a short moment.'

'Lucky all the same. You used to take the side of caution, always, didn't you Adam? You haven't changed.'

'Is it meant to be a contemptuous remark?'

'No, just stating the sad state of affairs.'

'What affairs?'

'Exactly, those that could exist but didn't.'

I pause.

'Silent again?'

'Don't want to impose myself.'

'What does that mean? This is moral shit,' she says, and finishes her glass.

I call the waiter and ask for a gin and tonic and a large vodka.

I look at Ana, trying to find out what goes on in her mind, sitting in front of me searching her bag. I think she loves searching her bag for no good reason; perhaps expecting a pleasant surprise. The gangs at other tables are bursting into bouts of laughter, silence and shouting.

The waiter comes with the tray of drinks and small bowls of peanuts and olives.

'I have been looking… forward to seeing you.' I say it with hesitation. 'I know this is corny.'

I take a big gulp of the vodka and chew some peanuts. They are stale.

'You have a funny way of showing it,' she says. 'You see, it wasn't that difficult to say it… and yet, you waited so long.'

'I am sure you were aware of it, weren't you?'

'I have been– always – but so what?'

'What do you mean, so what?' I say.

She picks up her glass.

'Cheers.'

'Cheers.'

'Do you remember the Student Centre?' Ana asks.

'Do I remember it? What a question! How come *you* remember it? It wasn't your sort of place to frequent.'

'I did go there once or twice.' She smiles.

'What stopped you?'

'Found it too lonely. The hedges, the green hedges, the circular pond always half-full, the gravel; more than anything else the green, the dark green was too cold for me, even in those hot summer nights.'

'So how is it you remember it now?'

'This is a package, isn't it? Apparently, we have come here to see each other after a long time, but in fact we have come all the way to meet our past. Don't you think? A past locked up in a box left in the loft. From time to time, when there is little else left to do, one goes to the loft, looks through the bits and pieces and mixes them up. Soon one is back to the sitting room, having left the past in the box.'

'But sometimes one sees something there he had forgotten about, he takes it with him.' I finish the little vodka left in my glass. 'I came here with the hope of seeing you,' I say.

'Me? Not the "me" you see now.'

'I wanted to see you, that's all.'

She takes a sip of her drink.

'Have you looked at my skin… the wrinkles? Are you still happy to have come?'

'You are too hard on yourself. You weren't like this.'

'Women lose their self-confidence as they grow old, they pay for their experiences… men gain confidence.'

'You are living in a world of false assumptions,' I say.

'I'd like to believe you.'

'It is true.'

'I don't know what the truth is, maybe only that we are here now, only what is here this moment,' she says.

'No ambitions?' I say.

She smiles.

'Ambitions! If I didn't know you, I would think you were a businessman.'

'I have my bookshop,' I say.

'Bookshop? So, my first impression wasn't that far away from the reality; when I saw you, I thought you were a teacher.'

'Disappointed?'

'No, I prefer to picture you in your bookshop than in a pinstriped suit. Where is it?'

'Oh, somewhere near the centre, you must come visit. It is a small shop but I like it.'

'I can imagine.'

'Could you live with it?' I ask.

'What do you mean?' she says.

'You know what I mean… let's talk about something else.'

'If you like… but what? Can't say this place is inspiring!'

'You seemed to have a good chat with Frank, though.'

'He is a gentleman. We have changed so much, but he has kept all those good things about him.'

'Should be difficult for him… I mean…' I say.

'He is not bothered a bit; it is more difficult for others.'

'Do you know? I never thought about it, but being here, looking at us I wonder how it happened like this… I mean how we, each one of us, ended up being what we are now,' I say.

'What a silly question, so what? You are talking like a sentimental teenager,' she says. 'Tell me, you say you have waited so long; you are here now, but you don't seem to…'

'There are things to be felt… and felt only; as if to utter them you have betrayed their innocence. I feel that I have already talked too much,' I say.

'I'm trying to understand you, but you must help me,' she says.

I pause; I look at her gazing at the empty glass resting on the table while holding it by both hands.

'Sorry but that's all,' I say.

'But things don't happen just by feelings; you need concrete thoughts… actions,' Ana says. 'One can talk endlessly about feelings, this is a self-soothing exercise… the "I'm the only one who knows… who feels… I'm the emotional one…", but this is not enough for me; at the end of the day everyone comes out of it bruised if not injured, damaged. In a way I do understand what you say… but if all your wishes are granted, I bet you will be disappointed. Can you ever imagine us living in the same house, a semi-detached refurbished house with fitted kitchen? Can you imagine coming down the stairs to have a hurried breakfast while the kids get ready for school? Could you imagine me combing our daughter's long hair? She comes in through the door with her long shiny hair combed and wrapped back… she comes in close and I see her eyes sleepy and her uniform ironed with sharp corners, white shirt. She brings her face close to you… a kiss for the day… the darling daughter… the father-daughter bond! Thankfully, that is no longer an option; this is the one time Mother Nature is kind.'

'You have taken this from a movie,' I say.

'Not one movie, you've seen many of them, but all end up with a sad ending… no one sees that side of the images though,' she says.

'There are good moments too, moments of satisfied dreams.' I say.

'Look at the real lives around us.' she says.

We finish our drinks.

'Another one?' I ask.

'Why not?' Ana says. 'Let's have some red.'

I call the waiter and see Helen talking with Roy and Colin the other side of the bar, but Frank and Maria have left.

Then I look at Ana again and notice wrinkles under her chin; her neck is covered by a black polo-neck.

'You had a moustache in those days, didn't you?' she asks.

She knows very well I never had a moustache. Beard? Yes, and that for only a short time. What does she want to say? That she didn't notice me then? Or does she want to tell me now that I looked ridiculous then? Does she want to hurt me now just like she did then? But now it only stays as an annoyance. It was stupid of me to show any interest in her anyway. But then, I always fall into this trap. I talk too much, that's it. I talk too much and give away too much. But then what does it mean if I don't express myself? What would a life be without expressions? Yet it doesn't put her in a good position with her way conveying a picture of supremacy. Perhaps she ignores the fact that she is not young anymore, that those days are long past. Perhaps she knows it too well, but she is also too aware of my feelings, so she can play her game. But it is not a game, is it? Talking about it, she gets into the mood of those times and she gets transformed into the person she was then. Who cares about the wrinkles around her eyes? She is in a different world now. And, where am I? Where do I stand? If the whole thing is as it was then, then I have no chance; I will act as I did before… as she is doing now. If I am experiencing this moment, this bar, then how can I relate to the old-young woman sitting in front of me expressing herself, stirring the memories?

Petals of the small red tulip on the table are drying at their edges. I hate these out of season pretentious flowers being thrown out at our faces. A single stem stays in the narrow-neck vase for several days until one day, around ten o'clock in the morning, the waiter remembers that he has to change it.

I touch my upper lip as I am sitting there looking at her. I ask myself what does she want from me? Her youth? And I smile.

'I have always imagined you with a moustache. You can imagine my shock when I saw you yesterday,' she says.

'You didn't show it at all.'

'Of course, I didn't want to be off-putting.'

'You don't seem to bother now,' I say.

We are close now, silly,' she says. 'When do you want to stop this game?'

'Game?'

'You don't want me to believe for a second that you are what you show, that your mind is so resigned, naïve, still naïve…'

'So, you do agree that I have been naïve.'

'One doesn't need to be an astrophysicist to know this. You were quite famous for it in those days.'

-15-

Can you think of places where background music is played all the time? The halls of eternal music! The lobby of hotels, airports. After a while, the music which is meant for relaxation becomes an irritation and then in a mysterious way, faints away... dies in oblivion. I suddenly became aware of the music as if someone had just started to play it at that moment. A song that you have forgotten, but you have always loved, one from those hidden alleyways of your past when you were walking with a mind full of images of "maybes" and unsettling desires. And now that music was in the air, filling the dim light of the bar.

'I have behaved beastly towards you,' Ana said.

I smiled. 'We are here now, and I have survived!' I said.

Her fingers drawing lines on the wine glass, then extending the lines on my hand resting on the table. Two dry skins with lines of veins next to red liquid touching the lips that have uttered so many words over the years and have ignored the words waiting to come out when the skins were fresh.

'Some events are meant never to happen,' she said.

'I'm not religious,' I said, 'and we are not dead yet!' I smiled.

'I wish you didn't smile each time you say something. It's full of sadness... some sort of despair... resignation. It is as if you want someone to assure you that what's happening around you... what has happened in the past is retrievable... ready to be rewritten,' she said.

The warm feeling of finding out that someone had thought so much about you, to have an analysis of you, was pleasing. No matter what Ana said, it was a compliment.

Even Helen, Colin and Roy had gone now. The barman was sitting at a customer's table, shuffling some bills.

'When you live alone for a long time, your outlook changes; sometimes I wonder if my perception of people... their motivations has anything to do with the reality. And as you continue to live alone with little close contact with people, you don't have a reality check,' I said.

'But you have a bookshop, you must see loads of people,' Ana said.

'Yes, I do, and I have all sorts of stories in my mind about them, and that's all... anyway, let's get back to our gang. Have you been in touch with the gang over these years?'

'Hardly!'

'I haven't asked about what you do,' I said.

'Good, don't.'

'I don't even know if you are married, have children.'

'What's the use of knowing? Does it change what we are doing now?'

'Well, no, but…'

'I've come here to be away from "buts" and "ifs". You have started with "ifs" and now we are getting into "buts".'

'Sorry, didn't mean to cause any—'

'Don't be clinical; we are here for a short time, it's best avoiding heavy discussions.'

'Would you like some fresh air?' I asked.

'Maybe a short one,' Ana answered.

-16-

The garden surrounding the building was well-structured but the cold and damp weather had its effect. There was a walkway with large stone slabs getting to a fountain with a stone statue of Bacchus. Walking away towards the boundaries of the garden, a couple of metal sculptures were standing non-symmetrically with faint blue light shining on them, casting shadow on the stones. Ana held onto my arm. We walked further into the garden; we could just see the walkway lit faintly by the light farther away at the hotel entrance.

'Are you content with your life?' Ana asked.

'I am happy now… nothing to complain about,' I said.

'What about the years past? Thinking about them… I've forgotten some of the names… doesn't it bother you?' she asked.

'I don't think about that.' I took her hand as it was wrapped around my arm. It was cold.

'You are cold,' I said.

'Yes… maybe we should go in.'
I stopped, there was a pause.

What is in a soft pressure on the skin? The pressing of lips? The smell of skin together with the smell of a familiar perfume reaching me in the cold weather, and you wonder where you had smelt that perfume before, as recently as a week ago on the street somewhere? But this one is mixed with an unknown smell of lipstick, sticky, stickier in the cold weather; thinking of prolonging the touch or stopping. Stop, and there is no guarantee of a follow-up… how can I stop after such a long wait? Years… and what if continuing in this cold weather is perceived as a sign of carelessness, insensitivity? Oh, she can hardly accuse me of insensitivity.

I look at her eyes as she smiles.

'Let's go in,' I say.

We walk back to the lobby. Ana slows down. Frank is standing in reception. His lips were dry as we went towards him and his skin was colourless. He looked much older than when I saw him across the table earlier. He had one hand on the reception desk. No one at the desk.

'My room is like a sauna, and the mini-bar is broken. I don't know what I am doing in this hotel,' he said, looking at Ana.

A waiter came with a bottle of water.

'Sorry sir, no one is there to deal with your fridge, but I hope this will do for tonight.'

The big bottle was misty.

'This looks chilled enough,' I said.

'That's what I need,' Frank said.

We walked to the lift.

'I am not sure if I will come down for breakfast,' Frank said.

My floor was the first one among us. I said goodbye while Ana was looking at me.

'Goodnight,' she said. Frank was rolling the bottle against his face.

-17-

The sound of the lift as the door closes and it starts going up as if it carries a heavy container. I walk slowly on the marble tiles. A large black vase with Chinese pattern sits on a pedestal with a tall narrow mirror behind it. There is a silence... the silence spreads from my head, leaves the whole building, extends itself... stretches out towards the woods surrounding the hotel. And then there is the faint noise of the card going into the slot on the door to my room. The door does not open. I try it again and again, putting it in by different face and side, but no luck. I go back to the lift and wait for it to come. I polish my shoes by the rotating shoe polisher next to the lift as I wait for the lift to come. I enter, expecting nobody in it this time of the night. There is a middle-aged Japanese man. He smiles politely and says hello. 'Hello,' I say, and stare at the floor of the lift waiting to arrive at the ground floor. It is a journey.

The man by the desk smiles. 'It happens sometimes. Did you have a mobile phone next to it?'

I touch my pocket. 'No, not really,' I say.

'It happens sometimes, sorry about that.' And he hands me the card again. He has done something to it. In the lift, I prepare myself for the card not working, let's avoid surprises. And there is no surprise. I enter the room, and straight to the TV, turn it on and drop on the bed. I do not look at the screen; I have muted the voice. I try to go to sleep; I have never *tried* to sleep. Bed means sleep, it has always meant sleep for me but not now, not tonight. A calm rain has started; I see it through the long glass window as the changing light of the TV screen reflects over the window. The silence comes back to my head. It carries with it, silently, Frank and his face… his thirst… and Ana looking at me getting out of the lift.

They must have been confused, the hotel owners I mean; just look at the design of the rooms, the corridors, the hall, everything. Did they want to create a modern hotel here? If so, they have completely failed. And as for a traditional hotel, something that I would have preferred, they have failed to do that too. We are talking about an absolute mess. Modern design for basin and taps, but they are so small that you cannot put your hands under the tap without hitting the basin! Card to get into your room, but you must look at the lampshades. It is as if you are in one of those tucked-away bed and breakfasts at the top of a small pub in the Scottish countryside. And as for the carpets, I'd better not mention them.

I stand up, take the TV remote control and change the channel. The remote looks new and flimsy; I have to press each button several times before it activates. Out of battery? I cannot turn the TV off, no, not now. I need to see some activity around me, someone to say something, anything, I do not need to hear it but just the feeling that something is happening out there just next to me is essential. I don't want to ask myself why on earth I decided to come to this so-called reunion. I want to do anything rather than thinking about people gathering here. But then, I remember the lift and its door as it closes.

No more rain, it is sleet now. I draw the curtain and imagine the grounds in the morning covered in snow. It will be cold and wet. I sit on the chair again and imagine all those people I had dinner with. Enough of Ana and Frank. Helen is the exciting one! Who did she go up with? Was it Colin or Roy after all?

-18-

I was sleepy, but I had no desire to go to bed. My back was aching dozing off on the chair. I moved a bit on the chair to find a comfortable posture. It is as if you are heavier when you drink, when you are sleepy. I turned the TV off and started to think about work and about my flat. There was nothing to be excited or worried about. Funny how each one of us ended up doing what we are doing.

Frank intrigues me. After all, manning a small shop is not an achievement, is it? He was so full of himself we used to call him Mr. Me. But this didn't deter us from liking him. OK, he is the owner of a shop, but my point is not about his position or the size of the shop, which is in a prime position in an affluent part of the town. The point is, I would have never guessed he would become an authority in the world of stamp collectors; finding the dough buying and selling stamps, and all that through a small shop. But there you are. And that's how he is dying away classifying stamps, living with them, looking at them, coughing away. I can imagine him alone in that shop, no assistants; as if the presence of anyone else in that shop would ruin his relationship with the stamps. I am sure he talks to them. *Ah, this one, this is rare, it doesn't show, does it? But it is rare, old and rare.* Sucking his upper lip anticipating. *Just look at the seal. Yes, it is red. Exactly! All these stamps have a black seal on them. And this one?* He would go silent as if he were in a chapel. He would look at the stamp for minutes. Then he would say, *Do you know how I got it? I bought it dirt cheap as part of a pack of stamps in a bazaar in Bangkok. Yes. Bangkok!* And he keeps on looking at the stamp for a while, then puts it in its protective cover, into a safe and locks it with a combination. Then he sits there looking outside the shop at people passing by.

He is one of those people I have difficulty picturing eating or going to the toilet! I remember when I was a child I used to ask myself, for a long time, if the kings and prophets ever had a need to go to the loo!

I wonder what his flat or house looks like. I am intrigued, and it is not because of him, but I wonder how men like me, single, over sixty years old, and not feeling it of course, live. How do they decorate their sitting room, their kitchen, their bedroom? Lonely men, they become odd. They start talking to themselves, don't they? Not in public, but when they are alone going home. I wouldn't admit it to anyone, but I have talked to myself, or worse, I have imagined people talking to me. No, no, I am not schizophrenic, but what does it matter if they really do or don't? I mean if I feel… if I'm convinced that someone is saying something to me, then that is all that matters, isn't it?

The room is getting cold and I'd better get into that bed; but it's so difficult to move from this chair to that bed, to move this short distance. It seems like a big job to do… it will be an achievement. I don't have to sleep, just the warmth of the bed is enough. I had imagined it differently while walking from the dinner table to the bar and then talking with Ana, my mind was working at a different plane assuming events to unfold differently… certainly not lying in the bed going over the events of the day; but there you are. I had prepared myself for a nice sleep after a pleasant encounter.

The room is getting colder. I think of Frank. He should feel better now, after that bottle of water. Funny how the rooms are… one too warm and one cold. I should be able to do something about it. I get off the bed and go to the gadget on the wall. A nub is broken. I imagine another guest trying to fix heating in the room, getting frustrated… pushing the nub… now the broken bit is in his hand. And then I go to sleep, two hours of interrupted sleep. It is still dark outside at seven in the morning. I go to the bathroom. I stand under the warm shower. I can stay here for the rest of this trip.

I have forgotten to shave. This disturbs me. I do not like to shave after the shower. What you do is, you take your shower, you dry yourself, wear what you have to wear and go out. But now, I have to stand in front of the misty mirror, wet the face again and shave. I stand in front of the mirror. Hair mostly grey, ear lobes drooping; eyebrows, nostrils, ear… all with unruly hair. I tell myself after all it is better to shave after the shower; the stubble softens under the water.

I get into the lift. It stops at one floor without anyone getting in. There is an unwanted quiet. I'd have liked to see people outside the lift waiting to get in, looking forward to their day of sightseeing. Sightseeing? Where? Here?

As I enter the restaurant, a short stubby girl with a maroon uniform comes towards me.

'Good morning, sir.' She takes me to a table next to the large glass windows.

'Is this OK for you?'

'Yes, thank you.'

'Could I have your room number, please?'

Her accent is welcoming. I feel better hearing her voice.

'253,' I say.

'Please help yourself, sir.'

There is a sharp smell of eggs and bacon mixed with damp weather. I look around me; an old couple at a table away from me are having their breakfast. That's all. So where is everybody? I know I am too early for a Saturday morning. But I expected to see someone here at least.

-19-

For me, sitting alone is dangerous. Walking on the crowded streets is OK, everything is in motion with you, there is no time for the mind to wonder on images, events. But sitting… you leave yourself open to the rush of memories.

'What are you thinking about? You look so remote… you scare me sometimes, it's as if you don't care about people around you,' Ana says, after a couple of drinks at the college bar.

Well, obviously, I have failed; if she thinks like this about me, I have failed. Silently, and perhaps somewhat aloof, I imagine Ana in my mind in all those moments of years gone by, when she would walk to the university library, search for the books, borrow one and leave calmly while I observed all her movements.

OK, let's say I try to be more sociable, what can I tell these people from the past? Tell them that I think about the bark of the trees at night when it drizzles, and the temperature falls to minus two? That I wonder where the birds go on winter nights where I cannot see them? Not all of them migrate. What happens to those who stay, or are left behind? A kid's question, and yet I don't have the answer. Shall I tell them I am thinking about the change in the daylight-saving regime? It is one of the advantages of being alone; I don't need to explain myself all the time to another person breathing in my flat. *What's wrong? What's wrong with you? You are not yourself today, have I said something? Is it me? It has to be something… you are not even denying it.*

Yes, it is an advantage being alone; I don't need to go home at a certain time thinking someone is waiting for me… that she has prepared food, waiting while watching TV, wasting time for me to arrive, that I don't need to buy food on the way for an early night. Early night! Why do we use such innuendo? Why don't we say, "timed sessions for an act of mutual consent"!

But then I arrive home. The walls of the flat are silent, silent and cold. I feel them without touching them. I go to the kitchen, drop on the table the ready-made food I've bought on my way home, go to the toilet, wash my hands, come back to the kitchen, turn on the small TV hanging solidly from the wall, take out the food from the pack, put it in the oven, wash the already-washed salad mix, bring out the plate and the cutlery, treat myself to a new patterned napkin I bought the other day, pour myself a glass of white wine from the half-empty bottle in the fridge, think about the taste of the new olive oil I have bought. I get disturbed by something they say on the TV, I change the channel, sit at the table waiting for the food to get to the fifteen-minute mark to take it out of the oven. I have already ignored the twenty-minute warm-up time and accepted, as the house rule, a fifteen-minute threshold.

Nobody's there to tell me *What's wrong with you?*, and I do not need to explain anything to anyone. But as I am sitting, not watching the programme on the TV, sipping the wine, I think I could've told someone what a terrible wine I was drinking, could've told someone the weather was getting colder, and that perhaps I should buy myself a warm scarf... Bob Dylan style, and could ask her what would she like me to buy her. Then there would be the dialogue... *nothing darling... oh, I don't know... you shouldn't ask me these questions... whatever you buy me is good... it is from you.* So, I have to think what I should buy her, something she likes? Or something she needs? And how could I be sure she would like what I buy her? I keep the TV going, it is essential. It is essential to have some noise, some activity in the flat. I can't explain why, could be a habit. I don't smoke, so I can have an addiction of my choice! *And what would be the one item of luxury you would take with you to the island?* Oh, how banal one can get? Not to be confronted with this question will be the best luxury, but when I walk out of the flat, the whole day is full of these questions. *Adam, have you read the new novel by...* the answer is no, I haven't; but I keep smiling, asking the question, how did you find it?

-20-

The walls of the hotel room look so alien to me. Sitting in the room, the words in my mind are tired, exhausted and, as minutes pass by, lazily stretch out of my skull, hang around for a bit and then precipitate in front of me, narrowly missing my shoes.

Buying a pair of shoes can be hazardous. Shopping is hazardous. You take home an alien, something you see in the shop window, something the shopkeeper brings you with a smile, convinces you of its qualities, and you buy it in a daze, you buy her words, you are convinced anyway, all you need is a push. And the push comes with another smile, a friendly gesture and the item is in a carrier bag. The design of the carrier bag is attractive too; you could do with the carrier bag alone.

'Do you want the box as well, sir?' do I want the box? What for? Could keep a pair of shoes in it, keeping the cupboard tidy. But the box in the carrier bag… the sharp corners of the box may pierce the bag, at best would stretch it. This is a dilemma. And this is only about a pair of shoes. And then, you put the key in the door, and you enter the flat with the bag in your hand. The sofa looks at you, the chairs, the walls. And you know you have shattered the calm, the tranquillity of it all. The flat was in complete balance, items were living in harmony with each other and with you… and now, you have changed all that; you have brought in a stranger. Yes, there is a silence, on appearance nothing has changed. But you feel it. You feel viscosity in the air, you feel dense particles stretching their territories. As you sit, the sofa is colder than usual, you feel the coldness of the walls, their colours have changed, slightly, but nevertheless there is a change. And you haven't opened the box yet. You don't know what the shoes think. Do they like the flat? Would they be accepted, eventually, by the present residents? You are stressed, you don't seem to be able to do anything right. Well, this is the price of growing old; you become more aware of everything. You continue but you carry this invisible weight of things invisible.

I open the box, take out the shoes and put them neatly next to the box. There is a need for moments of pause, moments for reconciliation about momentary disagreements; perhaps, after all, the shoes may be welcome. *Oh, look at those… I like the colour… but have you smelt it? I like the smell… the smell of fresh leather.* Wishful thinking on my behalf perhaps for a welcoming gesture from the seasoned residents. But I have exposed the shoes now, things are outside my control, I just need to leave the room, they can decide for themselves. And what about the shoes?

Yes, the shoes! They should be overwhelmed getting there… suddenly getting into the open in that room. Well, tough, this is part of growing old, you want to experience, and this is the experience for you!

I leave the room, go to the bathroom.

What a difference there is between the walls of… both of them are beige, both are silent, but are full of gossip. They murmur things to each other routinely, systematically. I am afraid of them, they are unreliable, they are full of stories. Things which are figments of their imagination, but they repeat them again and again to each other like a religious recital, and the words echo, get solidified in a strange manner and the outcome is clear, I'm condemned. But I have a sense of eagerness to hear what the walls say here in this hotel room. Perhaps, after all, I like gossip! Perhaps I like to hear them because they can't say much about me, not in this short interval of our acquaintance, but they will have all sorts of stories about people who have stayed there… perhaps have come back again.

I go to the bathroom; first a pause. The mirror is so large it has taken over half of the wall. I look at my face but ignore it fast, open my mouth and start to scrutinise my teeth. I take the toothpaste and toothbrush with the dark blue handle. I try to recall the different types, designs of toothbrushes. I tried to buy one the other day in the supermarket. The firmness or softness of the brush is a serious case to be considered. The curvature, the length, the width, of the handle is much easier to decide upon. I start brushing my teeth with the new toothpaste. I hope this one is not as abrasive as the last one. And then I imagine those people, and I have seen them, who brush and go. They don't rinse their mouth. Can you imagine? The small bits and pieces of left-over food mixed with the toothpaste formed into foam. And they swallow it.

Did I bother about this, when we used to sit around the big black table in the university coffee shop? Did I care if Ana had toothpaste in her mouth or had brushed her teeth at all? Now I think beyond the walls of this room, the hotel is silent, but as the morning light shows itself faintly through the closed curtains, I imagine Ana waking up… I imagine her standing in front of the mirror, perhaps with a pause. Does she ask herself why she has come all the way here? Then she takes the toothbrush and the toothpaste. The image freezes, and I look at the wall facing me with a sly smile.

All I wanted was to see how my folks have done over these years. But now, sitting in this room everything seems complicated. I need to energise myself to get ready to go out. I know… I know… once out, I'll be OK, the problem is me behind this door and me, with the time shredded into pieces, outside the door.

-21-

I often wonder about skin; it carries hidden stories of one's life. As if events, like particles of dust, imprint themselves in it. Concealed in this cover, our past lives walk around with us; when we shake hands, put a kiss on someone's skin, a hidden dialogue takes place through the touch, the skin whispers without us hearing. Sitting in the back room of the bookshop overseeing the main hall where the books are displayed in a central hall on tables leading to the corridors of books stacked in rows, I wonder what makes the skin attractive. I suppose, in a sense, my job is like that of a greengrocer… or a cashier in a corner shop who watches people coming in the shop, look around, buy things and leave. There are the usual customers and then odd ones who appear on the scene only once and then disappear; they might not be noticed at all, but sometimes, these entities… items… leave their own marks behind. The marks stay for days, sometimes forever. I remember them all. And it is not even strange to me that they enter my life, persist, and eventually stay there, permanently. The marks… the images… stay with me, stand next to me as I close the shop, walk with me home. They have their own style in staying with me. Some keep their distance, some come closer, but although they keep absolute silence, as if they vowed not to utter a word, I know what they want to say… all is there under that skin which has, very comfortably, placed itself in the image. It is not that they have amazing stories to tell, which they might have from time to time; it is the small sentences… phrases that they want to share with me, and perhaps with others. And these occupy my life; all to do with the whisper of skins. I look at faces, but it is the skin that confesses the totality of someone, not only as you see them, but as their life-story is entwined in them… a comprehensiveness of desires condensed in an expression that I cannot describe.

I watch the customers coming in, some determined, most in a leisurely fashion, go to the rack of books, take a book and get immersed in the words while, more often than one might imagine, they are followed by another person, unknown to them, watching them at a distance. And I know this is the work of the skin. These stalkers are harmless, while they take continuous mental notes; they enrich their life with those short sentences. But I don't need to follow anyone, or anything, they come to me.

So, I do ask myself why I decided to join this reunion. My life is rich enough not to want to know about Ana or Colin or Frank. My flat is full of images all the time. It is not that I am short of occupied moments in my life, what they consider to be the life of a "sad lonely man". I did think about it on the train coming over, looking through the side windows. As the country scenery passed me by, I remembered the images, and it was clear to me that they had played their role in me being on that train to the reunion, but why did they insist on proving their existence while present all the time?

-22-

Coming in, looking into my eyes, Ana says she is already bored, that it was a mistake for her to come all the way to this cold dreary place. Her long fingers with red varnish hide in her hair as she moves back her head to lean it on the sofa.

'What can I get you?' I ask.

'Just a glass of water, please.'

'Ice?'

'That would be nice.'

All those images that are moving quietly around me, disappear in Ana's movement as she holds the glass of water in her hand, her skin replacing silent images with sentences I can decipher trying to hide under the coldness of the glass of water.

'Ah, I needed this,' she says, smiling. She looks at her watch.

'What time is it? My watch seems to have stopped.'

Her watch is working perfectly, it is just that she wonders why she has come to my room and what she should do now.

'Have you read Dante?' I ask.

'What?'

'Have you read Dante?'

I see she is puzzled now.

'What's this question? Don't you have a better question to ask?'

'I remember you liked mystical writings,' I say.

'And Dante is a mystical writer? But I'm impressed you remember my interest.'

'I haven't forgotten things to try to remember them!'

She smiles.

'But things change, life takes you to landscapes you might not have particularly planned to go to,' she says.

'I hope not to purgatory,' I laugh.

'Yes, I agree, hell is a preferred option.'

I think she was in purgatory a minute ago… *what am I doing here…*

'But we go through all the stations all the time, don't you think?'

'Sometimes… but very often we stay in one for a long time,' she says.

'Have you been staying in one since we left university?' I ask.

'I haven't left any event since I remember… even before university.'

'This is intense.' I say it without believing it.

'I know. I think I wasn't decisive from the start; my mother loved to repeat to anyone she met, how many hours she was in labour until eventually they decided to do a caesarean,' she continued. 'I always thought she was indebted to me... I had provided her with something to talk about... drama in the boring life that she had; I suppose I am paying back for it. I have been paying back for it for a very long time... can I have another glass of water?' Ana asks.

I bring her the water, but I forget to add ice to it. She drinks it silently.

She has decided now, she stands up.

'Better be going.'

'You see, can't remain indecisive all the time,' I say.

'I guess you are right.' She picks up her bag sitting on the bed; it's red and small compared to the bags I see all the time these days. As she leaves, she says, 'I should've stayed.'

I don't say anything. She smiles and leaves.

I go back to the sofa and sit there looking at the glass of water she drank from. She hasn't finished it. I stay on the sofa. There is complete silence; there are no sentences and no images. Then there is a faint noise of a people passing through the corridor, and I go to sleep.

-23-

Have I been asleep all day? It's just a flicker of the eye. I am sitting on the sofa in the lobby and Ana is walking out of the lift while I think about Frank, his cough, his smile as I was talking to Ana… he is so dignified. What made *him* come all the way down here in the middle of winter? If he had any special relationship with any of us, I don't remember. Yet, he has coughed his way to be here with us. It seems it is just enough for him to see us, to see us moving around, talking, just being here around him. I think he, in a strange way, enjoys his state, both physical and mental. It is not a case of feeling sorry for himself, it is not a case of attention seeking either. I didn't ask about his family.

Ana sits across the coffee table. The waiter comes over. A button from his green uniform is missing and he keeps his left hand on the uniform clumsily to hide it. Ana asks for tea. I wonder how she could ask for tea when, only ten minutes ago, we came out of the breakfast room. I shake my head, saying I don't want anything, and look at Ana with disapproval.

'I wonder if Frank has married at all,' I ask Ana.

'He did, his wife left him a couple of years ago, just before he was diagnosed.'

'He should've had a hard time.'

'One thinks so, but apparently not, not at all. Actually, he started going to play tennis again, as if nothing had happened,' Ana said.

'So you have been in touch with him.'

'On and off, yes… more so recently.'

'But you weren't that close at university.'

'No, but you know how things are… you are walking in the street one day and you see a familiar face… a familiar smile, that dignified smile you know from somewhere… he comes closer and you say hello exactly as he says hello. You know then that you know each other.'

'It all seems romantic.'

'Not at all; actually, very comfortably real.'

'You mean romance cannot be real?'

'I suppose it can… I am not familiar with that scene. I deal with day-to-day issues. I prefer to see things in their context.'

'I'm not sure what you mean,' I say.

'If you work in an office dealing with people's daily problems, you don't have much time for romance.'

'You don't need to have a relationship to understand romance… to be romantic,' I say.

'In my line of work, to be able to do something, you need to deal with flesh and blood, to deal with skin… all the time you live in a state of reality check.'

'I am not sure if I know what you do,' I say.

'I am not sure myself,' she laughs. 'I am a counsellor.'

'Unbelievable,' I say.

'You think so? You think I am not made for it?'

'No, no, just that I suppose I am fixated on our university images,' I say.

'What would you expect me to be, then?'

'A lady of leisure… enjoying yourself… travelling… I don't know.'

'I do a bit of that, these are not mutually exclusive, you know,' Ana says.

'I suppose so; perhaps I was shocked when you said you deal with flesh and blood,' I said.

'And you thought I was a butcher!'

'Now, don't be silly; I thought you were a surgeon.'

'Perhaps surgeons deal with equipment, body parts… but when you sit there and listen to the people who come to you, talk with you about their life, that's when you see the flesh opening up, the invisible skin giving way to blood! That's when you see the obscure blood flowing, you see the blood that has flowed for years.'

She had a sip of the tea.

'This is cold.'

And then I saw Frank walking towards us. He appeared remarkably better than last night.

'May I join you?' he said.

'Please do,' I said. Ana was putting the cup on the table.

The eyelids move. There is no need for conversation. As if the stamps in his shop send texts to the books in my shop as we are sitting here looking at each other's eyelids.

'You know, I always wanted to get together with you, I mean with all the people of those years,' Frank says.

'And what do you think about it now?' Ana asks.

'Just seeing you, looking at your faces after so many years is amazing, the changes… I am yet to talk to you in any meaningful way, though.'

'You might be in for a long wait,' Ana said. 'You have gone quiet suddenly.' She looked at me.

'Just listening. I am not sure why I came over,' I said.

'Really? But do you have to have a reason for everything?' she said.

'You mean things are there just for the sake of it?' I asked.

'Yes,' Ana said.

Frank's face brightened with a delightful smile. Maria and Helen were coming over to us.

'It is getting better,' Helen said, approaching us. She just pulled out a chair and sat next to Ana. Maria was standing.

'Don't you want to join us?' asked Ana.

'Is it OK? I don't want to disturb your—'

'We weren't having a top-secret meeting,' Ana laughed.

'Maria is so prim and proper it gets boring,' Helen said, curling her right foot under her on the chair.

'So, what's the plan for the day?' asked Frank.

'Colin is dealing with it; I think we will be going for a long hill-walk,' Helen said.

'This time of year?' asked Ana.

'Yeah, all was in the e-mail,' said Maria.

'I guess we all live in hope. Look at the weather,' Ana said.

'The sun has come out, it will be a nice day out here,' said Frank.

'Are you going with them then?' asked Ana.

'Yes, doing something different,' said Frank.

'What is it that everyone wants to do something different? What's wrong with enjoying the warmth of the room, having tea – OK, whisky – watching those cold branches from inside?' Ana said.

'Nothing's wrong with that, but it's not enough to be content with "nothing being wrong",' I said.

'So, Mr. Adventurous is talking now?' said Helen.

I said nothing.

'Some people are fixated on their university image, but fail to deliver,' Helen continued.

Colin arrived in full gear, rainproof overcoat, thick gloves and a woolly hat in his hand.

'Come on, folks, it is ten sharp – ready to go?'

'Well, people are having second thoughts,' said Helen.

'You are not serious! It's beautiful out there,' Colin said. 'Which people?'

'Ana and Adam,' said Helen.

'Well, Roy is waiting outside. I'll be waiting with him for whoever wants to join us. We'll wait ten minutes tops, go get the right gear! I guess Maria and Frank are coming too?'

Colin started leaving. Frank stood up.

'Are you sure you want to go?' Ana asked Frank.

'It might be good for me,' Frank replied.

'Stay with us,' I said, assuming Ana didn't want him to go.

'Yes, stay with us, we shall go to the town,' Ana said.

'No, better be going with them, you have a good time in town.'

And the three of them walked away; there was silence. Ana and I sat there saying nothing. And the silence kept us both busy. We didn't try to resist it, so it went on for a long time. Looking outside, the party had left. From inside, it was as if it was a cold gloomy day outside. Then Ana said, 'Going to the town then?'

'If that's what you want,' I said.

'Better go to the town, she said.

'I'll call a taxi.'

It was only a ten-minute taxi ride, but most of it was through the countryside, the narrow road spiralling through tall hedges, then suddenly passing by a couple of garages to arrive at the town. We got off at a small square, the bottom end of the main street.

'This is where you want to be, anywhere you need to see starts from here, just go a hundred yards and then turn left, that's about it,' the taxi driver said.

We started walking down the street, and then turned left, faithfully following what the taxi driver said. We would have walked anywhere. It seemed the silence was following us. We stopped by the shops, window shopping, small souvenir shops with worthless pieces hanging from the ceiling and placed on large tables. We walked through an apparently new shopping arcade with modern shops, bright windows; something unusual for a small town.

The arcade's floor was coloured marble throughout the two-storey building with several fashion shops; the famous names, a big jewellery shop, two coffee shops and an antique shop – this one, I thought, was very strange in this place. The arcade was very cold with only a few people walking through. Some shopkeepers were paging through popular magazines like a timed ritual. We walked silently, on the ground floor, stopped in front of the shop windows in a strange harmony, and then walked through the wide stairway to the next floor. There were more fashion shops, of less stature, a big restaurant, a tailor shop, a vegetarian café and a hairdresser where two girls in white uniform were talking under halogen light.

'Coffee?' I asked.

'Not in this vegetarian café, whatever it means,' Ana said.

We ended up downstairs in the smaller coffee shop.

'Two cappuccinos,' I said.

'And an almond croissant,' Ana added.

We sat at a rectangular light pine table with a metallic tissue paper holder. The tissues were thin and small with a crispy sound as you cleaned your hands.

'This croissant is too oily,' Ana said.

'Do you want something else?' I asked.

'No, just wanted to have something with the coffee.'

We stayed silent a bit longer.

'I was surprised that Frank decided to go with the gang,' I said.

'He thought fresh air would do him good,' Ana said.

'And it brings him pneumonia… the state he is in.'

'You exaggerate, he is fine; you seem more concerned than he is,' Ana said.

'You think so?'

'Yes, there are too many preconceived ideas about cancer,' she said. 'It is good he doesn't see you every day, not good for his recovery.'

As she was talking, I started looking around the shop; something I never do back home. But here, with a feeling of isolation, I seemed unpredictable to myself. The walls were painted light yellow; there were mugs for sale with patterned flowers and some castles printed on them, transparent packs of fudge, local cheese and bottled herbs. There were some flyers on the counter advertising country pub walks, a local performance of *Twelfth Night* and a small wind band. I stood up.

'I need to go there,' I smiled. 'I'll be back soon.'

'I hope so,' Ana laughed.

As I was standing in the toilet, I had an image of the cloudy day outside drizzling. Had I come miles away from my bookshop to be standing here in this cold toilet while Ana was waiting? There was a dripping noise from the tap and the hand drier cloth roller had jammed. I looked at my face in the mirror before going out.

'So, what do we do now?' I smiled.

'Nothing much I suppose, perhaps we could just walk about in the centre, have lunch and go back.'

'Seems reasonable,' I said.

Just the thought of walking beside her alone with nobody else around could keep me busy for days. Now with our skins dehydrated, her hair tired and mine mostly grey, things are different. It seems that particles of time have settled deep into our flesh, and as blood follows its route dutifully but not as smoothly as before, our desires have surrendered themselves to the passage of time… have decided to sleep under the dust of memories… and as this blanket gets thicker and thicker the voices of the old wounds come out only as a whisper from time to time. Ah, those eyes I remember… that smile… and look at those fingers I loved to touch.

As we walk, the mall gets busier. Young mothers with their children in pushchairs stop to wrap up their children tighter, old women walk slowly going to the hairdresser and teenagers are sitting in coffee shops chatting away. There are hardly any men here, and as for the women, there is a big age gap. What does that young woman do all day? Her dialogue is mainly with the child who cannot speak yet; it is a one-sided dialogue. The other side responds with a muted glance, but when it gives a hint of a smile, the hormone-release in the woman is a flurry of joy, there is a biochemical revolution in her that keeps her going. And she then takes the baby home, unpacks the shopping, tells herself how the handle of the pushchair can be useful for hanging shopping bags, pours herself a cranberry juice and takes the baby out of the pushchair.

The thought comes back again – what am I doing here? I have promised myself to visit at least one museum every year, one museum in a different country – and this year? I have betrayed myself. *What am I doing here?* This looks like a nightmare; instead of walking up and down an obscure, intriguing museum, I am walking down a mall in a cold wet provincial town. Yes, I am walking with someone I loved to walk with, but that was years ago; yes, this is a mismatch of desire and eventuality of what happens to the long-awaited desires. The repeated speculations ruin the moment when it arrives years later. Now, I miss the silence in the museum rooms, the unseen, unheard chaos of the noises in the onlookers' minds as they stand in front of a piece, walk past it, admiring it, ridicule it, try to interpret it – all in silence – and then someone drops a book, a momentary break in the silence. I miss all that in this moment, not Ana's hands that I so much loved to touch, just a breeze of her skin.

'I'm glad I came over,' Ana says, 'aren't you?'

'It all happened suddenly, I must say; I am still trying to adjust myself,' I say.

'Adjust yourself? To what? What a big deal! It's just a short trip for goodness' sake. You've seen me now, after such a long time, is it not exciting?' She smiles.

'That's for sure,' I say, 'it wouldn't have happened if I'd had time to mull it over, though.'

'Are you always so intense? Those times, I used to put it down to your shyness,' she said.

As we walk, we go through the tunnel of smell again, the whiff of egg and bacon lingering in the wet.

Ana stops at a shop window. It is a knickknack shop.

'What?' she asks me as I look at her, 'you think I shouldn't stop here?'

'I think you have a reason for it,' I say.

'Ah! Now you are talking, you think I am a calculating person?'

'No, just thought you want to buy something for a niece or something.'

'Do I really look like a person so domesticated?'

'I don't see anything wrong with that.'

'Well, I do. If I wanted to get involved with that sort of thing… I would be mother to a university student by now, I wouldn't need to look at fluffy bears.'

The small bear was sitting in the corner of the window; all the toys, bits and pieces were in good shape. I could imagine the old woman standing inside the shop leaning towards the window would clean them meticulously every day.

'Do you like the bear?' I asked.

'No!'

This had a ring of her youth; I remembered her defiance when people asked her something and she would simply say no with a sense of victory.

She said no, and yet stayed in front of the shop window. The old woman came out, smiling.

'Would you like to have a closer look, dear? Why don't you come in?' she asked Ana.

And Ana went in; she didn't even look at me. I followed her.

'How long have you been working in this shop?' she asked the old lady.

'Oh, since my husband died some thirty… thirty-five years ago, dear,' she smiled. 'I was a woman of leisure then; but it all happened so suddenly… anything catch your eye?'

'I am just looking; I suppose the shop wasn't like this then,' Ana said.

'Oh, no! There was no shopping mall then,' she laughed, 'but I survived all the changes; they are about to make a gym here now. I might sell this and go… go somewhere nice and warm after all.'

'Isn't it a pity to lose the shop, with all its memories?' Ana asked.

'You don't need to have a shop to keep your memories, dear, but you always lose some and you gain some. This is the name of the game; some people learn it too late. I hope I have got the message eventually, just in time.' She laughed again.

'Could I see that?' Ana showed the woman an item on the glass shelf.

'Of course, dear.' The woman took a small key from the pocket of her light blue woollen jumper and opened the glass cover of the shelf. She took out carefully the elliptic pendant and kept it in her open hand.

'This was brought here two years ago, and the reason I remember it so well is the young girl who brought it here.' She closed her hand.

'She was a thin girl, perhaps twenty, twenty-five, not more than that. She gave it to me and said take it. What?

I said. She repeated, take it. This is for you to keep. No, no, no, I said. It doesn't work like this, young lady, I said. Let me have a good look and then you tell me how much you want for it. But, no! She said you can have a look at it as much as you like, that's yours. Of course the first thing I thought of was drugs. I thought the poor girl was on something, but she didn't want money for it. But why? I asked her. She said that's the price you give me for it. You pay me by not asking. This is the price! She smiled and left, so fast I couldn't thank her for it. So I kept it here, wasn't sure to sell it or not. Then I told myself if someone asks me, I will tell them the same thing. You see? It is beautiful.' She opened her hand.

'You can get a better chain for it, but the pendant itself is gold with fine carving.'

Ana took it from her and had a close look. She wore it and looked at me.

'What do you think?' she asked me.

'Well, it looks beautiful,' I said. 'I agree… a new chain will make it look even better.'

'How much?' asked Ana.

The woman smiled.

'You know how much it is, my dear,' she continued. 'The price for you is not to ask!'

'But—' Ana started.

I interrupted her. 'Perhaps you have a good necklace that could go with it? I would be interested,' I said.

'Well, of course I have, my dear,' the woman answered. She opened a drawer and in it, very carefully, a range of necklaces of different sizes were laid out.

I went around the stall and looked at them.

'What about that one?' I asked Ana.

'It is really nice, but—'

I interrupted her again.

'We shall have that one.'

'You have good taste,' the woman said, looking at me.

'I am discovering it,' I said with a smile.

'Do you want me to wrap it?' she asked.

I looked at Ana.

'No, I'd like to wear it.'

'We shall keep the old chain though. It will be a good reminder.'

We came out, and walked towards the corner of the mall and the main street.

'A very practical woman,' Ana said.

'Sometimes events drive you to become practical… but I think she was both practical and romantic,' I said.

'I still think when the shop goes, the memories go with it; you are a hopeful man! What's the use sitting somewhere reading a paper, washing a cup, then suddenly remembering the shop? When you have lost it, you have lost it… no matter how much you try to convince yourself. Perhaps all that remain are the agonies,' Ana said.

'But you are selective here, if you have the sorrows, you have the joys as well,' I said.

'Maybe… but all these are somewhere you cannot put your hands on. When there is a shop, you know you will get up early enough to get there in time to open the doors, dust the counter, tidy up things, wait for customers to arrive; but what is that momentary thing you call memory? That is a disturbance, an escape from the moment at hand.'

'I guess this is where we differ. Memories for me are alive, they are part of the moment; they are not impositions... memories wait there, listen to what we say, see what we do, and they wait patiently for the right moment to express themselves,' I said.

'I'm not sure if I understand you... these are all airy-fairy to me,' Ana said, 'but the woman knew what she wanted.'

'She was a woman of stories.' I hinted at the necklace that Ana was wearing now.

'I really like this, thank you for it, there was no need.'

'It was *my* need,' I said. 'There was a peculiar thing about the whole encounter there, don't you think so?'

'Perhaps,' she said, 'but still, you didn't need to buy me the—'

'That was my need, as I said.'

'You are a strange man,' she said.

'Maybe I have strange ways of expressing myself, but I am not a strange man.' I smiled.

'A bit early, but perhaps we could grab something to eat,' I said. 'It is getting colder.'

'Yes, I wonder if it will snow tonight,' Ana said.

-24-

It was early for lunch, but the restaurant was half-full already. We sat by the wall and the waiter had to squeeze himself to pass by our table and the one next to us. As he was passing, he put a couple of menus on our table. We hung our coats on the back of the wooden chairs. Ana's long black coat with fur collar swept the floor. She took the menu. 'I am not sure why I am so hungry, it is too early for lunch,' she said.

'Eat when you're hungry, sleep when you're sleepy, these are the wise words we've heard,' I said.

Ana laughed. 'You are a teacher by nature. I don't care that you have a bookshop, you are a teacher.'

'I didn't want to lecture…' I said.

'No, I know, it's just that there is a big difference between what the wise say and practicalities. Socrates said if you need to go, do it even if you are in a bazaar! Well, everyone knows it is a relief to let go when you need to, but there are circumstances that dictate themselves to us… oh, I love pork belly!' she said, looking at the menu.

The waiter came over. Ana looked at him with a smiling face.

'I'd like the pork belly, please,' she said.

'Could I take the drinks order first, please?'

'Oh, that's easy,' she said, looking at me, 'red and sparkling?'

'Yes, we'll have a bottle of sparkling water and a bottle of house red,' I said.

'And I'll have the pork belly!' Ana said.

'Sorry, we don't have pork belly today,' the waiter said impatiently.

'Oh, what a pain… what will *you* have?' Ana asked me.

'I was thinking of a club sandwich,' I said.

'Boring!' Ana said, and looked at the waiter, who looked indifferent.

'OK, I'll have a club sandwich, too.'

As the waiter was leaving, I said, 'But you don't need to have it, there are other dishes.'

'I cannot be bothered,' Ana said, and continued, 'somebody said do what you want when you want.'

I laughed. 'And? I can see protest is coming my way.'

'It's obvious, isn't it? I wanted my pork belly, I didn't get it!'

'And?' I said.

'You portray a life without any problems, you want it – you have it! But even on that Socrates "Bazaar-relief" case,' she laughed, 'I bet you are unable to do it, you cannot have what you want… you won't do what you want!'

'I agree with you, but that is desirable.'

'What is desirable? For whom? For you, maybe; although I doubt it too. Fancy doing it while people are looking at you with disgust!' she continued, 'and… and… I am sure it is not desirable for the one who witnesses it or gets a hint of the splash!' She laughed again, she was angry.

I poured the wine for her and myself. 'Let's drink to us. I am so happy you came, I wasn't sure till the last moment if the whole idea was interesting to you.'

Her eyes have the old shine, even now with the wrinkles around them. Her eyelids look heavier, have lost some eyelashes… and her fingers holding the glass… they look thinner with the dry skin… what's so different since thirty years ago when we first met?

'I wasn't sure whether to come at first, then, I don't know… it was something about the past, perhaps hope of reliving at least some moments of it,' Ana said.

'And have you?'

'No, not really, it is like an old wound, there is a crust and you are here to scratch it off… you don't know why, you know if you do, it will start bleeding but still there is an urge to do it. And eventually, when it has all healed, there is a scar!' she said.

'For me, it is to do with the desires, where do they go?'

'Oh,' she smiled, 'that is easy, haven't you heard? There is a planet where they end up. They don't need a spacecraft, and they don't get affected by time as they go faster than light. They reside on that planet, they have no problems living there, but the point is, when they go there, they start their own life, so much so that if they come back, they will be unrecognisable by us. They are young and refreshed while they are there, but if they come back, their skin cracks, their blood becomes red dust.' She had a gulp of her drink and took my hand. 'Adam, I know what you are living with, better leave it on that planet, it is best.'

'Oh, this is so biblical, is that a paradise you pictured?' I asked.

And her hair? A dark shiny brown, dyed in a hairdresser she has known for years I suppose. A transition from long black to shorter brown a statement about thirty years' gap. Yet the combination of the skin, the hair, and the way she moves about… is her, is Ana fixed in time; this is for me, and I know this is only for me, my experience.

This entity of the past vacillates, disappears in Ana sitting across the table and reappears confidently, she carries with herself untouchable long hair! Ana looks at me, and I have the assurance that I can caress her hair any minute now if I wish to, say something, and hear something back. But with that entity, everything is so elusive. I caress her untouchable hair, in a daze, I feel the softness of the long black hair, the mixed smell of her hair with her skin, and yet I cannot say how or why, I relate, but the elusive image leaves me when Ana starts talking.

'It wasn't bad… the sandwich,' she says.

I was suddenly relocated to the realm of flesh and sounds. I poured some wine for myself. I forgot to fill her glass.

'It will be even better with a glass of wine,' she smiled.

'Oh, I am sorry,' I poured the wine for her, 'let's drink to old wounds,' I said.

'We are grown up now, no need to be melodramatic!' she said.

'Are we so drawn up into the world of logic that we cannot afford moments of emotion?' I said.

'You are continuing to be melodramatic,' she said. 'Sure, we can have the emotions, we are here now, aren't we?'

It was the time for silence, and it came so naturally, not only to me, but also to her. We both turned our eyes to the door of the café.

'OK, we had our one-minute silence, to remember the past,' she said. 'Now, time for the pudding!'

Her eyes looked childish, but my silence was continuing with my smile and my words to the waiter, who came with the menu again without us asking him to do so.

'A sticky toffee pudding for me and a spoon for him,' she laughed and showed me to the waiter.

'Thanks for making my life easy,' I said.

'It is not always easy to remember things. When you call them, they do not come alone, they come with their baggage,' Ana said.

'Now who is melodramatic?' I said.

'You do not need to be revengeful in your old age,' Ana said. 'Be kind to me.'

'I wasn't, and what has it got to do with my age?' I said.

'We have less time for good things, so we should spend the moments wisely,' she said.

'I am trying,' I said, as I was pushing the spoon into the pudding, 'but as you can see, I have a problem.'

'What's that?' Ana asked, taking a spoonful to her mouth.

I pointed to the cake. 'Believe me, I do want to have a new start, but each time I try, something stops me.'

'And this time is a hard cake?' she asked.

'You know me,' I said.

'Yes, you are your own enemy, you were your own enemy, and you are now,' she said.

'How do you say that?'

'Everything seems to be a struggle for you, not an opportunity to try, you are too proud,' she said.

I was standing under the old plane tree. And she was sitting on the wooden bench next to me. The night was summer. The trees were summer. Her body was a summer breeze in her light outfit, and her face asked for a word from my skin. Oh, I kept silent, silent through frozen moments, and the summer was short. Now that I remember it, it was too short for me to grow up, to grasp, to hold the smell of her hair in that pulsating night.

'I know you are right, but it is not a case of pride, it's a case of lost chances, events gone; and it is a case of mismatch between the desires of the moment… the totality of the moment, and what goes on in your heart. Now every move I make is shaky. I don't know if it's me who does things or it's me following a line of dust on a windy day,' I said.

'Have you considered writing?' she said.

'Why is it that the moment I start talking about my feelings, people tell me to write?'

'Oh, I thought these were the impulses of the moment… that you are sharing your feelings with me, not that you had rehearsed them several times before with others,' she said.

'You prove me right,' I said, 'I'd better keep silent.'

'Now we are going to ruin a lovely day, and so easily,' she said.

'No, I am enjoying it very much, even this non-sticky, sticky pudding,' I said.

'I have to agree with you here; this is more like dried-up chocolate than sticky toffee.' She laughed.

'Time to go?' I asked.

'If you like,' she said, looking at me.

This is the way they are; once they get hold of your emotions, your sensitive point, you've had it. That's when they start looking at you with a loving glance; putting their hands under their chin glaring at you. And you think you have found new love. You might think it's too simplistic, but it's true.

In the taxi going back, we didn't talk. Ana was looking out of the window, and I was looking at the winding narrow road as the taxi driver drove through it as if he was driving on his private drive with a guarantee that no car would come the other way; and it didn't.

-25-

Frank was walking in the front garden of the hotel when we arrived. The small snowflakes looked suspended in the air with a cold breeze, and it was much colder than in the morning when we left.

'He looks like someone with plans, walking like that,' Ana said.

'Good afternoon, good people!' said Frank.

'You need to be inside, not out!' Ana said.

'Fresh air is good for you,' said Frank.

'How much fresh air do you need? How was the hill-walk? You must've had enough of it,' Ana asked.

'Oh, well… very good… as expected. Colin has put lots of effort into this get together.'

'So, are you staying out there? We are going in,' Ana said.

'I can come in with you now, I've had sufficient fresh air,' said Frank.

'Who's the lazy one?' I asked, laughing, as I saw Colin on the sofa in the hotel lobby with a pint of beer in his hand.

'Look who's speaking; you missed a good walk. I'm here to enjoy myself in this glorious, wet, cloudy, muddy place. I don't care, soon it will end,' Colin said.

'We had a good walk in the town, it's only a few miles away,' Ana said. 'There is a big mall…'

'You've seen one, you've seen them all; what's so special about a small town up north? I guess your highlight of the day was a cup of tea in a new arcade,' Colin said.

I laughed. 'Not far from reality, Colin, but good to see it anyway.'

'If you say so. I like my beer,' Colin said, 'sipping away in quiet.'

'I see that. You could do that back at home anyway,' Ana said.

'Why don't you join me?' Colin said. 'Don't just stand there.'

We both sat next to him. Frank was still standing.

'We can squeeze, come Frank, sit next to me. Adam is sitting too wide!' she laughed.

'Actually, I need to go up, will be back soon,' I said, standing up. 'Don't go anywhere!' I laughed.

I open the tap and put my head under it, with difficulty. I let the water run. What do I want from myself? What was I doing in that mall, in here, miles away from my flat? I could be lying on my bed, reading the newspaper, I could have a cup in my hand toying with the idea to go to the Saturday market… buy some cheese, perhaps a pot of basil for the kitchen window… one leaf a week when I make my customary pasta, my beloved ritual… Oh… I have acted as a fool coming here. I don't blame Ana for wondering why I have come, that is, if she even thinks about it… probably not! The water is still going, now getting warmer – it took so long for it to get warm – all this piping in the large hotels. Why did we come here anyway? What was wrong with a nice cosy bed and breakfast? It's all Colin, isn't it? With his loud voice… and we all went with the idea. You know what? It's because we are lazy. Him and his pint o' beer! Better get back to the lobby… as if they are waiting for me! Come to think about it, my life is the bookshop. Who cares if everything goes – has gone – digital? I will stick to the books. There are still some people interested in taking the books in their hands… to carry the books with them, to feel the weight of the book, feel the books getting old in their hands, in their suitcases. Mind you, there are other people too… people who treat the books as if they are a piece of jewellery. The books in their hands are newer than the time they bought it! I wonder how they eat, how they sleep, how they sleep with someone. Any fun, my dear? Have you creased your underwear? Hah… can you imagine? Ana, have you met them? How would you respond to them? I close the tap. The bathroom is steamed up.

Returning fast to the lobby, as I was going down, I saw Ana standing up.

'I'm going to bed,' she said.

I said, 'What? Now?'

'Yes, any objections?' she laughed.

'I thought we were going to have a gathering, all of us, now that Colin is here, all are bound to converge!' I said.

'Not really,' Colin said, 'I'm off too.'

'Ah!' I said, and sat next to Frank on the wide sofa.

It had started to drizzle again.

I watched Colin leaving.

'There is something – I don't know what – about the dark, cloudy days,' I said.

'Romantic, eh?' said Frank.

'You are right, perhaps that's it, but I can't imagine some people being romantic on any occasion. Take Colin, for example, can you imagine him in a romantic scene? Can you?' I asked.

'Well, appearances could be misleading.' Frank coughed. 'Are you a romantic?' he asked.

'Well, hum… it means a different thing to different people.'

'Well, exactly… but this is just an innocent question, didn't mean to pry,' he said.

'I don't mind, it's just that I want to give an accurate answer,' I said.

'OK, I'd say, most people are… some hide it, they think it's adolescent stuff, some are not even aware of it, but they are romantics. Have you noticed how excited Colin is? I know he talks loudly, and behaves abruptly, but I think he doesn't know what to do with himself now that he is here. Don't forget he was the one who suggested and arranged it all,' Frank said.

'Yes, I know what you mean.'

'In my view, being loud has become a personality trait for him, but it's also a hiding mechanism, a protest against being a romantic.'

'Some psychology, eh? Have you thought of taking a course?'

'I think most people are, nowadays, some sort of a psychologist, that's why psychology courses are so popular,' Frank said.

'And are *you* a romantic?' I asked him.

'Oh, so you want to hear a story!' He leaned back in the chair, and smiled. 'You know, after university, I was in a state. I needed a change. Ana had told me about Iran, and I was fascinated. I don't know why, exactly, it was all a feeling, perhaps more my imagination of something I had desired. To get away from it all… to see another part of the world… and Ana, of all people, strangely, had described it to me. I had read something about it, the poetry, the wine, the gardens, the deserts, and of course the people. So the next thing, I found myself in Tehran's busy streets going to a restaurant with a couple of people Ana had introduced. She had given me some contacts.

'They were a lovely couple, talkative and curious, proud to see a foreigner was interested in their culture. And I was captivated. I went there for a short holiday, but I stayed well over a year!'

'A year?' I asked, surprised.

'Yes, a year,' Frank replied.

Helen and Maria were talking, entering the lobby. They came straight to us.

'You look as if you're trying to explain a complex problem to an absent-minded student,' Helen laughed, looking at Frank.

'Hi folks, can we join you? I hope we are not bothering you?' Maria said.

'Oh, no, not at all. We are talking about Iran,' Frank said.

'What? Iran? Don't you have anything better to talk about?' Helen asked.

'It is a fascinating country, and when I went…' Frank said.

'What, you've been to Iran?' Helen asked.

'Yes.'

'How did you survive?' Maria asked.

'It was years ago, but you should ignore what you hear in the media. The mullahs are a breed of their own, nothing to do with Iranians. It is a country in siege. Anyway, I was…'

Helen interrupted Frank. 'Let's hope so! In any case you've been courageous. So what was your motivation?'

'Nothing particular, just travelling,' Frank said.

'We are coming from a trip of a kind too, walking up the hills. I must tell you all about it!' Helen laughed.

'So, tell us all!' I said.

'You should've come! This was a "once in a lifetime" chance!' Helen said.

'This looks ominous!' I said.

'Indeed,' said Helen.

'Own up then,' I said.

'Just Colin walking, Roy making fun of him, and the punch-up.'

'What?'

'Yes, a punch-up on the cold hills of the snowy land!'

'Do you want to come out with it or not? You are being cagey,' I said.

'Not at all, look – we started to go up the hill over there. It looks close enough, but it's not, it's a good couple of miles away. By the time we arrived, Maria and I were exhausted.'

'I don't know how you did it,' I said.

'Yes, you were always at a loss,' Helen laughed.

'I mean with all that smoking,' I said.

'Only a few here, a few there, Adam, be kinder to yourself, you are too uptight,' Helen said.

Maria asked, 'Where is Ana?'

'They have already lost her – again!' Helen answered.

'She has gone to lie down for a bit,' Frank said.

'She was always delicate!' Helen smiled.

'So what have you been doing all these years?' I asked her.

'Making a man miserable, procreating twice, looking after my creations… I've been quite busy. What have *you* been up to?' Helen asked.

'Avoiding all that. Books are more attractive to me,' I said.

'Mm… I thought so, you are incurable,' Helen said.

'That's great, though,' Maria said. 'What sort of a bookshop? Specialist or general? Where is it?'

'Well, all sorts really, so you could say general, but with emphasis on fiction and travel. You should come and visit, it is quite central,' I said.

'I will,' Maria said.

'You were so intrigued to see what happened on the walk, and now you have forgotten about it,' Helen said, 'it's typical.'

'Talking of the devil!' I said.

Roy walked over. He had a handkerchief in his hand, wiping his nose. He looked at it, and quickly put it in his pocket.

'What's this punch-up people are talking about?' I asked.

He took a chair and sat next to Helen.

'Nothing much, a friendly reminder not to be too hasty accepting invitations to reunions!' he said.

'It seems everyone is getting a bit too dramatic!' Frank said.

'Helen was telling us what happened up there,' I said.

'He thinks he knows everything,' Roy said.

'Colin was just saying the way the business world is going, we will face another stock market crash,' Maria said.

'A load of university mumbo jumbo! He thinks he knows it all, he doesn't know a thing about business. Better stick to his maths and geography!' Roy said. 'And… and… he shouts all the time. The herd of sheep could hear him a couple of hills away.'

'So, you had to punch him!' Maria said.

'He wouldn't stop,' Roy said. 'I'm the one with a bloody nose.'

'And Colin is in bed I think, he went to his room, so unlike him,' Maria said.

'Let's not get too dramatic about it,' Helen said. 'Boys like a lively debate with occasional handiwork!' she laughed, looking at Frank.

'I think I need a short nap too, before the evening drinks!' Roy said. 'I'm off.'

Helen said, 'I'll be off too, then. Maria, are you coming?'

'Actually, good idea.'

I looked at Frank.

'Don't look at me! I should be the first one to go to bed, but I don't feel like it at all. What we started with – talking about Iran – has taken me far away,' Frank said.

'I don't feel like going to my room either,' I said. 'It's great you are here, Frank. I am so happy to have seen you again.'

Frank smiled.

'Drinks?' I asked.

'Why not? A very good idea, let's change the scenery, let's go to the bar.'

And we did. No one was there. A waiter saw us walking to the bar and came over.

'The bar is closed for now, but I can bring you drinks anywhere in the lobby if you like.'

'Oh, yes, please,' I said. We walked to a corner, and chose a small table with two armchairs.

'Can we have a couple of large whiskies?' I asked the waiter.

'Yes, of course, anything else?' he asked.

'Some nibbles, anything, but lots of it, please!' I smiled.

'No problem,' the waiter said.

We sat on the comfortable black leather chairs, silently looking at the empty small round tables. Then I said, 'Even in the winter, when there are not many people around, and there are not many varieties of flowers, they have put flowers on each table.'

'The flowers don't look happy, but you're right; a woman manager?' he asked.

'Or perhaps a business-minded man looking at flowers as a business opportunity!'

'Mm...' Frank responded, 'it is too easy to fall into what they classify... stereotypes, boxes...'

'I guess we do it all the time, it affects our relationships,' I said.

'But then, if someone is like you or me, he will see through it, perhaps in a hard way... but sooner or later.' Frank paused, then said, 'Do you know? Before coming here, I was thinking... I was thinking for a long time... it wasn't a very joyful train of thought. When you are alone, and you assess, revisit, your relationships that have passed you by, you come across things as if they have emerged from nowhere, but they have been with you all the time, eating you away, eating away silently pieces of your mind, your... your... whole being. And then you come face to face with it, saying to yourself, *I* am responsible, I am responsible for all that. For years, I was a martyr, I was the one who had the bad deal in relationships. But then one day I was rearranging the stamps, and then it came to me out of the blue, I found suddenly... I told myself, look, *you* are responsible. In all my relationships, I made people behave the way I liked them to behave, not the way they were, the way they wanted to be. I encouraged them to pretend to be someone else. A character in my dreams, but an artificial one, a façade created by me, by my subtle but unwitting impositions. And one day they had enough, the characters revolted. And I felt

I was betrayed, but I was the one who had deceived myself. I lived in a bubble, and it was inevitable that one day it would burst. What emerged from the bubble was a miserable martyr living in another bubble, this time a bubble I created to feel pity for myself.' Frank stopped to clear his chest with a cough. The he said, 'Once you see you were responsible, the pain starts to gradually penetrate into every bit of your body. You're sitting there watching people passing by, but something keeps telling you, how could you be like that? How could you behave that way? What were you thinking? It's like being put in a boxing ring with strict instructions to stand still to receive the blows… not to respond, not to escape. And the funny thing is that you feel better for it. Because eventually, you are physically so much in pain that you forget – only for some short moments – the feeling of guilt. And yes, it does come to your mind to seek forgiveness. But whom are you asking forgiveness from? Everyone? That's easy, put a column in the newspaper. "I would like to apologise to all those whom I hurt, I ask forgiveness… I apologise for making a mistake between you and the one I had created from you in my mind. I apologise for my arrogance, I didn't let you live the way you were, and I responded as if you were someone else!" But this is not it, is it? The point is *you* really need to forgive yourself in a relationship, not the other side. The other side has moved on, the events have gone, but you are sitting here with flesh and blood reminiscing about the past. Now, others are merely elements triggering your emotions, memories that hurt you. You need to come to terms with your emotions, your responses; and this hurts, and that's why it's so difficult to forgive. It is difficult because you want to remember the hurt, to blame yourself, to live in a condemned world. Yes, it's so soothing to hurt! You see, Adam, no matter what you do, you are condemned to suffer in pain.' Frank had a gulp of his whisky.

'Don't you think you are too hard on yourself?' I asked.

'If anything, to the contrary,' he said. 'We haven't seen each other for some years, Adam; properly anyway. So, you cannot say what I am. After coming back from Iran, I was very disorientated, to say the least… for some time. Days would pass me by as I sat in the shop gazing at the stamps without looking at them, only to have my stupor broken off, from time to time, by the ringing of the phone, a customer coming in asking for stamps of a certain ceremony, a certain occasion… and then I would go back to my mingled thoughts about my time in Iran. It wasn't much about Iran really, although I couldn't separate it from events, but it was mainly about her. Images… images of those moments kept coming back to me. Walking on busy streets, inhaling dry polluted air, she would tell me about what they called good old days, when sitting in beautiful air-conditioned coffee shops on summer days, which intellectuals frequented with copies of English newspapers under their arms, discussing Sartre and Camus, sipping their drinks. Imagining those days, we discussed classic music against pop, jazz against blues.

We listened to classic Persian music while she tried to translate the lyrics for me. I kept on seeing myself looking at her, thinking of her as the descendant of some forgotten king, reading a handwritten old book with broken spine, reciting poetry. Sitting in some characterless café, I almost always asked her, "Another coffee?" She would look at her watch and say, "OK, a quick one." Then – this time – she said, "Not really, no," and I didn't insist, just asked for the bill. Outside, I waved a taxi for her, and she left. Then I went for a long walk through the crowded streets of Tehran. By then I knew the streets, the ones I needed.

'Walking through the long street with the long row of old plane trees on the two sides, I remembered giving her a scarf; it had a navy blue pattern on a deep red background. "I bought it for you after the first time we met, but I didn't – just couldn't – give it to you," I told her, as we were walking in the park. She opened it, looked at it, and put it carefully in the same wrapping. "Get rid of the wrapping," I said. She didn't. "Thank you," she said, "but why didn't you give it to me earlier?"

"I don't know," I said.

"You weren't sure, were you?"

"It's not that, it's just…"

"Don't worry. I wonder why you give it to me *now*? I also had something for you then… but I threw it away." She looked at me with her eyes somewhere else, watching with hidden aversion. She repeated, "I threw it away," as if she wanted to make sure I had heard what she said.

'I didn't ask her why, or what it was.

'As we were walking, entering the park, I remembered the last time when we had met. I thought I was trying hard to keep us together; I didn't see how she tried, tried hard to get away.'

'So, what happened? Was that it?' I asked Frank. 'It sounds like a radio soap opera. The audience is impatient to know what happens next!'

Frank looked at me, smiling. 'You might say that, but it takes me away, somewhere somehow familiar, but far away as if you want to touch a bubble, and yet you don't in fear of bursting it.'

'Anyway, that *was* that. I left Iran shortly after that. We met a couple of times, but with other people around. In fact, I saw her husband at one of the get-togethers. He looked like a serious official, I think he worked in a bank or something like that, something to do with money. The last time I saw her, was actually at a party. I didn't tell her I was leaving, I told her on the phone the day after. I just phoned her to thank her for inviting me to that party, and then said, "Oh, by the way, I am off to London, tomorrow."'

'What did she say?' I asked.

'Nothing, nothing much; of course there was a silence. Then something like "Have a good trip back, keep in touch," one of those things you say, just to say something, but you don't mean it,' Frank said, 'and I didn't see her until, oh, some five, six years later in London. She had come over from the States for a short visit to see a family member, and we met for an early lunch. The restaurant wasn't busy, there was a nice sunny spot by the large window where we sat. She seemed jolly to me, but rather distant. She wore the same perfume she had worn years back in Iran. I had forgotten about it, but the images came back to me with that smell. "What have you been up to?" I asked her. She told me that she left Iran for the States soon after I left; that she ran a big travel agency with a friend of hers in the States with most of her customers wealthy Persians, travelling to the Caribbean or South America, and wealthy Americans travelling to Iran to rediscover the mysteries of 1001 nights! She said she was making good money, and insisted she was happy with her life. We exchanged some pleasantries like "You are very much in form", "I see you are keeping well too", "Can't complain". Clichés like that, then her face tightened. "Well, what doesn't kill you, makes you stronger, isn't it what you people say?" she asked me. I thought I was handling a delicate situation well, but suddenly I realised I was wrong. "Have things been that bad?" I asked her. "You should know, shouldn't you?" she asked. "Know what?" I asked. "Oh, come on! It was easy for you to fly out, you people always do, your motto is when things get difficult, move on," she said.

"I thought we were going nowhere. I thought *you* were seeking a way out," I said.

"*You* didn't want it to go anywhere... and you know it, don't pretend otherwise. Anyway, it was a difficult time for me," she said.

"I cannot understand, I really thought we had good times, you and I, but you didn't want to continue with it, for some reason," I said.

She had a sip of her red wine she had kept in both hands. "What reason?"

"Something you didn't want to share," I replied.

"I stand by the door. I have arrived home after we met, after those moments… the small lamp is on in the corner of the room with its faint light and he is sitting next to the lamp, reading. He does not raise his head, I do not ask how he is, how his day has been. I go to my room," she said.

"I don't understand, I thought it *was* the case, you didn't appear to be a typical married couple," I said.

"Oh yes, a very comfortable assumption. You forget it was *me* who, at the end of the day, had to go back, and tolerate the miserable atmosphere of that room," she said.

"Had to? What sort of a relationship was that then?" I asked her.

The waiter brought the starters.

I had a gulp of the wine; it was my favourite, but it felt sour.

"Is the wine OK?" I asked her.

"Perfect," she said, "as good as old times."

We paused and looked at the people around us. Then I asked, "So, what do you do these days?"

"I am a lady of leisure!" she said. "At last, doing something for myself."

"What happened to painting?" I asked her. "Do you still paint?"

"Oh, I do sometimes." She paused. "Only when I tell myself pull yourself together!" I thought obviously she has thrown away all her painting gear.

"So, nothing to complain, but you seem to carry a lot of heavy baggage in your leisure," I said.

"Better say scars, do you know? Scars never go away. The wounds heal, but leave a reminder. You can leave your baggage in a waiting room, and forget about it," she said.

I had another sip of the wine.

"You don't seem to like it," she hinted at the wine.

"It doesn't have the good taste it had."

"Why have it? Order something else, you men are good at it."

"It is good to experience the sour taste!" I said.

"You have become courageous in your old age, but punishing yourself is not a way to redemption, no matter how much you believe in it," she said.

"Old age?"

"OK, middle age. Some say nothing matches the merits of old age," she said.

"You seem to have the experience, is this one of the opportunities the life of leisure has brought you?" I asked.

She ignored my comment. "Where is lunch then?" she asked.

The restaurant had become busy and all tables were full. I called the waiter, but he acknowledged from afar with his sign language, saying lunch is coming.

She finished the last pieces of avocado in her dish. Then she said, "Well, it was odd when you left. I had to struggle with myself, keep on going home late as if no routine had changed. But it had to change, I knew it, but I didn't know what to do. Then it happened, and it was weird. I would never have thought that he could have an affair. After all, who would go out with an old, gloomy lecturer? Well, a young blonde did! When I found out, my first response was loud laughter. I tried to say it was all for his money, but he was such a stingy bastard. Then I thought perhaps he was a gloomy stingy old loser only when he was with me. I couldn't contain myself, I made such a scene, I made life hell before divorcing him. I had felt guilty every time I looked at him just because it reminded me of the time I had spent with you. But do you know? By the end, I felt relieved, not only because I was free from seeing his miserable face every night. I felt great because I was free… not only because of getting rid of him, but because I was free of guilt."

"I thought you were happy with me," I said.

"Typical, men are all the same. All you thought about was yourself, and your obsession to have me. Well, you did have me, but the sad thing is, you lost me as you had me," she said.

"I never thought you had such feelings about our relationship. I thought it was something different to what others have, something special," I said.

"Now you are deluding yourself; what was so special about dinners together, a couple of drinks, and a hasty time?" she said.

"Well I'm so… so… sorry. I thought ours was something different, all those times… but if that's what you think, then you are right, I *was* deluding myself," I said.

She continued eating her steak. "Don't kid yourself! It's unbelievable, even now, after all this time, you cannot see the reality. You know why? Because you are so vain. Everything must revolve around you and your selfish dreams. But I don't care… you can think whatever you wish. When I found out about him and that totty, I felt relieved because I found he was unfaithful like me, it was as if a heavy weight was taken off my shoulders." She had another bite from her steak. "Have something, you need food!" she smiled.

"This is so new to me, you are so melodramatic now. I thought we had an understanding, that you didn't care about all that pretence, the facade people have, all those sanctimonious friends around us pretending they were faithful," I said.

"Understanding? Understanding what? That I am just a figment of your imagination? That I don't exist as I am? As I *really* am? I had told you I was traditional, my appearance was a façade. I told you, didn't I?" she said.

"Yes, but I thought it was a wrong image you had of yourself," I said.

"You see? You are an arrogant man, what makes you think you know me better than myself?"

I smiled, had a sip of water. "You are full of hatred," I said. She said, "No, I had this urge for a long time to see you one day to tell you what I feel… what I felt. Do you know, after you left, I had to see a counsellor? I went to a shrink."

Her accent was fake American now as she referred to the shrink. I thought, *of course, what else. You cannot be truly part of that culture without having a shrink. Perhaps he had told her to throw away all she had kept from the past, go to yoga and pilates classes, do a trip to Las Vegas, and wear comfortable clothes.*

I told her, "I bet you go to tennis classes." She looked surprised. "How do you know?" she asked.

"I thought your shrink had recommended you," I said.

She laughed. "You are funny," she said, "we did have a laugh or two, didn't we? But yes, you are right, tennis classes were *his* recommendation."

Then I thought, I was sitting across that table witnessing the corpse of my memories disintegrating, corpses of moments of my memories, corpses that didn't want to leave quietly, like the other times when they came out randomly, but persisting, without notice, attacking me like hot steam with a mixture of smells when you arrive at a busy popular, no frills Chinese restaurant.'

'I can't believe you have remembered things from the past so vividly, with so many details, line by line,' I said.

'There are things that stay with you… time flows smoothly, jumps, flies, but some things stick to your skin, penetrate your flesh, flow in your veins, occupy your mind, cut through your mind, and the scars remain, imprinted somewhere deep in you. I am a man walking with these memories, sitting with them while talking to others.' Frank stopped and looked at me, and I was dazed looking at far away, looking at his images floating in my mind.

I said, 'Sometimes life is a big misunderstanding, so many feelings get lost in a heap of misplaced images.'

He had a bout of coughing. Then he cleared his throat, and said, 'And there was no drama after that, we finished the lunch, talked for some time, talked about how the streets had changed over the period we hadn't met, the shops, and the small cafés where we used to have coffee. She had a flight back in a couple of days. We had a kiss goodbye as you knew something was broken. All that time, since I had returned from Iran, I had this faint hope that things might be good between us. Now I had realised that things were never good, like a fake stamp... so masterly faked that no one could identify it, but then, suddenly, all is so obvious. You can blame yourself for being ignorant, stupid, naïve, but these are all simply adjectives... words... nothing can explain your feelings. I walked through the streets without looking, without looking at anything. I just walked, and walked... and then I found myself outside my shop. An old customer was waiting outside the door. The "Closed" sign was there, but he was waiting.

"I knew you would be back after lunch," he said.

"You took a risk," I said, "you must have been waiting here a very long time."

"I don't mind, I knew you would come. The stamps I've bought over the years have something to tell me about you," he said. "After all, I have nothing else to do. It's either here or a walk through the park, watching people taking their dogs for a walk."

"So, waiting is risky, but wise," I said. "Nice contradiction."

"Not always… not always, my friend," he said.

And I opened the shop.'

'So, was that it?' I asked Frank.

'Well yes, more or less. I met her a couple of times later at parties, I rarely went to parties. So, it was strange to meet her on those occasions, particularly as she used to come over for very short visits. We only exchanged short pleasantries while chatting with others. But then I met her by chance once more. I had gone to a shop to buy a newspaper after lunch, and there she was, buying a pack of pocket tissues; she had a bad cold.

"Fancy seeing you," I said.

"Yes, how are you?" she said.

"Better than you," I said, looking at her taking a tissue out of the pack.

"Just a cold…"

"Do you think a glass of hot tea could help?"

She looked at her watch. "Why not? Good idea."

There was a cool breeze. We went to a small coffee shop with light metallic chairs in the small park nearby. We drank tea in silence.

"Unusually cold today," she said.

"Perhaps you feel it more because of your cold," I said.

"Maybe."

There was another silent episode. She appeared uncomfortable sitting in the chair. She wore a light pink dress with large light blue flowers. I thought how does this match her mentality… the mentality of someone running a travel agency. Then I thought of my stamps, specifically, a stamp with a large blue colour, and that normally flower stamps are not valuable items. Then I started talking to her about my stamps, the rare one that I acquired with some timely actions. She was looking at me with a smile, a smile that a mother gives her son when he is back from a sports day with muddy shoes. Then I thought I was as much of a fool as I was in those years. I was assuming she had the slightest interest in what I did. But I was embarrassed as I was again selfish, just talking about myself, and she was sitting there with a cold… and that I would not see her again probably. Her smile was telling me I was the same old fool,' Frank said.

'And now? Was that it?' I asked.

'Now what?' Frank laughed. 'You *are* the romantic one, Adam.'

'It seems to me there is something unfinished,' I said.

'Nothing finishes, you want to create a happy ending to things, but nothing ends, and that's the name of the game. There is no "endgame", even when I go, you will live with this story… with me… won't you?' Frank said.

'Well, well, we don't need to be melodramatic now,' I said.

'Sometimes reality is more dramatic than drama,' Frank said. 'But actually, there was nothing melodramatic. I got married several months – maybe a year or so – later.'

'But how could you do that?'

'I understand your point, but things happen,' Frank said. 'You might think it was a reaction to the episodes I had… and you might be right, too, but it just happened, and appeared very logical at the time.'

'Anyone I know?' I asked.

'No, not at all, but now you will see how Ana has been instrumental in my life, in the events in my life. A few months after that last meeting, I met her in the street going to my shop. She said she had a group of friends coming, and would I like to join them for dinner. We hadn't met properly after I had returned from Iran, and she wanted to know what I felt, what my experiences were. I didn't tell her about my affair, though. It wasn't intentional, it was just that I wasn't on those terms with her. I went to her small party, and it was there I met Judy, my ex-wife. We had real fun together for several years, you know. But things changed gradually, typical! We both tried hard, but it didn't work.' Frank coughed.

As I was asking the waiter for another drink, I saw Ana coming over.

'So, that's where you are hiding,' she said, laughing. 'I needed that shower. What are you two chatting about? You look like conspirators sitting in this corner. People are gathering for drinks at the bar. Come on, let's go.'

'We are just enjoying ourselves, must we go?' I said.

'Yes, and that's an order!' she laughed. She was refreshed.

We stood up.

'I have always followed you, Ana,' Frank said.

'And you haven't regretted it I hope, although…' she stopped herself.

'Of course I haven't. I was just telling Adam how instrumental you've been in my life,' Frank said.

'Now, now, let's not get too melodramatic,' Ana said, as we walked to the bar.

'What is it with you two?' Frank said. 'Just a minute ago Adam was telling me I was melodramatic.'

Ana laughed. 'If Adam says that, then it has to be true. You know? He is a very well-read man, he has this cute bookshop, as you know.'

'Yes, I want to become a regular reader frequenting the bookshop!' Frank said.

We arrived at the bar.

'Here they are! We are a full house now,' Colin said to Helen, Roy, and Maria. 'The first round is mine!'

We were the only ones in the bar, but it didn't feel cold and impersonal; it had a cosy atmosphere. And there were rounds after rounds of drinks. We were all tipsy now.

'Let's have a game,' said Helen.

'Oh, come off it, Helen,' said Roy, curling his oily hair around his index finger.

'Look folks, we're here after so many years, we are allowed to feel young again; let's be mischievous for a change,' Colin said.

'No change for some of us then,' I said, laughing.

'So what do you have in mind, Helen?' asked Ana.

'Nothing drastic… just a game… something to feel we are close again,' replied Helen.

'It might be fun,' Maria said.

'What about going over what we wished then, and what our wishes are now?' Helen said.

'This is mischievous… deep!' Roy said, grumbling.

'Surprised you felt the depth!' Colin said, laughing.

'Now, now… boys you must behave!' Ana said. 'Who will start, then?'

'Must be brave!' said Maria.

'I wished I could become a pilot,' Roy said.

'What? Studying history, becoming a pilot?' Colin said. 'I always thought there was something odd about you!'

Roy finished his double vodka in a gulp. 'What's wrong with that? It was a wish, unfulfilled, but a good fantasy. You know, my wife worked for BA.'

There was a silence. Roy continued.

'And then she died, she had to die. All was good, you know. She gave me a large model of a TAMIYA 61112 Lancaster B MKI/III. I have it on my desk, we had a good life together. Several times she organised for me to go for some fancy flights, just sitting next to the pilot. I didn't.'

'But why not?' asked Maria.

'Mmm. I would've betrayed my own fantasy. I could be a pilot one day, but sitting next to a pilot as a visitor for a birthday present? No. I loved Sarah, but I couldn't betray myself. She never understood it.'

'And now? What do you desire now?' asked Frank.

'Oh, that's easier to say. I'm waiting to retire.' He raised his voice. 'I'd like to retire young! And I can. I've been slaving away in that hell-hole for twenty-eight years now, do you hear me? Twenty-eight years in the City. I can say goodbye anytime. But I like to suffer. I'll wait for another two years. Then I'm off.'

Maria asked, 'What do you mean, off?'

'Off means off, practically!' Roy said. 'I will turn the lights off in my office for the last time, and I'll go to the pub with the office gang. After that, it will be a potbelly life! From hell-hole to potbelly!'

Colin said, 'No problems mate, you are already there,' and he laughed.

'You ain't seen proper potbelly yet,' Roy said.

'Anyway, count me in… pub crawling we shall do!'

'So, after that exciting chapter, who's braving it next?' Helen asked.

'You!' Ana said.

'OK, no sweat.' Helen let her shoe drop as she folded her left foot under her body. She was clearly excited to talk.

'Comfy chairs, aren't these? I wish I had one at home,' said Roy, looking at Helen.

'I loved that Student Centre… I really did.' Helen rearranged herself sitting on the chair. 'I didn't want to leave that place. I know… I know it's sad, but I loved it. So it wasn't only Led Zeppelin… I was besotted about everything in those days, but the Student Centre was something else. There was something magical…'

'Those are called boys!' Roy laughed, but others kept silent.

'Oh… it was everything. Of course there were the boys too! I loved them all whatever they thought or did. But there was one, always one I…'

'Pray tell!' said Roy.

'You don't need to know that, but I can say it wasn't you.'

Now we all laughed, not Roy.

'So, what is your wish now?'

'Not much, it's good I came over, we met again, all of us.'

'Just to remind you of those times?' asked Maria.

'Yes, sort of. Living alone has its benefits, but it's good to meet people from the past sometimes,' Helen said.

'But you are the last one to be alone,' Roy said. 'I'm sure there are loads of people out there waiting to see you, meet you.'

'Sure, but I am alone. There are people out there, but sometimes you want to share a drink with someone without prior arrangements, without texting them to come over,' Helen said.

'I remember when I was a child, staying with my grandmother back at home, people would come over just like that, no notices, no nothing. There would be a knock at the door, and there it was, one of her friends. They used to sit in the garden, grandmother would bring tea, cucumber and cheese. I can still smell the freshly watered soil, the smell of petunias in the evening, and the radio that was on in low volume in a corner, a popular singer singing away. That radio would never lose its battery power,' Ana said.

'That was in Iran, right?' Frank asked.

'Oh yes, of course, where else? You wouldn't have it here; the weather is so different.'

'But is it only the weather?' I asked.

'OK, so many things are different, but for me, that scene popped up suddenly as Helen was talking. It's as if I am there, or that event is here… I don't know,' Ana said, then continued with a different voice, 'What is it with you, Adam? Can't one talk about something and you… you… not bringing some philosophical questions… some points to dig in?' Ana asked.

'I just asked if it was only the weather that was different,' I said.

'Yeah, your questions are always innocent, so-o-o innocent, but then there is something that niggles immediately… if not immediately, it bothers one later.'

Frank laughed. 'This is hardly a bad thing, Ana, and we love him for it.'

'Oh, you might,' Ana said. There was a silence.

'I am sorry, I really am,' I said.

'Where is that drink? Colin asked loudly.

'Which drink? I didn't hear anyone asking for more,' asked Helen.

Roy raised his hand and called the waiter. 'We want more.'

And suddenly we all started, 'We want more, we want more!'

The waiter laughed. 'Are we desperate, gentlemen?'

'Not only the gentlemen, the gentle ladies are desperate too,' said Helen.

'It seems it's Ana's turn to say something... what were your wishes then?' Frank asked.

Roy said, 'Don't overdo it, just one wish... one.'

'I guess you mean before I came over, you mean in Iran.'

'Whatever. Just tell us,' Roy said.

'I don't know, it seems so far away. They were building a cinema near us. They had advertised the movies to come a year before the cinema was to be opened. It took ages for me. I used to pass by the cinema in the school bus every day looking at the semi-finished building, thinking why doesn't it finish. I wished to go to see the film the first night when it opened to public. It never happened, of course. I went to see the film a month later with a friend. We used to go to private English classes together, and the cinema showed movies in English on Monday nights. We were so happy to see the film in its original language. It was a Western with John Wayne. We had our ice-creams melting in our hands and happy with a feeling of superiority being among the so-called highly educated audience! We were going to show off to classmates the next day, but my friend couldn't come. She had flu; didn't come for a week. By then, the whole feeling had gone, but I still remember the movie. Mind you, John Wayne was much better when dubbed! They would add funny lines to what he said, very much in line with the theme of the movie and his character of course,' Ana said. 'Those lines added so much to the movies.'

'How our wishes change as we grow up!' Frank said.

'Our wishes change every day,' said Helen, laughing.

'And then comes a time when you don't have any wishes left in you,' Frank said.

'Now that's morbid!' Colin said. 'This is not allowed, not in this weekend.'

'OK then, we consider this as your present wish when it's your turn,' said Helen.

'So, let's not get distracted, what is your wish now?' asked Roy. 'I hope it's more exciting than your youthful wish.'

'Steady! The lady is still young,' said Colin.

'Do you think I care?' asked Ana.

Helen replied immediately, 'Yes, *I* do.'

'But then we are different,' said Ana.

'Anyway, what is your present wish?' Roy repeated.

'I want a quiet life, I want a small cottage outside a village in green, lush countryside,' Ana said.

'That's easily doable,' Frank said.

'I want a small river passing by it, my bedroom window opening to the garden with the river running where the garden finishes.'

'Now that's a bit difficult,' said Frank.

'That's such a beautiful idea,' said Maria.

'What would you do all day?' asked Helen.

'She can do all sorts of things,' Frank said.

'Like what? Fishing from the small river?' Colin laughed out loud.

'Don't be ridiculous, she will take on knitting… she will sell her patterned jumpers in the local market,' Roy sniggered.

'Interesting how people have become critics of her wish,' I said. 'She is entitled to her wish, you know.'

'So? What's it to you? I sense personal interest here,' Roy said.

'I can defend myself, thank you, Adam,' said Ana.

'What has happened to us? We were fun to be with. Other students always tried to join our group… look at us now,' Frank said.

'I try not to… too many wrinkles!' Helen said.

'That's the last thing I'm worried about.' Frank coughed.

There was a silence. Then Ana continued.

'I tell you how I will spend my days. I will go for long walks along the river before breakfast. I will read most of the day. In the evenings, there's glass of good red, and music…'

'Come on, you do this and die of boredom, it will then be down to us to come and collect your forgotten corpse,' said Colin.

'You are so morose, can't see good in anything,' said Maria.

'Oh I can, it's just that the picture Ana portrays is a momentary dream… it lacks a simple thing: reality,' said Colin.

'Mm… dodgy word… try to avoid it, Adam will take you to strange abysses you regret you mentioned,' Frank said.

'Who do you warn? Do you think just because I'm a teacher, I am ignorant?' Colin laughed loudly.

'Perish the thought, I just know that when Adam detects prey, he goes for it. He looks innocent enough, but when it comes to anything to do with philosophy, he goes berserk!' Frank said.

'Thank you for the introduction, Frank,' I said.

'What's so philosophical here?' asked Maria.

'Don't worry,' said Roy.

'What do you mean? asked Helen. 'I find this sexist.'

'Oh go away…' said Roy.

'Come on folks, let's have a drink!' Frank said.

'Now you are my man. *This* is the reality,' said Ana, 'and is momentary too!'

We had another round of drinks, and there was a silence. Then Ana said, 'Well, you don't think I will rot in oblivion, do you?'

'Who are you asking?' asked Colin.

'Does it matter?'

'Yes it does, if you want a straight answer,' Colin said.

'Well, I ask you then,' said Ana.

'To be perfectly blunt, I think it's an irrelevant question.'

'What do you mean, irrelevant?' asked Maria.

'As I said… simple, nobody thinks about anyone when we go back. There's nothing special about you!'

'Why do you say that?' asked Ana.

'Because I know, I know it is very easy to say something when you are miles away from home in a strange reunion… going back to those dream times… thinking about hypothetical things in the future. But when you go back home, and look at the bundle of post behind your door, most of which is rubbish, you change your mind. Actually, I stand corrected, by that time you have forgotten all this completely!' said Colin.

'Do you have to destroy? Destroy even our dreams?' asked Helen.

'Well, reality stinks!' said Colin.

'Don't worry, he is entitled to his views,' said Ana.

'OK, whose wishes next?' asked Helen.

'You are really keen on this, aren't you?' asked Roy.

'Why don't you tell us about your old-time wish, Colin? You don't look shy, are you?' asked Helen.

'I don't see why I should share my wishes with you, with you of all people.' He was drunk now.

'You are sharing it with us, Colin,' said Maria.

'OK, I wanted to leave uni, escape from it all, but my father didn't have any of it. I had enough shit from those calling themselves "lecturers", all they knew was to satisfy their ego, to show off, and look at me now! I am a teacher. A teacher! Could you imagine in a thousand years?'

'You look to me to be a good teacher,' said Maria.

Colin smirked.

'Leave uni doing what?' asked Maria.

'Nothing, being out of that place was a wish and a half itself, heh! Some wish. And of course, I stayed there to the bitter end!'

There was a silence.

'Shall we move on?' said Roy. 'What is your blooming wish now?'

'Oh, shut up for a second, would you?' Colin stood up, wobbled and paused. 'I organised this because I wanted to see you all. We've had our differences, but all things considered, I was really looking forward to meeting you people again, see what you are up to. Being married for… what? Twenty-five years, having a lovely wife, and two kids, you don't have time to see your old friends. I thought to myself, it is now or never. And I suggested this place because I wanted only those who were keen, to come. After all, who goes to a God-forsaken place like this in winter? But you did… we all did! And I want to thank you all. It was my wish. That's all.' He sat down.

'Oh, how nice, I am so touched, I really am,' said Maria.

We kept drinking for a while. Then Frank looked at Maria.

'Perfect characteristics for a nurse,' said Frank. 'I think you told me you are a nurse.'

'Well, after social sciences, I needed to take another course,' replied Maria.

'But it was a big change, no?' Frank asked.

'It was all because of social studies disincentives. It was so demoralising. Anything I read was disappointing; at one point, I was about to leave uni.'

'None of us knew about *that*.' Looking at us, Helen was surprised.

'Well, it was more an impulse of the moment, but then there was my granny. I loved her so much,' Maria said.

'Grannies are much dearer than mothers,' interrupted Helen.

'When she fell ill, I was the only one who cared, and that took me to nursing, to take a course,' Maria said.

'So that was your wish?' asked Colin.

'Mm, in a way, yes. When I saw my granny in a helpless situation every day, being there for her, I felt there was something more real to do than talk about far-fetched Dickensian problems of the society, remote from my daily life. It wasn't a burning desire to become a nurse, but it was – in a strange way – somewhat natural to me.'

Frank was listening eagerly. 'And now?' he asked.

'My wish now?' Maria asked.

'Yes.'

'I have really felt so good seeing you all again. I feel like someone who has found her long lost family. I wish we will remain in touch now that we have found each other. I wish to see you again, perhaps we could meet for a coffee, or arrange to go to events… not to lose each other again.'

'Have you forgotten how rotten Roy can be?' Colin laughed, and we started telling jokes.

'Well, this guy…' Colin said loudly, 'listen to me… this guy went to the pub, asked for an old bottle of wine. The barman brought him a dust-covered bottle. As he touched it, a genie came out of the bottle…'

'Oh come off it, it is one of your silly jokes again,' Roy said.

'Let the man finish what he wants to say,' said Helen.

'Well, the genie said to the man, "You may have two wishes."

The man said, "Why two? There's always three."

"Just because!" said the genie, "take it or leave it."

"Well, it's my luck, when it comes to me, only two! One is lost!"

The barman told him, "You idiot, take it, there are two wishes to be fulfilled."

"Well OK then… mm, I don't know, what can I wish?" he said.

"Lots of money… beautiful women with insatiable passion… position in high places…" the genie said.

"None of these," the man replied, "you think I'm stupid? The only thing these bring you is misery, suggest something different."

"OK, what about a never-ending pint of beer?" the genie uttered jokingly.

"I'm not a beer drinker, but yes, that looks to be a good idea."

Immediately a pint of beer appeared, full to the rim.

The man was stunned.

"Is it really…"

"Yes," the genie replied, "drink it."

The man drank it to the last drop, and put down the glass. As soon as the glass was put on the table, it got filled up to the rim.

"This is a miracle," the man shouted.

"Well, there you are, now quick with your second wish, I have to go," said the genie.

"OK then," said the man, ready to announce his second wish. "I wish another one like this!"'

Colin started to laugh first, directing all to laugh out loud. Only Roy said, 'Ha ha ha, you consider that funny?'

Colin ignored him, but Frank said, laughing, 'I must say, this is not only funny, but it's philosophical.'

'Oh, don't you start that, Adam will not leave us in peace!' said Ana.

'It is psychology, just think about the man's behaviour,' said Maria.

'Now it's Maria's turn to get on the bandwagon, and we thought she was the silent one,' said Helen.

'Really, just look at it, the man is not a beer drinker, but just because it's free, he accepts it, and then… and then… he wants more of it!' Maria said.

'But most people are like that,' said Ana.

'Yes… and that's sad,' Maria said.

'Oh, you get sad about anything so quickly, Maria, cheer up!' Helen laughed.

'But philosophical? Of course it is,' I said.

'There we are!' said Roy.

'From the start to the end that joke is a philosophy gem,' I said.

'OK, can we move on?' said Colin.

'I am very interested in what Adam wants to say,' Frank said.

'Belief in miracles, to start with… from a beer bottle to the essence of religions! This mythological hope that things happen suddenly, without any precedent… giving false hope to people… just look at it! How many people buy lottery tickets?' I said.

'Mm… some win, though!' Helen said.

At this moment, the young barman came over with an old bottle of beer in his hand, smiling.

'I couldn't help listening to the joke, so I thought I'd bring you this bottle. This is on me, enjoy it!' the barman said, smiling.

Helen said, 'What if a genie comes out of it?' looking at the boy admiringly.

'He will be bound to satisfy your wishes,' the barman replied.

'What's your name?' asked Helen.

'Ralph,' he replied.

'I will keep you posted,' said Helen.

'Of course you will!' Roy said.

Franks said, 'We are deviating. Adam was saying?'

'And take the other element, greed! The man has the never-ending pint, and yet he wants another one of the same. I would say this also reminds me of religion; it promotes greed!' I said.

'I'm lost now,' Maria said.

'Let's continue with our wishes. Ralph, can we have another round? Not of your beer bottle though!' said Ana.

'Whose turn is it?' asked Maria.

'It's my turn,' said Frank, looking at me. 'Well, I must say I like this… game, for me, it blends fantasy with reality.'

He had a sip from his glass of water.

'Of course, it depends on how far back one can go with a good memory of that time. I remember… I was a child, can't remember how old, perhaps five or six. I had passed the desire to have a rabbit or a kitten, or a bicycle. I was fascinated by birds; not that I had seen many birds. I had come across a film on the TV of some birds migrating, and there was this small bird, I cannot even say what it was… it wasn't a sparrow or a swift, it was perhaps a finch. But I was mesmerised. So that was my wish, to have a bird, but I never mentioned it to anyone. I didn't ask anyone for it. Somehow I liked to keep the wish to myself; I created an imaginary bird and talked with it at times when I was alone during the day, but usually at night in bed before going to sleep. This is the first time I am talking about it, it is odd to talk about something of your childhood you have never talked about before.' Frank stopped, and had another gulp of water. He had drops of sweat on his forehead.

'I have a bird, you know,' Maria said. 'It's not difficult to have one, but you need to be committed, it gives you so much love.' She looked at Roy. 'You might not believe it, but it's true, you can understand what they want… and they know what your feelings are.'

'You bet they know what they want… they want out! You know that too, but you keep the poor bird! And you are the most goody-goody one among us,' Roy said, and raised his voice. 'So, what is your wish now? Not the bird, not the birds of that sort, I hope,' Roy laughed aloud.

'Well, we move on… and our interests change too,' Frank said. 'I like all kinds of birds now.' He laughed too.

'But you will be surprised how absorbing the world of stamps is. You look at a stamp, the picture, the colour, the stamp mark, the indentations, how intact a stamp is, how it has changed hands without losing its value, in fact gaining value… you think about previous owners, who they were, what was their motive in buying a particular stamp, why they sell a stamp? It is an attractive job, sitting in your office in the shop, meeting these eccentric people, not necessarily wealthy, although they often are… talking with them about their wishes. Their wishes are always for a unique stamp. A stamp which is unique to them. I am not talking about the famous stamps that people are after for their market value, looking at them as investments. I am talking about particular interests,' Frank said.

'So are you one of them? Is your wish having a particular stamp? Perhaps a stamp with the picture of a bird?' Maria asked.

'No, not at all. I tell you what my wish is. I was sitting in my office, it was some… I guess twenty years ago. I had come back from Iran, and was very much entangled with my thoughts and emotions. It was difficult for me to separate myself from those images – images that haunted me – then this young woman, perhaps around twenty-eight, thirty, came in; you know. my customers are – mainly, perhaps all – men. She came in, and walked directly towards me. "I need to talk to someone expert in historical stamps," she said. I said I was the sole person responsible for the whole stuff, and might be able to help her. I must say, I was a bit taken aback, but didn't consider her to be serious. But she was… I felt her eyes could pierce the wooden counter, the steel. I learnt, while she was talking, that contrary to my assumption, she did not have a degree from Oxbridge. She was a self-taught person who lived alone, and spent her time reading. Reading different things, mainly history and philosophy, and she listened to music, mainly classics, with no interest in current affairs. She took me through a journey of Middle East history from Mesopotamia to Iran, and then asked me about the stamps. I can't tell you what I felt while she was talking.'

'Did she buy stamps? That is the main question,' asked Roy.

Frank ignored him, and continued, 'She asked about some rare stamps. I told her I could perhaps get hold of them, but it needed time. I told her I could introduce her to some people I know who might be able to help her further. We talked for a while, and then she left. Perhaps some of you know my weak point about Iran. When she was talking, I had my mental images about Iran, with her face, mixed together, I could see her walking in those streets with her hair loose over her shoulder…'

'What a strange imagination, Frank,' said Ana.

'Not really, just put two things that I liked next to each other,' said Frank.

'And she didn't return?' I asked.

'No,' Frank replied.

'But it doesn't mean she won't return,' Maria said.

'If she is really keen on stamps,' said Ana.

'But I'm not the only one – do you know how many stamp traders there are? Not to think about the "on-line business",' Frank said.

'Still, there is hope,' Maria said.

'OK, now it has to be Adam,' said Helen.

'I'm afraid my childhood wishes are rather boring, like any other boy's. I was craving for a bicycle, but I had to wait years to get one, and even then, it wasn't what I wanted. It was a couple of sizes bigger for my age,' I said.

'"It's best for you, it helps you grow taller," my mother would say.'

'So I had to do acrobatics to ride that bike,' I said, 'but mind you, I learnt things to do with the bicycle that others found difficult.'

'At least you had got what you wanted,' Maria said.

'Well, not exactly. First I had to wait for what seemed like ages, then something that was different to what I expected. The point is, when I look back, anything I wished for didn't happen the way I wanted, there was always an issue,' I said.

'Don't be such a martyr! What a spoiled child! Now that you talk, I remember… you were exactly like this during our time at university. Spoiled!' said Helen.

'And he is the one you were after,' said Roy emphatically.

'Correction, one of many!' Helen laughed. 'It was his "intellectual" demeanour, the way he had a book under his arm walking like a suffering thinker, someone whose shoulders are bowed under the pressure of worry about human suffering!' said Helen.

'That was the time when Marx ruled the corridors, and Engels the doors to the classrooms!' said Frank.

'Also the time of our lives! Those were the days…' Helen started singing and Colin joined her while Ralph was watching from the bar.

'So, what is your wish now?' asked Ana.

'It is simple, and easy to say. I have wanted, for a long time, to write a novel. Sitting in that bookshop all day, watching people coming in flicking through the books, it's as if at least some of them are in love with books. I want to know what goes on in their minds when they turn those pages. And I think of myself writing a book – my mind going through the unwritten pages – seeking those characters, finding them, starting a life with them.'

'Wait a minute, Adam,' said Helen, 'is it your wish to write a book or to see what other people think when they read your book?'

'What does it matter?' asked Colin.

'It does matter, it's so obvious,' said Helen.

'I like the whole thing, can't separate,' I said.

'So it's a wish. When are you going to do something about it?' asked Roy.

'Sometimes one is happier with an unfulfilled wish,' said Frank.

'Ah, but that is desire, not a wish,' Ana said.

'Come on folks, things are getting too convoluted for a reunion party. Where is this handsome waiter? We are drying up!' asked Helen.

Frank raised his hand for Ralph to see. He was behind the bar, leaning on a magazine. He came over.

'I thought you were taking care of us,' said Helen with a smile.

'How may I be of service, madam?' asked Ralph.

'You don't need to be so formal. Are you making fun?' asked Helen.

'Can we have another round, please?' asked Colin.

'He is desperate, he said *please*,' Roy said loudly.

'Perhaps not for him, he is already there,' said Colin.

'Talk of yourself, actually, bring me a large one this time,' said Roy.

'I think I'd better return to my room,' said Ana.

'Please don't,' said Maria with a low voice.

'But I'm not sure where this conversation is taking us,' Ana said.

'Should it take us anywhere?' I asked.

'You know what I mean,' said Ana.

'We haven't talked about our regrets,' Maria said.

'Oh, for goodness' sake,' said Roy.

'But this is true, we have wishes, and regrets, and what better than living with them again in this reunion?' asked Ana.

Suddenly, Colin said with a loud voice, 'Haven't we forgotten something?'

'Yes, to ask for another round!' Roy said, drunk.

'Wake up, we just ordered,' said Helen.

'But I mean it, we totally forgot,' Colin said.

'What?' Roy shouted.

'We are invited to the village party,' Colin said.

'Thanks for reminding us, but aren't you the organiser?' Helen said.

'We can still go, there must be some booze,' Roy said.

'It's too late now, I'm not going anywhere,' said Ana.

'It is quite cosy here,' said Maria.

'I need some fresh air,' said Frank, standing up. 'We'll be back soon.'

'I can do with a break too,' I said.

'This is getting too formal! Shall we reconvene in fifteen minutes?' Colin said. 'Gosh, I love this!'

I followed Frank, who was heading to the hotel garden.

'I'm not chasing you,' I smiled at Frank.

'I needed to have a moment with myself,' Frank said. 'I'm sure you have the same feeling… when one lives alone for long time, it's difficult to share group conversation.'

'Sure.' I walked towards a different part of the garden. It was dark and cold; the clouds had gone and I could see the clean starry sky and hear the pebbles under my feet in complete silence.

Here you are standing in the cold carrying your days, your empty spaces in your flat, the image of yourself in the train going back, putting the key into the door, making tea for yourself before anything else, only a little post has dropped in your flat, most of it adverts. You think of getting ready to go to your bookshop. Now the smell of the books…the smell of the books penetrates the cold of the night. When did you decide to open the bookshop? What possessed you? You love it… of course you do, but all the same… do you want to get stratified like all those books on the shelves? You are already an old man anyway.

Old? I am not! Watch what you say!

And what about the books on the large stands? Autobiographies! Do you want to write one? Who's going to read it? Who's Adam? Adam what? Who's interested in your closed, puny life story? Look at the books… I'm sure you've looked at them hundreds of times, whether you wanted or not. A creature of habit! Look at those books! A book of travel, books on cooking, on baking, on sewing. What about those on how to lose weight in thirty days? Have you seen "A gym in my flat… avoid getting fat?" Can you imagine someone spent time, did some background research to write that book? Do you know what to eat? You are stupid having so much sugar. And what about philosophy? I am what I eat! And what about all those magazines? Do you sell them too? Healthy eating. Keep Fit! And so much on fashion. Ah… Ana has kept well, hasn't she? I'm sure she looks after herself well, she knows what to eat and what not! Ah… those days, can you remember yourself in those years? Can you remember when you asked yourself again and again should you go talk to her, ask her out? What a prude… Roy is right after all, you were a waste of time.

I look at the other side of the garden. Frank has his hands behind his back and is looking at the sky. A man with a stamp shop!

Can't you see how similar you two are? Two men and their shops! One plays with books, the other with stamps! You are perfect examples of boys frozen in their childhood… with their old fantasies changed shape… from bicycle to book, from football to stamp! I guess we are similar in a way, we have grown similar. The fact that we all have come here, in winter, suggests we have something in common.

Do we? What is common between me and Roy, for goodness' sake? Just look at Helen. I don't need to contemplate... no need... where is the similarity?

You idiot! It's the past, the past you all share, it's your past you want to somehow relive. Just wait, go back to that bar and all of you will start by saying how good those days were! You even romanticise vomiting at the lamp poles. Oh, those late nights. You haven't talked about those yet, have you? And, of course you, so decently so far, have avoided talking about your feelings then, those days. Where was Ana in your life?

I walk towards the metallic gate, but then change my mind, and turn back to go in. Frank calls me. 'Adam, let's talk for a minute.'

'Sure Frank, it was a bit stuffy in there,' I say.

'Yes, had to come out. Things get too serious with these people,' Frank says.

'Well, we haven't seen them for a long time, perhaps we've forgotten how they were,' I say.

'And how *we* were,' Frank says. 'Listen, do you think I was, well, I was too arrogant in those days?'

'What I think now is different to what I thought then, Frank,' I say.

'Mm, I know. Perhaps you know me better now, although we haven't been in touch all this time,' he says.

'Of course, I think the same is true for you,' I say.

'I did come across as an arrogant man in those days, didn't I?' Frank asked.

'We loved to categorise people. I remember you and Ana were considered the same sort,' I say.

Frank coughs. 'I admired her.'

'You weren't alone,' I say.

She was standing alone by the wall on the right-hand side of the big hall at the university as we went in. She had on a red roll-neck and a check patterned skirt, her hair wrapped behind her.

Go! Talk to her!

It was good sunshine out there. I had to stand in the long queue to get to the tables to register; alphabetical registration. I followed her quietly, but we ended up in different queues. Frank had his scarf loose around his neck, although it wasn't cold. I had seen him earlier that day. He looked at me seriously.

'What is the sound of one hand clapping?'

I was thinking if Ana and I would end up registering at the same time; her queue was longer.

'What?' I said.

'The sound of one hand,' Frank repeated.

'I don't know. Have you registered already?' I asked.

'Yes, I have a useful family name, not many family names start with Z.'

'What's your course?' I asked.

'History, yours?'

'Engineering.'

'Oh,' Frank said.

'Yes, I know.'

'I didn't mean it in a bad way. For some reason I thought you would do literature or arts,' Frank said.

'Appearances can be deceptive!' I laughed. Then I looked at Ana's queue. She wasn't there. How could it be?

'Listen, I need to go, see you later,' Frank said. My queue was moving very slowly.

'Do you remember her long hair?' Frank says.

'Well of course, but I remember her bag. It was part of her body, inseparable! Sometimes I wished I could have a glance inside. It seemed she could not live without it, and quite right too.' I feel revived. 'Whatever you thought she needed was in there. I was intrigued how she could find things in there,' I say.

'It was years before mobile phones, we could check her vices if she had the bag now,' Frank says. We laugh.

'Yes, I wonder. I thought she would have it still, or at least something like it,' I say.

'But she doesn't have long hair either,' Frank says.

'True,' I say.

'I feel cold. I'm going in,' Frank says.

'I'll be with you soon,' I say.

From gravel to gravel. A cold night in the garden of the hotel, a mild night in the courtyard of the Student Centre, and the moment's gone... moments fused together as if nothing has gone, as if I have created all those moments just now with characters sitting in the bar of the hotel just images in the past breathing in this moment.

'Adam, Adam, is that "Catcher in the Rye" you carry with you all the time these days? Do you like it? Easy reading. I finished it overnight.'

Her hair was long and she looked at me as if I was transient, a man who has just arrived from a nearby town, and is flying to lands far, far away.

'I read very slowly,' I say.

-26-

'Are you mad? Standing in the cold talking to yourself?' Helen is standing at the door to the lobby. 'Come in, we want to continue our game.'

And it continues, Ana, it continues. I still have the book. You wrote on it: 'Adam is a slow reader!' Yes, I am slow, not only a slow reader, I am slow! What's so special about the fast ones? What is their amazing achievement?

'I am coming,' I say. And I go back.

All are laughing, and Colin is standing unstable with a glass in his hand looking at me.

'Now that the missing culprit has returned, we can resume our contemplation of past and present!'

'We have exhausted it to death,' says Roy.

'Come on, Roy, don't be a party pooper,' says Helen.

'I have an idea,' Maria says.

'Let's hear it,' Colin says with a hiccup.

'What is our biggest regret, then?' asks Maria.

'What?' Roy asks.

'Well, we talked about our wishes, now about our regrets.'

'Oh, come on! This is turning into a silly sad game,' Roy says.

'It's not a game, Roy, it's what our lives have been. Look at us, a sad group of people. Losers,' Maria says.

'Steady! I'm not a loser! I've had some regrets, but loser? This is too depressing,' Helen says.

'*I* had a regret,' says Ana.

'You've been so silent, now you come back with a regret!' says Colin.

'Interesting what a stir this has this question. I've been struggling with it for many years now. So, it's easy for me to voice it, I've lived with it. I came out of Iran when I was young. I didn't have the chance to see the country properly. I remember bits and pieces when I was a child. For me those days were the good days, though some people still have a different view on this. Anyway, I remember the green hills, a river, the village cottages, houses, the angry drivers,' Ana said.

'And your regret is what?' asked Helen.

'As I said, I didn't have a chance to see my country properly,' said Ana.

'Is that all?' Helen said.

'You can't decide for people what to regret about!' I said.

'It's an observation, Adam,' Helen said.

'All I have with me are images. A garden with a round pond and fountain, with geranium pots around the pond alternating with jasmine and petunia. I remember watering them in the evenings. My grandmother would say "Don't water them when the sun is hot!" I never asked her why. I had so many questions to ask her, but she died only a month after I came here. I regret not asking her when she was alive, when she used to sit by the pond next to the jasmine pots. I used to make necklaces for her with jasmine flowers, and I used to pick a petunia flower and taste the end bit of the flower, it was sweet. We used to sit together, saying nothing. I regret not talking with her. I want to fill in the whole space with my voice, my words, as if talking will keep her alive, would have kept her alive, to read poetry as she did while sitting by the pond.

'There were a couple of bakeries. I knew all the people who worked there. What happened to them? I didn't say goodbye to them. It was late at night. I was in bed at that time, usually, but not that night. It was as if nobody wanted to go to bed. Grandmother walked slowly to me and put her hand on my hair. Her old fingers were cold, they had the smell of a soap I liked. I didn't say goodbye to anyone, and I didn't go to the doughnut shop for the last time. Oh, they had all sorts of fillings from minced meat to cabbage to jam to cream, and I didn't go there. All I remember from the streets is in a haze now, with noises of people shouting, and their shouts getting louder and louder. I asked myself why are they so angry? Why do they shout Arabic words? Yes, I regret my ignorance.' Ana stopped.

Frank said, 'In a way Ana's regret is our regret too. The people and the places are different, but the feeling is similar.'

'What is *your* regret then? You are so clear in your mind about what is regrettable,' Helen asked me, but Roy shouted, 'I regret being here, folks, it seems that anything can turn into an argument here.'

'Cool it off, Roy,' said Colin. 'We are enjoying this, aren't we?'

'I've been looking forward to coming here and seeing you all, it was a nice feeling for me when I decided to come. It didn't take much time for me to decide, and I am happy I am here, having seen you all. When I go back, I might not see you again, who knows. At this moment, I am enjoying all the feelings from the past fused into here and now, this moment. And I would like to thank Colin for having arranged it all,' Frank said, and raised his glass. 'I said, I would like to drink first to Colin, and then to you all,' said Frank.

There was a silence, then Ana said, 'Oh Frank, I am so happy that you've come too, and am excited to see you all. When I say I regret not having seen Iran properly, my mind is all over the place. Sometimes I think I am a wreck.'

'I wish I were a wreck like you! You are the most elegant, you've changed the dreary mood of this place,' Maria said.

'Let's go back to the regrets, shall we?' asked Colin.

'What is yours, then?' Helen asked.

'Oh, I still think about it sometimes,' said Colin. 'When I was twelve, thirteen, I loved football. I still love it. I was good at it, you know? It was my left foot. I was in the school's, and then, when I was eighteen, in the county's top teams. We used to play regularly, every week.' He paused.

'And?' Roy asked.

'In one of our county games, this guy came to me and started chatting during the break. I hadn't seen him before.

"You're not doing badly, I've been watching your game, you have it in you," he said.

'I was very shy then,' Colin said.

'How one changes!' Roy laughed.

'Let the man finish,' Helen said.

'Well, I didn't say much, of course I was chuffed, but then chickened out when he suggested I should go and see his boss in the club. I won't tell you which club it was, but it was a Premier League club. Do you know what it means? What a leap it was? Well, could've been.'

'But what stopped you?' asked Helen.

'I don't know what has possessed me to tell you all this. I would never mention it anywhere else. Well, I've said it now. I just didn't think I was good enough, I thought I had creeped myself up to play at the county level. I don't know, I thought they were kind to me because my father was a council member.'

'Oh for Faberge's sake!' said Helen. 'Enough of self-pity, you are OK, Colin!'

'Yes, you have a good career, I am sure a good social life, that's what matters, isn't it?' asked Maria.

'Well, among other things,' said Frank.

'Shall we forget this topic now? Let's move on to something fun,' said Roy.

'My regret is that I was too shy,' said Maria. 'I should've talked more with people.'

'You are not a bundle of communication now either!' Helen laughed.

'I know, but I think I'm better now.' Maria wrapped her jumper tighter around her chest.

'Communication is not only talking. We have seen so many chatterboxes with little to communicate!' said Frank with a cough.

'Well, this regret can easily be overcome, thinking about what you haven't lost, but have actually gained by being shy!' I said.

Colin stood up.

'Thank you, sir, for your revealing statement! Now, who's next in this fantastic session? Who's oozing with desire to share his regrets?' Colin wobbled.

'So, you think that only men are left with their desire to share?' Helen said.

'It's bloody language,' said Colin.

'And you are the teacher!' laughed Roy.

'Don't push your luck, Roy, otherwise I'll fail you, although this doesn't have much novelty for you!' said Colin.

I look at Frank looking at Ana.

I can live with my regrets, hoping I will remedy what happened. Yes, there will be times when I tell myself the damage is done, cannot reverse it, the water has spilt, and all that crap. But what about Frank? Any regrets he has, will stay with him, will go with him.

Frank started talking as he was looking at Ana.

'I have no regrets!' He smiled. 'I look at you, Ana, and remember all the good times that we all had. Our group… you might say, what group? But for me it doesn't matter, I had this group in my mind. And look, Colin must have felt the same, sending that email to gather us here, and we must all have had the same feeling, otherwise why come here in this cold? I have no regrets; my mind is full of memorable moments with you lot. You might laugh, but when you are driven to think about your life as a bundle of events, your perspective changes. You go beyond momentary worries and grudges.'

'Have you considered a job at your local church?' Roy sniggered with a hiccup.

'Memories become stories, stories that you like reading again, wondering what happens to the characters after you read the last line. By the way, what is the first thing you do when you go back, Roy?' asked Frank.

Roy didn't respond.

Maria stood up. 'I just remembered the Rolling Stones' "I can't get no satisfaction". I like this so much. It's still the same. Does anyone want some water? I'm going to ask for some.'

Helen stood up. 'I'm going to the toilets, I'll ask Ralph on my way.'

'Who's Ralph?' asked Ana.

'Such a short memory, Ana. Ralph is our barman!' said Helen.

'Oh, don't we know that!' said Roy.

'I see Ralph is in luck!' smiled Colin.

Helen smiled back. 'Do you want water or not?'

All hands went up. 'Sparkling for me, please,' I said.

Helen was now standing by the bar talking to Ralph. She laughed and stroked her hair while Ralph smiled.

As Maria sits, I ask her, 'If you were not shy, what would you do then?'

Maria looked at Frank and went red. 'I would ask Frank to lend me his books.'

'Is that all?' asked Roy. 'For goodness' sake! Somebody help me!'

'You are beyond help, Roy,' I said. 'Can't you wait for people to finish what they say?'

Roy stood up and came over, standing over me. 'Who says you are the manager here? I say what I want to say, when I want to say it.'

'Well, that's the problem,' said Colin, 'you haven't learnt to shut up when you must shut up.'

'Folks, let's not argue, we have only a short time together after so many years,' said Ana.

'Indeed,' said Frank. 'Maria, it would've made me so happy had you asked me then, but if you'd like to borrow any book now, that is if you are still interested, you are welcome.'

'Oh fantastic, it will be a treat, thanks Frank.'

'Do we not want to go to bed?' asked Ana.

'Is it a proposition?' asked Roy with a hiccup.

Ana ignored him. 'I am quite tired,' Ana continued.

'But we are waiting for the water, and we haven't heard Adam's regret, and Helen's regret.'

'What regret would Helen have? She managed to, to, you know,' said Roy.

'I think that's your regret you weren't one of them, if that's what you are implying, Roy!' said Maria.

'Ha ha ha! That was below the belt, Maria. I see you have overcome your shyness,' said Colin, laughing away.

Ralph came over with a big tray of water. As he was putting the glasses on the table, Helen came over. 'Oh Ralph, you are already here! Now this is what I call service.'

Ralph smiled.

'I am sure the water is super tasty, too!' sniggered Roy.

'I am glad you will reap the fruits of my effort, no one had the energy to act. You would've died of thirst if I hadn't asked for water,' said Helen, laughing.

'So what's *your* regret, Helen?' asked Maria. 'Only you and Adam are left.'

Helen tucked her legs under her. 'I loved travelling, but all I did was to go to Glastonbury. It was such fun, I went there every year for five years. I should've followed groups on their tours, seen the world. But didn't, don't know why, just didn't. I guess there were too many boys around!' She laughed again.

There is something sad about her as I look at her curly brown hair, red lips with a cheap lipstick, and her dress. I keep on repeating in my mind "shabby as before". How did she bring up two kids? Two kids! The Helen I knew would not go near a family-structured life, any structured life. Sitting there in her own old fashion, she is a mixture of what has happened to her and what she still dreams will happen, to continue the time she had with us, in her mind a mixture of Led Zeppelin and moments of looking at the mirror applying red lipstick carelessly.

'Where are you, Adam? Miles away? North or south?' Helen laughed. 'Won't you help me see why I didn't go about places with the groupies?' asked Helen.

I had a sip from my drink. 'I'm not clairvoyant, Helen,' I said.

'You know what I mean,' she said.

'And you overestimate me,' I said.

'OK folks, let's not bicker, this is supposed to be fun,' Frank said.

'Some fun talking about our regrets,' said Roy.

'Well, let's get it over and done with. It's Adam's turn, anyway,' said Helen.

'My regrets? Where do I start? The point is, if you live enough with your regrets they lose their intensity. It is like when you live with someone for a long time, the relationship changes. This is not negative, but things change and become – sort of – milder. Their urgency disappears, they become part of you.'

'OK, OK, tell us about your regrets,' said Roy.

'I will. In a sense it is boring, boring because it's like anyone else's. You see a girl when you are young

– high school young – and you fall in love, but never tell her. You regret it for a long time; at first, it's like a melancholic novel, then it becomes a short story, then a line that appears and disappears in between the layers of your memories, and life goes on with events happening all the time. Then the regret becomes a memory point, it might not be a regret any more depending on the events that have happened after over the years.'

'Are you telling us a story? It is simple, what is your regret?' asked Roy again.

'I like what Adam says,' said Maria.

'You just said what my regret is, Roy. I have always dreamt of writing a story. I even started one, but then tore it up, tore it into pieces,' I said. 'I didn't regret that though! The act was a gift to the literary world!'

'But running a bookshop should help,' Ana said.

'On the contrary,' I said, 'going to the bookshop every day, meeting those people who are so interested in reading and writing, some of them telling me about what they are writing, let alone the classic books I read, those have convinced me not to write. My writings look naff to me.'

'So, what's the regret? You think your writing is naff, and you haven't written. So, you must be happy!' laughed Roy.

'Come on, Roy, you don't have much to say, only making ridiculous remarks,' said Maria.

'But you know I am right; I can only see one "regret" scenario in what Adam says,' Roy said.

'What is it, then?' said Colin.

'Ah, good morning Colin,' said Roy, 'did you have a good nap? Adam's regret is that he hasn't written to give a hard time to his readers!' said Roy. 'He says he's been charitable to the literary world, but deep inside he is boiling with revenge.'

'Come on, Roy, you are reflecting your own feelings; just look at yourself. Since we have arrived, you have been attacking us. What's wrong with you? After so many years, we are here meeting up, revisiting all our memories. Who knows, we might not meet again, can't we have a good time together? A good memory at least from this, this, gathering?' Ana said.

'Reunion,' Maria said.

'You are all under this illusion of the past, as if whatever happened then was rosy, that we liked each other. You live in a world of make-believe. I'm fed up with this goody-goody image you all try to portray. One very polite, one – the goddess of water – (he sniggered) trying to be elegant, but bleeding inside for the memories of her childhood. One, one thinks he is still at uni with his Sartre under his arm, bending over as if he is carrying the pain of humanity… should I say more? OK, another one thinks hippies are still running the show, another, oh, a picture of 1950s obedient mum you see on washing powder adverts, and of course one who thinks he's in control, but what he controls is the kids in his mind's classroom, he has to speak so loud those kids won't hear. But hey, even if they hear you, they won't listen to you; can't you get it?' Roy said.

'What about you, Roy? It seems to me then, that *you* are the free soul among us! But if anyone bends, it's you. You bend or break under the grudge you are carrying within yourself,' said Helen, and had a big gulp of water. Then she said, 'Anyway, Adam, there is still time, why don't you start writing now? You should've collected many ideas from this, from us here.'

'I wish things were so simple,' I said.

'It's time for me to say goodnight,' Frank said, standing up, 'and it's nearly one in the morning. We need to be sharp and ready tomorrow.'

As he left, Helen asked, 'But we haven't had dinner yet, anyone hungry?' We ignored her.

'Frank's such a gentleman,' said Maria.

'And good company,' I said. 'I haven't been a close friend, but I want to be, now that I have seen him. I wish I had kept in touch.'

'Another regret?' sniggered Roy.

'What's your problem, Roy? Everything seems to be a problem for you, you have to attack everything. Have you had a troubled childhood?' I said.

'Ha ha ha, don't you regret, another regret, you haven't done psychology? But no, you are a natural, taking a course is a disservice to you, betraying your natural talent.'

I called Ralph, who seemed to play on the computer at the bar stand. He came over quickly.

'Can I have another one of this?' I hinted at my empty whisky glass.

'Sure, anyone else?' Ralph asked.

'Let's get another round,' Ana said.

'Good for me,' said Roy.

Colin was dozing off.

'What about dinner?' Helen asked again.

'We will go to the restaurant,' I said.

'I'm afraid the kitchen is closed now,' Ralph said.

'It's Saturday night!' I said.

'Yes, but the kitchen closes at ten, sorry.'

'I'm famished,' said Ana.

'Me too,' said Maria.

'I can make you salads and some sandwiches, if you like.'

'I knew you were my saviour, Ralph,' Helen said.

'Indeed,' Roy said with a smile.

'So, repeat your drinks as well, while waiting for food?' asked Ralph.

'Yes, just ignore that one,' Helen hinted at Colin.

'Now that we are awake, let me tell you a story,' said Helen.

'Oh no! Adam will be jealous!' said Roy.

We all ignored him.

'At the graduation ceremony,' Helen started, 'I was totally pissed. And you lot were all over the place; apart from Frank, who left early.'

'Like tonight,' said Roy.'

'Give us a break, Roy,' said Colin, half-asleep.

It's time to resort to the half-empty glass in front of me, a simple tall glass can take me away from all this. So much bickering, and we've been here only for a few days after so many years. Now I appreciate my nights alone with myself, with a book, a glass of whisky, certainly a better glass, and better whisky. They say the glass affects the taste. I vouch for that. No, I don't regret having come over, this has helped me with my state of mind! It's been good for my health! It is good for my health. Ah! Now I'm talking like that woman I met once, where was it? Whatever it was, it was a short encounter, nothing special, wouldn't say it was all for sex but perhaps it was. "You're like any other man," wearing an open top shoe with her toes coloured dark grey. I looked at her fingernails, shiny red, a silver cross hanging from her neck. Her hair was thin for a young woman. She looked at her watch. As we were having a drink before going to my hotel room in a very traditional way, she told me, "Do you know how long it is I haven't had sex?" I didn't have an answer. Before saying something she said, "It's six months! It's not good for my health, you know." I should've stopped there and then. I should've asked the barman to bring the bill, I should've developed a dizziness, or something. I should've excused myself, ordered a taxi for her and rushed to my room as fast as I could. How could I sleep with a woman who was going to have sex with me for health reasons? Was I a witch doctor? But I didn't say anything. I just continued drinking. Well, perhaps she was bringing reasons for herself, to convince herself what she was doing was OK. But why do people need justification all the time? Oh they do, they do. Imagine her going back home. Her husband in deep sleep. She had showered in the hotel, so she wasn't worried about signs. I would say, that itself is a sign, being too clinical. The husband awakes, murmurs, "How were your friends? Where they OK?" She gets alarmed. She says, "Yes, all were in good shape, nothing special, as usual." She wouldn't see "the friends" for a while, now that her health, after that short remedy, was not in danger anymore, at least for another six months, perhaps. She wondered how long it would be for, perhaps she might need help from another "friend".

My hotel room was hot, and the windows were sealed on the sixth floor. The air conditioning was struggling to work, it was noisy. It reminded me of the bus trip I had in Morocco. I felt fake. I was a fake tourist in a country with fake artefacts for fake memories. And as I lay on my bed, I felt fake. I went to the large glass window. The lights that I could see standing behind her were flickering now.

"What are you looking at?" I asked.
"That's the park I go to everyday for jogging," she said.
"You take care of your health beautifully!" I said.
"Shouldn't I?"
"You have every right! Let's go eat something," I said.
"Has to be quick, I need to go back."
"Something quick in the lobby?"

As she walked to the open car park, I followed her up to the gate. She was hesitant, walking slowly. I stopped and looked at her putting the key into the car door. There were only few other cars under the car park lamps with their short, narrow shadows. I returned to the bar and had a drink. As I went back to the room, I remembered I couldn't open the window. I went to the large window and looked outside. There were fewer lights on, the sky was beginning to brighten up. I dropped myself on the creased bed, and I thought about regrets.

-27-

A hand touches my hair. I open my eyes. It's Ana.

'Good morning,' she says, leaning over my head; I can see the bar-stand behind her with a tray of used glasses.

'What do you mean, good morning? Where are the rest of the gang?' I ask.

'In bed by now,' she says.

I sit up on the chair.

'You dozed off. We kept Roy away, he was intent on waking you up. Colin was also half-asleep. So people decided to call it a day.'

'You should've woken me up, it's so embarrassing.'

'Well, I just did… don't be silly, you always wanted me to wake you up like this… didn't you?' she looked at me with a smile. 'Shall we go?'

'Go?' I ask.

'I guess we can stay here all night, but perhaps better to find a bed!' she continues, smiling.

Her room is the same size as mine, but a mirror image of it. Her windows open partly to the garden and partly to the hotel entrance. I splash some water on my face. As I come back, she has put a couple of mini whisky bottles from the mini-bar on the table next to the TV.

'Do you want some? Or something else, vodka perhaps? Or gin?' she asks.

'I'm OK actually,' I say.

'Just want to stand there watching me drinking?' she asks, while sipping the whisky from the small bottle.

'That's an attractive option. I have other ideas, too,' I say.

'Now, that's the boy I like,' she says.

I look at her as I move the pillow under my head to raise my head as she draws the thick curtain. Then she turns on the bedside lamp. I watch her movement as she walks from the curtain to the lamp.

The taste of whisky as absorbed by her lips, and the warmness of her face standing in the middle of the room… as I sit on the bed, the taste changes. I feel the warmth of her skin, and I think she feels the coldness of my hand… my fingers… she moves away, drinks up the whisky, and takes the other bottle. I look at her skin with wrinkles at places… places I look at now without shy eyes. And how much I craved for this moment years ago when I didn't make a move… didn't move an inch to say something… to express my feeling… but I'm sure she knew. The viscous movement of her body takes me away from the past to the present. I wouldn't feel this feeling then… I wouldn't have the ability to look, to pause on her eyes… her skin… her pulses. Now every movement is a labyrinth sucking me into whirlwinds of emotions I didn't think existed. And they think about youth, fresh, tight skin… do they know what they miss? No! They are not aware of the charged skin carrying the invisible loads, each attracting a mixture of emotions.

'You look like a dreamy young boy,' Ana says, with her thigh caressing the mattress.

'I hope not; their dreams are raw… lack refinement.'

'So it was best we didn't…' Ana says.

'Yes.'

'And what about now? Would you have taken the initiative if I hadn't?' she asks.

'No.'

'You are too proud, proud people carry a suppressed life!' she says.

'I am not sure if it's pride. I just don't like to hear "no"!' I say.

'Then you are presumptuous… how can you assume people's feelings?' she says.

'I've grown up thinking that way,' I say.

'Yes, I should know… you were the same at university.'

'But we agreed it was best I didn't express myself then. Didn't we?' I say.

She moves in the bed, with the duvet pushed away, she talks with all her body under the early morning light penetrating through the curtain.

'What do you think now? You don't need my answer, do you?' she says.

I move closer to her, and take her hand.

I'm absorbed in the contour of her body… the faint, but persistent smell of the perfume grown old… mixed with the smell of her body… and the strings of her hair stuck to her temples after a long-lasting sweat.

'Did you fly over or came by train?' I ask.

'How romantic!' she says, and she sits up on the bed.

And I think about the university courtyard when I saw her first.

Ah… look at those eyes… and her hair hanging loose over her shirt… white, and her fragile arms naked… holding a book in her hand, standing there in the queue waiting to register.

"What are you reading?" I ask.

She shows the book to me without talking.

The Stranger.

"So, you like Camus?" I say.

"Is it a blemish?" She laughs.

Before I answer, the girl standing with her in the queue moves forward, and she follows her.

As she is sitting on the bed, wrapping her flabby arms around her curled feet, she says, 'Do you read a lot?'

I nod. 'It's the effect of the bookshop, I think.'

'Never thought you would be a bookshop person,' she says.

'Is it a weakness?' I ask.

'It's nobility!' she says, laughing.

'I am happy I came over,' I say.

'But you didn't suggest coming up here… you could be deep asleep in your bed now,' she says.

'But I'm not. Sometimes one needs a suggestion, a push. It was good of Colin to organise this,' I say.

'Yes, but sometimes one needs to act… moments pass us by, you know.' She stands up, the early winter morning light enters the room, and her body moving under the dim light is a dance, her contours forming and dissolving.

-28-

I had my breakfast alone; none of our group was in the breakfast room yet. An old couple were sitting next to the large window. The man was holding the woman's hand across the table, and the woman was looking at me. I turned my eyes to the waiter, who had started clearing the table next to theirs. Another waiter brought a plate of bacon and eggs with hash browns for the man. He left the woman's hand and started eating. The woman had a sip from her cup, opened a small book, the cover showing a green hill, and started reading. I thought, who comes here all the way for sightseeing? This place is only good for revisiting your past, it has nothing in common with you and your life; it pushes you to go back to your past through your own memories – in our case, with the help of us sitting around the tables with our drinks – the entities from the past, reminding ourselves that we haven't lived. A bunch of sad middle-aged entities in search of what? We don't know! What glum thoughts to start the day with. I selected some food quickly. I could feel the cold air penetrating through the window frame near the table where I was sitting, mixing with the heat in the room, but in doing that, getting to my skin. I did not move though, I sat there with the glass of orange juice and scrambled eggs as the breeze touched my skin. The egg was dry and bitty, and the coffee was too watery. I had some butter and marmalade with the orange juice while having a cursory look at the newspaper headlines. Outside, there was a drizzle, and the cypresses were bending under the wind. My mouth was dry. I had some water and went to the lobby. Frank and Maria were sitting on the leather armchairs further away.

'Good morning!' I said, 'you are already settled in. Have you been up long?'

'I have, I came down early, and Maria joined me shortly after,' said Frank.

'I should've come down earlier, I didn't sleep much, but was afraid nobody would be there,' Maria said.

'And you were right,' I said. 'It seems people are enjoying their sweet dreams!'

'I'm not sure about sweet,' Frank said.

'You were sleeping so innocently at the bar last night; even Roy didn't have the heart to wake you up,' Maria said.

'I just dozed off,' I said.

'People should be here soon,' said Frank, 'or else we'll be late for the trip to the distillery.'

'Indeed, but I'm afraid I don't know the details,' I said.

'Colin has the details,' Maria said.

'That's great, where is it though?' I asked.

'Apparently a distillery nearby,' Maria said. 'I think a bus is arranged.'

'I would've preferred to visit a tourist site, ruins of some sort,' Frank said.

'Like what?' I asked.

'I don't know… anything but drinking!' Frank said.

'It won't be a repeat of last night, Frank,' Maria said.

'Don't be so sure,' I laughed, 'but it could be fun.'

'I know what these things mean. You enter innocently and leave totally damaged, and have no one else to blame but yourself,' Frank said.

'But Frank, you are the most "prim and proper" person in this group,' Maria said. 'Sorry Adam, I didn't mean to—'

'Don't worry, Maria, in fact I agree with you. In a sense you are a close competitor,' I said.

Maria blushed. She always blushed when people mentioned the slightest thing that involved her. I'm sure it was not only the sensitivity of her fair complexion; I remembered her in those days, with her plain, somewhat rural, flowery outfits.

I saw Roy and Colin going to the breakfast room, followed by Ana and Helen.

'I'd better go and see what Colin has in mind for today.' Maria stood up.

'I hope they had a good sleep last night,' Frank said.

As Maria was walking away, Frank said, 'She is a nice girl.'

'Nice woman, Frank!' I said.

'Yes, I still see her as a girl at university,' Frank said.

'And I think she likes you, to put it mildly,' I said.

'I know. Living alone, I'm sure you agree, makes one look at things in more detail. This can be hurtful at times, but it has its own merits. One can see things,' Frank said.

'But I've also come to believe that one becomes more selfish, egocentric. They feel the whole universe owes them something, feel they are martyrs carrying the cross,' I said.

'Are you like that?' Frank asked.

'I don't think so, at least I hope not, it's the bookshop… seeing people all the time, somehow I don't feel alone.'

'Well, I can tell you I don't feel being a martyr either. You might have a point. For me it's the shop too.' Frank paused. Then he said, 'Maria… she wants to look after me.'

'I'm not surprised, has she actually said that?' I asked.

'Not in so many words, but she has hinted. There is this humanitarian look about her… she displays a picture of innocence,' Frank said.

'And what's wrong with that?' I asked.

'Nothing and everything,' Frank replied. 'I would've liked it if I were healthy, but now, I'm not sure about her motive. I don't want someone to look after me, I'm not a good subject for charitable acts.'

'What's wrong with that?' I asked.

'Everything… everything,' Frank said.

Colin was coming over.

'That was a quick breakfast,' Frank said.

'How long do you need for English breakfast? We should get ready; the coach will be here in half an hour.'

'This is for the—' I started.

'Yes, the grand whisky nosing and tasting all of us were waiting for,' said Colin.

'How far is it?' I asked.

'Not far, around half an hour, perhaps less. The place is a major attraction, part of the history in this part of the world,' said Colin.

There was a faint sunshine out there.

'Let's walk a bit, while waiting for others,' Frank said to me.

We walked to the garden, close to the statue of Bacchus. Lichens had grown on it, and traces of snow persisted at its base. It was strange to have such sculpture in this place… in this hotel.

'I suppose the owner must be Italian,' Frank said.

'Or an admirer of whisky!' I laughed.

'You know, Adam, this was a very good thing for me, this reunion. I was looking forward to meeting up with you. I've been living alone for most of my life, and want to keep it that way, but it would be good, if you are happy too, for us to meet up every now and then back in London. Perhaps we could talk about the books we've read.' He didn't wait for my reply, he just continued, 'Maria is keen… keen for us to meet, perhaps to be together. But I'm not that way inclined, not any longer. I don't want someone to mother me.

She's such a nice woman, caring, accommodating… you've seen it here, you've seen how she responds to comments. I've lived alone for some time now, and want to live alone. Anyway, I didn't find it exciting when someone else was breathing down my neck at home. The shop was a bliss… still is.' Frank said.

'I am fascinated by what you say about your shop.' I said.

'I can imagine you would; after all, you have a bookshop; we are much closer mentally than anyone else here. We stopped walking; he took out an old small moleskin wallet from his jacket. It was something between a wallet and a notebook. He opened the zipped part carefully and took out a small semi-transparent envelope. Then he pulled out from it a large stamp, using small tweezers. 'Look how exquisite this is.'

The stamp was square, with no indentations on its borders. There was a circular picture inside the square, leaving sides of the square blank. Each part of the four blank sides was in a different colour.

'This looks to me to be a pretty unusual stamp,' I said.

'You bet it is!' Frank said. 'I take it everywhere with me, I just can't leave it alone!'

'You must be in love,' I said.

'More like possessive… or obsessed!' Frank said.

'So, this is it?' I asked. 'How can you carry this everywhere with you? You can lose it, someone might steal your wallet, throw the stamp in the gutter, and take the money! The stamp can be destroyed, vanished,' I said.

'Don't be so hasty, my friend. Do you judge everything so quickly? What do you know about stamps?' Franks asked.

'Oh, come on… you just explained everything I needed to know.'

'Yet I didn't tell you that this one is *the* stamp; in fact, this is a bad replica. Look at it carefully, look at the colours, the circle,' Frank said.

'I don't know these things, how can I say anything? I haven't seen the original,' I said.

'And yet you decided it was the stamp, and that I was carrying it carelessly,' Frank said.

'So what's the story then?'

'Simple. This is a replica, in fact, it is worthless. Well, I'm a bit harsh, at best, perhaps a few grand,' Frank said.

'And that's for a fake one?' I asked.

'Oh, yes! The original is much more expensive,' Frank said.

'So why carry it with you with such ritual?' I asked.

'Why not? It reminds me of the real one,' Frank said.

'I suppose like rich women wearing their fake jewellery when they go out,' I said.

'No! They do that to trick burglars,' he said.

'You're doing the same.'

'No! The motive is different. I don't want the real one be destroyed. There's an increased risk taking it with me all the time,' Frank said.

'Well, I think this is sad to have jewellery in the safe, wearing fake, what's the point?' I asked.

'Yes, but this is how things are… beauty locked away, imitation showing off!' Frank said.

Colin shouted from the gate. 'Come on, folks, the coach is here.'

-29-

The red-faced fat driver wearing a thick loose grey polo-neck is jovial. Looking at Ana as she climbs the bus he says, 'Come here for the good weather, love?'

Before Ana can say anything, Helen jumps in. 'No, she's come here to see you!'

'Good choice!' the driver replies, laughing.

'OK, OK, enough of the tittle tattle! Give a rest to your tongues and prepare your noses! We are in for a treat! The brewery we're going to visit is an old one. I mean a really old one,' Colin says.

'How old?' Frank asks.

'I don't know, ask the manager when we get there. Difficult to believe, but older than you, Frank!'

'Why do you pick on Frank?' asks Maria, but her voice gets muddled in the group's loud singing "Get me to the church on time".

'What rubbish are you singing?' Roy shouts, but no one pays attention to him.

Ana is sitting next to me, but talking to Maria, who is sitting the other side of the coach. I have the window seat, looking outside through the glass covered by drops of rain.

'It was OK half an hour ago, but it had to start raining,' Helen says loudly.

I look out of the window. Large balls of hail start hitting the window with a rhythmic noise. The grey sky, the greyish shower and the dark grey of the hills further away takes me to something I had read, but I cannot remember the details.

Easy to lose memories? Selective loss of memory? How long will it take me to count all my memories? People like to boast about the earliest time they remember something. I bet Roy would say he remembers it when they cut his umbilical cord! As for me, the point is that when I remember an image, I cannot remember how old I was! What's the importance of it anyway? Some of the memories I recall, I am not sure about their details; and as for other ones... I doubt if they ever existed. Perhaps they were figments of my imagination. Now they say our memories are changing all the time. Well, as for me, many of them have faded away. I know there was something, something did happen, but have no image of it, it has all perished. Perhaps it is better this way.

Yet, I start remembering. Her skin was rough on the back of her hands, with veins showing. I used to follow the path of the veins, but they disappeared quickly as they moved up the wrist into her forearm. The skin was soft, though, at the front of her hands. I used to sit there, look at her while she turned the rosary beads with her thin fingers. I used to count the beads, the rounds, and always would get distracted by something. She had an old wooden icon in her bedroom next to a mirror on a table, and a book I couldn't read. The carved wood had lost its colour, with only traces left in the grooves, a dusty blue, a faded red. And the face of the man with the beard was fierce. "Do you eat well?" she would ask me, turning her rosary slowly. "Yes," I would say in a low voice. "You should... you should, you are growing up fast."

'What are you gazing at? Haven't you seen rain?' Ana smiles. I remember the smile, that mischievous smile matching her eyes, her fleeting, but piercing glance.

'Oh, I was miles away.'

'Not somewhere as cold and wet as this, I hope.'

I heard Colin's voice, loud, coming from the front of the bus.

'Can I have a moment of silence, please? We will soon be arriving at our exquisite destination! May I remind you that any sort of indulgence, particularly "liquid type" is clearly permitted, oh, in fact is mandatory! But before then I want you all to clear your throat for a very common and happy song to sing together, for the one and only Mr. Roy, the pilot to be! I am sure you didn't know today is Roy's birthday. Oh, yes, the man is getting one year older, but don't think for a second wiser!'

As we started singing, the bus swerved suddenly. We jolted to the left, then the right, and left again. The driver had good control of it, otherwise we would've rolled down to end up at the bottom of the valley. He quickly stopped the bus just behind an old tree at the edge of the road. He was clearly shocked, but tried to compose himself.

'Could be his last day too,' the driver said, laughing it out.

'It is an omen, Colin, remembering my birthday,' said Roy.

'How on earth did you remember his birthday?' asked Helen.

'Never you mind!' said Colin.

'Is everyone OK?' asked Maria, looking at the driver.

'We are fine,' said Helen, 'we can't not be fine before having our drinking session!'

'May I advise you that we are going for a "nosing" experience, not a tasting one? This is a whisky distillery, not a vineyard in Bordeaux!' said Frank.

'Ah, but you forget the genius of Colin! I have arranged for us – after we have put our long noses into each and every orifice in that distillery – to taste a range of their whiskies from earlier days to the present, from single malts to exquisite blends,' said Colin.

Helen walked to Colin and pinched his cheek. 'What would we do without you, Colin? We would be lost in the misty winding roads of the cold land,' she laughed.

-30-

Helen is talking to Martin. She started talking with him the moment he introduced himself as our host today.

'Welcome everyone, I am your host today. My name is Martin,' he says.

'What a sexy accent,' Helen said.

I thought a robot could do what he was doing.

Martin smiles, 'Thank you,' and continues, 'but first things first, and that's a bit of housekeeping and safety!'

'Oh bollocks!' I see Helen murmuring to herself, standing next to him.

'If you need to freshen up, you need to go through that corridor, and it is on your left-hand side. If you hear the alarm going, it is real, it's not a drill, it's not Wednesday! So please walk calmly to that door, yes, that door, and you are out. Please do not gather next to the door, just walk to the parking where you arrived, where your bus is parked.'

'Can we take a bottle before leaving?' Colin asks, laughing.

'Of course we can!' Roy shouts from the other side. 'If there is a fire, nothing will remain, so we might as well take as many as we can!'

Martin ignores the comments and continues, 'Please follow me.'

He moves to a door behind him and we follow through a wide corridor into another door which opens to a courtyard, and then to a hall. We stand at a corner.

'Do we need to do this?' Roy mumbles.

'We store raw barley, malted barley, and also distillery waste, there are samples here. Please feel free to examine them, not the waste! It's just to see what they look like. We sell them to the farmers!' Martin says, laughing.

'He thinks he's funny,' Roy says.

'No, he knows we are stupid!' laughs Helen.

'Speak for yourself,' Roy says.

'He is excited to see us; this is a lonely place,' Maria says.

'You think so? Forget about the dull day, not everybody's idea of holiday is like ours. Come over in summer, and you'll see. They don't have a moment to sit.'

'My heart is bleeding! So what? He goes to work, then home, like us, the chores, nobody says we are lonely,' Roy says.

'If nobody admits it, it doesn't mean we're not,' says Frank.

We enter a very large hall with a high ceiling. There are eight tall stills extending from the ground floor to the first and second floors.

'Well, after the fermentation, this is where the main activity happens. Do you want to go up?' asks Martin.

'Not really, we have jumped through steps anyway,' says Roy.

'So, you are familiar with the process? asks Martin.

'My father was very keen!' Roy smirks.

'You are right, we need to go faster. We are a bit behind, the days are short,' says Martin, 'let's see the casks.'

We follow him, I think like school children on a day out. I do not listen to him any longer as we go through some other halls and end up in the room where we had arrived.

'That was a wasted journey,' whispers Roy, but loud enough for me to hear it standing next to Ana.

'At last, we can try water of fire, fire in water!' Martin says. 'I am sorry to have rushed you through the tour, I thought you would be more interested in trying the real stuff than to see how it's made!'

'You're not wrong there!' Roy says loudly.

'We are eagerly waiting,' says Helen.

'Today we have lined up a special collection of delightful vertical *and* horizontal samples for you to examine and enjoy.' He shows whisky glasses and glasses for water on a table against each chair.

While pouring, he talks about the history of the distillery, the family tree of the owners. My eyes wander around the room, as his words move to the background. There are memorabilia items to decorate the walls and shelves of whisky enthusiasts. T-shirts with images of the countryside showing the distillery building in the background, crystal glasses, a wall-hanging calendar, and some knickknacks. There is a bronze sculpture of an eagle with its wings stretched out. Not for sale.

'What's wrong with a pigeon? Or a swift? What is this obsession people have with hunting birds?' she asked me, and it was the first time we had met.

'Well, I suppose for different reasons,' I said.

'Like what?'

'I mean different people like them for different reasons.'

'What is it that you like about them?' she asked.

'I didn't say I liked them,' I said.

'But you do, don't you?'

'Yes, but—'

'I knew it. It was all so obvious,' she said.

It was so absurd, I thought. It was the first time we were talking, and she was already accusing me of something I liked, and the whole thing was so ridiculous!

'So, what if I liked them for whatever reason? It is not a crime, is it?' I asked.

'Why do you think something must be a crime to be wrong? It *is* wrong, but it is *not* a crime! You see? People have these set opinions and carry them all the time,' she replied.

I thought, *but you have a set opinion yourself, look what you are saying about the birds.* But I didn't say anything. Her eyes were shining while talking. She was my first… first… I cannot bring myself to say my first love.

We were on the train going away for the first time. A weekend away. 'Look at that bird on the wire, quick,' I said. She was too slow.

I wish I could remember her face. I can describe it, but it doesn't satisfy me, as if something is missing. I feel I have lost her image. I watched too hastily not to miss the moments with her, but the moments moved faster than my glances. A picture? No! I do not have a picture of her, we were together practically for the best part of two years, but no pictures, strange… I know. But it wasn't the decade of mobiles, decade of taking pictures of anything that moves or doesn't move! And after all, who needed a picture? Somehow, none of us thought of eternalising those moments in photos! I think of her name, the moment when I asked her for her name, the way she answered, but I keep all this a secret. Funny, what secret? It is stupid, I know. But I feel if I utter her name out loud, I will wipe out the little else that has remained of her in me. But thinking of her, it brings me pages after pages of drawings, and her fingertips tinted by colourful chalks.

'I will draw you one day,' she says.
'No, thank you!' I say.
'Do you think I'm not good enough?' she says.
'I think *I* am not good enough!'
'I'm not with you for your looks, you know.'

'I hoped you'd never say that, what's wrong with my looks?' I say.

'Nothing, but you're not exactly Burt Lancaster or Sean Connery!'

'Hey! Don't forget, it's all about animal magnetism. Jean-Paul Sartre and Picasso weren't a David reincarnate, you know!'

'But they had that attraction, that mesmerising effect men don't understand, cannot understand,' she says.

'Of course, and women do!'

Well, I should've known, should've known the thing between us would go nowhere, but the shine in her eyes and her smile kept me persisting. There was some sort of contradiction in the way her eyes talked to me in those silent moments, and the way she behaved when we were with the others. And I was young – we were young. When someone says this, it means he is going to bring an excuse for his naïvety, his behaviour, his actions. And it is exactly the case here. We didn't continue… I didn't continue… I didn't continue.

'You are somewhere else again,' Ana says. This time there is no smile.

'Funny how small things can take you to places you haven't visited for many years,' I say.

'You are still there, far away. You speak in codes,' she says.

'I am fascinated by that eagle,' I say.

'Oh, that kite? It's the company logo,' she says.

'I wondered, why kite?'

'Why not? You look mysterious now!' she says.

'Mysterious?'

'Yes, your face looks like a man coming from an emotional funeral.'

'You are clairvoyant, Ana.'

'I know,' she says. 'I am a gift, too!' She laughs.

-31-

'This was a non-event,' Ana tells me as we enter the bus going back.

'What did you expect?' I ask her, but I agree with her. I don't know how the whole trip went so fast. I can see Martin with his gestures, his movements, the faces looking at him, Colin drinking, Roy's fat red face with his nose poking into the whisky glass.

'It's near two and it's getting dark,' I say.

'What do you expect?' Ana smiles.

'Are we drunk enough for the pub?' asks Helen.

'We are hungry,' says Roy.

'And drunk,' says Colin.

'Do I hear pub?' asks the driver, and I think he looks like Roy!

'Yes, is there a good one around here?' asks Colin.

'Is there a good one? Is there a good one? What a question. You must have heard of the Red Eagle.'

'As much as I would love to say yes, the answer is no!' says Colin, 'but is everyone happy with pub lunch? Alternative is back to the hotel.'

There is no answer.

'OK then, I take it we are all happy to indulge! So, off to the Red Lion.'

The driver says, 'Eagle.'

'OK, Eagle… Lion… whatever you say.'

'It seems it's birds' day!' says Ana.

There is a calm in the bus, only the noise of the engine, and snoring of Colin and Roy, mixing, blending with the scenery outside passing fast, but reassuring. Feeling the warmth of people being around you, a strange feeling of warmth in the winter, winter scenery. Frank is reading a book. He told me it was more like an essay about the state of stamps during the Second World War, and the decade after the end of the war. Helen and Maria are both sleep.

'I thought Martin at the distillery was OK, didn't you?' I ask Ana.

'Yes, can't imagine an exciting life here, though.'

'Perhaps he likes it exactly for the same reason,' I say.

'Probably, but he hasn't seen much else.'

'Some people are content with what they have, a wife, a husband, a couple of kids, a secure job… what else would they want? They go to work, take the kids to and from school, see a movie, watch TV, save to go on a ten-day holiday somewhere sunny… you know? That sort of thing. And they grow old… that happens fast. They look forward to their grandchildren,' I say.

'You are too presumptuous!' Ana says.

'But true, don't you think?'

'Life has its interesting things as well for everyone, but something exciting for other people might not be for you!' Ana said.

Mobile rings. It's Maria's. She opens her eyes quickly and tries to find the phone. Others don't react.

'What? When? Oh no! I cannot believe it… how did it happen?' She lowers her voice. 'Please… yes, I think that's the best… yes. Oh, thanks Jane, thanks. Yes… I will call later, bye… bye.' Maria closes the cover of her mobile.

'Is everything fine?' asks Ana.

'My budgie just died,' says Maria.

'Oh, what happened?' asks Ana.

'I had never left her before, only this time, only once. It was a beautiful green and blue budgie. Oh, I loved her so much.'

'So sorry, it's difficult to keep birds,' Ana says.

'She was in very good shape, I thought only a few days couldn't harm her. I asked my neighbour to look after her. She is so careful, a kind old woman,' Maria says.

'Well this could've happened any time,' I say.

'There is no excuse, I shouldn't have left her alone.'

'So, what could you do? Not come over?' I ask.

'Oh, don't know… I don't know.' She takes out a handkerchief from her small handbag. It has small colourful embroidery with a small flower pattern in a corner.

The hearse was stuck in the traffic, and it was hot. The smell of dusty diesel mixed with burning plastic was in the air, and the cars had come to a complete standstill.

'Do you want chewing gum?'

'No, thanks,' I said. I was thinking of the flower they had laid on her coffin. What would be the shape of the spade the man uses every day to throw earth on the coffin. From where I will stand, will I hear the sound of the soil hitting the wood? And flowers... what about the flowers? Why should they be buried? My mother liked flowers, but never bought one. She would cut a small white flower from the garden, stick it to a letter with Sellotape, and send it to me. I have her letters somewhere. I am not sure why; I never look at them, let alone read them. They are sitting there, somewhere, I am not even sure where they are. All I know, they are somewhere. And her grave?

'Are you sure?' My aunt offered me a pack of chewing gum.

'No, really, thanks.'

'It'll be a long day, you know,' she said.

My mother never bought flowers... but then, one day, I saw her with some special thin pieces of fabric, all colourful, and some tools. She'd enrolled in a flower-making course.

I didn't like artificial flowers in those days. I didn't ask questions. My childhood was a sequence of silent moments that evaporated easily, only few moments are left. I keep dried flowers in my office at the bookshop, but not artificial ones.

I love this feeling of suspension... being suspended in the air... have you seen those big birds? Have you seen how they hold their wide wings, letting the air do the rest?

I made kites from colourful paper, and most of them nose-dived.

Frank has moved from his seat and is comforting Maria. 'There are things in life that are inevitable.

Look, this has happened while we are all around you, you are not alone, you do not need to witness this alone.'

'Thanks, Frank, you are a good friend.' She holds Frank's hand.

'Perhaps you will get another one on your next birthday, when is it?' Franks asks.

'Let's not be so melodramatic, a bird dies… long live other birds!' says Helen. Ana frowns at her.

'What? This is life, you know? Shit happens. Thankfully, it's not one of us, it's a bird.'

'Are you saying that life is not as dear for different beings?' I say.

'Yes! And if you don't, your brain needs to be examined!' Helen says.

'Wait a minute, surely, it depends how close you are with something. You might have a relative that you have little in common with, a pot plant that you live with every day, take care of,' I say.

Helen interrupts me. 'I can easily ignore you, you and your words. You are a man of words; when it comes to real stuff, you chicken out. You haven't changed an iota. In fact, you are worse.'

'Maria, what is your friend going to do with it now? Is there something we could do?' Frank says.

'My neighbour has a good-sized garden. She asked me if I liked the idea to have some sort of – I don't know – praying for her. She said she can bury her near her rose bush by the wall. I said yes,' Maria says.

'I think this is a good idea, you always know it's next to you, Ana says.

'Wise decision,' Frank says.

'What are these voices of approval? What could have happened in the few minutes I closed my eyes?' asks Colin.

'The first thing that happened is that we couldn't do the same because of your snuffle, and with that of your mate… he is still snoring! What a duet!' says Helen.

'Maria's budgie died,' says Ana.

'Is that all?' Colin says.

'What do you mean is that all? Do you have any feelings?' Ana says.

'Don't you lecture me on feelings, lady! My kid had a rabbit, she died. We replaced it for him. He was upset for a couple of days, but then he loved the new rabbit much more, and, and, learnt to look after it better. Despite all these years, I remember it very well.'

Maria pressed the handkerchief between her fingers.

'I know, I should've done better.'

'All I'm saying is that you can always have another one!' Colin says.

'I'm not going to keep anything anymore. I don't want a replacement; she wasn't a lamp to replace when burnt,' Maria says.

'You don't need to do anything now, give it some time, you can then decide,' says Frank.

The bus turns into a short narrow gravel road.

'We're there,' the driver says. 'Eagle's landing at the Red Eagle.' He laughs.

We stop at a big car park; I think what a waste of land for a pub in this tucked away place.

We start getting off the bus, but Roy is still deeply sleep.

Helen went to his chair. 'Wakey wakey! The Eagle is waiting for you,' Helen says.

Roy opens his eyes. 'What?'

We laugh. Helen says, 'The Eagle, the Red Eagle, can't you remember?'

'What are you talking about? Where are we?'

'Let's go, we are famished,' Ana says.

The pub is heaving. I see from an angle there is more parking space the other side, completely full. We manage to get a place, just, in a corner. There's a nice smell of wood burning, mixed with whisky, and beer. I sit next to Maria in the corner of the table. Frank and Ana sit in front of us, while Helen sits at my other side next to Roy and in front of Colin.

'Let's celebrate,' says Roy.

'Celebrate what?' Colin says.

'I don't know, anything,' Roy says. 'I've had a good sleep, and feel like celebrating.'

'And while you were snoring your life away, Maria's bird died,' Helen says.

'Now you are pissing me off! Do you have to be a killjoy?' Roy says.

'You have the sensitivity of a rhinoceros! I'm sure a rhino snores like you!' says Helen.

'But Roy doesn't know what has happened,' says Frank.

'Doesn't matter, he's still a rhino!'

'What's the matter?' Roy asks.

'My budgie just died,' says Maria, and this time she starts crying.

'Oh, I'm sorry, Maria, really, you must've been very close to her. When my wife died, I was away on a course by the company. It was terrible, I know what you go through,' Roy says.

'I'd better go get a menu or something, I'm not sure if they're still serving lunch,' I say.

'Don't worry, I will, you can't come out of that corner easily,' says Colin.

Ana says, 'We are used to ignoring things around us, things dear to us. We ignore them, ignore them until something happens, and then, it seems we feel them more than when they were near us, accessible as if forever.'

Maria nods.

'Time to see what we want to do for the rest of our stay,' says Frank.

'Indeed,' says Roy.

'Let's wait for Colin to come back,' Ana says.

'They will bring us some ploughmans, that's all that's left. We can order our drinks when the food comes,' Colin says.

'This corner reminds me of the pub at university,' Helen says. 'Do you remember the cosy corner in the Rooster's Arms? The red sofa over there, the other four comfort chairs?'

'I remember you were good at crosswords, dark horse of the group,' says Frank.

'I remember it, I remember when I beat you to it, Frank, it was such a joy!' Helen says.

'It was a miracle!' says Colin.

'A coup!' says Ana, laughing.

'Let's not overdo it,' I say, 'I put it down to luck!'

'We had good times then,' says Maria.

'No reason not to have it now,' says Frank.

'Why not get together when we return? We can meet up for a pint or something every now and then… perhaps once a month,' says Colin.

'Good idea, let's see,' says Roy.

I look through the small window. The light from a lamp shows the rain pouring down. The waiter comes over with plates on her hands.

-32-

Back in the hotel, I touch the card onto the plate next to the door to my room hoping it works, and it does.

'Can do with some water,' Ana says.

'So do I.'

I increase the temperature in the room. It has gone cold since morning after the cleaners did the room.

That was winter with the unexpected white Christmas. The best present I had was a set of colourful pencils with a big pad of plain white paper all packaged together in a colourful plastic box. When I opened it, I was fascinated by the white pencil, but my drawings with the pencil would not show on the paper. I grabbed a used magazine and tried the cover which showed colour bits of a forest, but the texture wouldn't take the pencil colour. I took the box to my bed with the white pencil in my hand, and I went to sleep.

'Do you want to go to sleep like an innocent boy, for me to wake you up? I think this is your desire the way you are fixated looking at your bed,' Ana laughs.

I look at her with a smile. As my fingers touch her skin, I think of the colourful pencils, the white one… what happened to them? I kept the white one in a box together with screwdrivers, a small hammer, and pins of different sizes, some of them bent, used and reused.

'Hesitant?' Ana asks.

'Oh… far from it, far, far from it,' I say.

It has been raining, nonstop since we were at the pub, and it was only Ana and I who remained in one piece; all resigned to their rooms.

'Would you like a cup of tea?' I ask.

'Love it,' Ana says.

'I know so little about you, Ana, you are still a mystery to me.'

'Mystery? Why?'

'Since university time, there hasn't been an occasion we could talk about you… us.'

'Perhaps there was no need for it,' she says.

'Yes, I'm sure, but I always wondered… there is a sense of stories untold.'

'Now, this is your bookshop sense, nothing amazing to tell though.'

'Do you know how many books we receive and dispose of without being read by anyone? How many stories gather dust waiting to be destroyed? Sometimes I think they're like those who are condemned to death, awaiting… they are in a death row. But then there are even more, many more stories untold.'

'Does it matter at all? If they are to be destroyed, then why write them?'

'It is like saying, why should we be born, as we will die anyway,' I say.

'But we don't need to humiliate them by throwing them into the rubbish bin, or, at best, recycling them to make newspaper to be used as a wrapping for fish and chips takeaway!'

'But that's life! I look at you and… and… you know what goes on in my mind. We will be together in that exploding moment of glances scanning our totality, skin, form, movements, pulses… and yet we are sitting here… again… this time having tea. Should we not do it? Can we not do it all?' I say.

'With you everything turns into a philosophical discourse. I feel I am in Athens!' she says.

'I hope you're not disappointed in this journey!'

Ana stands up and moves towards me. She ruffles my hair, standing behind me as I remain on the chair.

'Not at all, that journey has prepared me for another one!' I stand up and turn to look at her… her full body.

-33-

'So, you were going to tell me something about yourself.' I face her as she is lying on the bed with her hands under her head. I think this is a masculine pose. She takes my pillow, and puts it over hers to sit leaning back on them.

'I'm not sure what you want to know. People have their lives with the usual routine,' she says.

'But people want to know about each other too, while they live their routine, as you say.'

'It depends on whose lives we are talking about. There are all sorts of people. Some prefer to talk about a piece of art, a play, a performance than to talk about themselves and whether the life they've had has been catastrophic or privileged,' she says, and throws the cover to the floor as she stands up.

Her contours against the dim light in the room, her contours against the light as she moves gently. I imagine her walking between the rows of books in the bookshop. Oh... the books... the books in the bookshop are silent without me. They accept the particles of dust, solemnly... the rays of the sun, and their pages go yellow… ever so slowly… so tenderly as her skin has folded on itself… slightly… under her chin. She wears silk scarves now, beautiful ones, but I like her skin as it is now, and as it was before. I like all those memories that I cannot recall! They remain abstract, elusive, but I know they are there. They breathe without me seeing them, touching them… they touch me, call me when I am least prepared.

Ana has taken her shower now, walks in the room naked. She sits on the edge of the bed. There is something alluring about her posture, not sexual anymore, but attractive.

'OK, I decided to tell you about myself. I really like you to unravel me as we go on, bit by bit… but you prefer to have a box opened for you with the instructions on how to use the items inside. You do read, carefully, "Handle with care" sign, unlike most others, but all the same, you want easy answers. This is the sign of people gone tired, this is the sign of our time. So, I will tell you about my life, but I will tell others too, perhaps best to share it with the reunion gang!'

'You don't need to be like this, you really should know what I mean when I say I like to know about you,' I say as she quickly dressed up.

'Let's go,' she says.

'Go?'

'Yes, they should be down there at the bar talking about the pub, or the budgie.' She laughs.

'Do I see a trace of sarcasm here?' I say.

She wears her shoes. 'It's in the air, Adam, it's in the air.'

When was the last time someone called my name intimately? I cannot remember. There must be a time, but I cannot remember. I fear it's all in my imagination as a boy's imagination, so severe he believes in it. What is there in a name? A name uttered with passion, with a feeling of being wanted? Now, I only remember Ana calling me.

'Are you coming, or is the room so engaging you cannot leave it?' Ana laughs again.

-34-

The gang are sitting in the bar, have put some short, round tables next to each other, and formed a large sitting area. As we walk in, Roy says, 'Eventually! We thought you'd gone back to London!'

'Rubbish, we've just arrived ourselves. We never thought you would leave the cosy intimate air of the rooms here for noisy London!' Helen says.

'You are full of insight,' I say.

'How are you feeling?' I ask Maria.

'Much better, thank you, Adam.' She wears a bright red jumper.

'OK then, enough of pleasantries, let's order.' Colin calls Ralph, who is standing at the bar watching us.

'I am so happy we have done this, getting together,' Maria says.

Does she want to give a portrayal of a tolerant woman? She was clearly upset by the death of her budgie, now she wants to show herself as a tolerant, suffering woman. A typical Christian. Look at her jumper. She hadn't worn that one before... now that her budgie has died, she wears shocking bright red! Maybe she is, deep inside, happy about the bird's death. She can go places now! She did say it was the first time she had left the bird behind. Maybe she is guilty about it.

'What do we want? Whisky? Beer? What?' asks Colin.

'None of that,' says Ana, 'time to give ourselves a rest. I want a large hot pot of tea. Do they have clotted cream here?'

'Of course we have,' answers Ralph, who is now standing behind Helen, facing her.

'That's great, I'll have afternoon tea then,' Ana says.

'I'll have the same,' says Helen.

'Me too!' says Maria.

'So that's the women's choice,' says Colin, looking at Frank and me. 'What do *we* want? I tell you, a cold beer will do me nicely.'

'For me too,' says Roy.

'Just Darjeeling for me, Ralph, with a slice of lemon if possible,' Frank says.

'I'll have tea too, any tea will do,' I say, looking at Ralph. He has a short golden chain with a cross around his neck, I hadn't noticed it before.

'Martin knew his stuff, didn't he?' Helen says.

'You would say that,' Roy says.

'Meaning?' Helen asks.

'Nothing, obviously you are in the know,' replies Roy.

'Are we set for another fight now?' asks Ana.

'It's like a family, we have our fight, bickering, we have come all the way eagerly to meet up, to be together, albeit for a short time. But all this is a bit confusing for me,' Maria says, 'we are behaving as high school kids.'

'Don't let it confuse you, Maria, there is nothing unusual about it. We are here because we've been bored with our day-to-day routine. Colin's suggestion was very welcome for us all, but now that we are here, after all these years, we want to relive those days. It's role play, we like to imitate our past,' Frank says.

'Is it getting warmer here, or is it me?' asks Helen.

'It's you, darling… it's always been you,' says Roy.

I see Ralph coming over with a large tray. As he looks at us, smiling, he trips over and falls. The drinks splash all over. One scone topples, and strawberry jam smears the floor. Ralph stands up and looks at his outfit. He is red in the face.

'This is the first time in my life, this hasn't happened to me before, ever,' he says.

'No problem, Ralph, not a big issue,' says Helen.

'You'll get over it,' says Colin loudly.

'I want my beer,' says Roy.

What was going on in his mind the moment he dropped the tray? Was he thinking of his family? Whether he would get a good tip from us before we go? Was he thinking what a loud, rowdy group from down south? Was he thinking of Helen's hints? Perhaps the floor was slippery.

'Sorry, sorry, I will bring your order soon.' He went back.

Yes, a boisterous group from the south, in this quiet isolated hotel in the north, in the middle of winter, each in their own world, their worlds colliding… splashing noises… mumbling words.

'That's not a big deal, so what? Something dropped. You can wait for your beer, you won't die!' says Helen.

'Do you know at this moment how many stars, planets, galaxies are colliding, being destroyed? Life, or whatever you call it on them, ruined, vanished, gone?' says Frank, leaning back in his chair. He looks very relaxed.

'Do you have to make everything so physical?' asks Roy.

'He has a point, it's exciting actually!' says Ana.

'Exciting? Do you get excited so easily?' asks Roy.

'If you had my background, perhaps you would get excited too,' says Ana. 'We are talking of destruction, devastation, damage, death… we don't need to go to other planets. Look at us, the earth, all that destruction… war. Do you know what happened in Iran? You weren't there, *I* was.'

'Oh, oh, wait a minute. For goodness' sake! Someone just poured my beer and your tea on the floor, made a mess out of it. I want my beer, you want your tea. Full stop! You Iranians are so melodramatic! You think you are the only one with emotions,' says Roy.

'Interesting, the first time you have mentioned me as Iranian in all these years. You are making a fuss about a glass of beer, and *I* am melodramatic? My country is still in a mess. It went through something people called revolution. For me it was a massive murderous destruction of so many things that were created over the years. Have you ever seen someone with blood gushing out of him just in front of you? Of course not! Do you know what death means? You love your macho outbursts, and your pint of beer.'

Ana looks flustered. This is the first time I've seen her talking about Iran in this way. This is the first time I've seen her so angry.

She stands up. 'I need some fresh air,' she says, and leaves, heading to the lobby. I follow her. She sits on a comfortable chair facing the counter. I sit next to her.

'That idiot can't think of anyone else but himself. A rhino is more sensitive!' she says.

A young couple arrive and go to reception. The boy is puny with a skeletal face and red hair. The girl looks older than him, wears a thin dress, but carries a thick black coat. She looks around and monitors the lobby.

'Look, don't let this change your mood, our mood. I think, after all, this getting together has been great, at least great for us, don't you think so?' I ask Ana.

'Something has prompted me into this. I am miles away now. Somehow all those events when I was very young have affected me, they've come back. I had put them in a safe place, I thought, somewhere there was no need to go back to, but suddenly, so unexpectedly, they exploded out of their calm quarters.' Ana looks calm with her misty eyes. 'Anyway, you wanted to know about me! Now you do. I remember the smoke, the smell of burning. My grandmother and her Quran – it was so small you could hardly identify the words – and her rosary. I loved her, her wrinkled skin, her thin grey hair, her thin body – I don't know how she could go thinner – the smell of her skin, so intimate. And I hated all that was happening around me, the shouting, the radio, the television, and the arguments between my parents. I was going to start at university, and I considered myself very much in a relationship. Relationship! I had met this boy, went out with him for a year, and we were going to continue in the same university. But then he started behaving strangely. It wasn't only him. One of our relatives, who had been living in the States for fifteen years, hurried back, went to this religious town to repent from all his sins, then quickly married a mullah's daughter, and started inviting to his house the students of the religious school to provide them with lectures by some religious figures that I didn't know ever existed. I hear he is a very successful businessman now! And my boyfriend started talking about Sartre's plays and the importance of the people's revolt against forces suppressing masses. But my outlook on life was more like internal revolt against a cosmic force, a Sisyphus, Prometheus, Eve! Have you thought of the nobility of Eve when she gave the apple to Adam? If seducing someone brings him awareness, so be it, what better than this? Don't you agree?' Ana stops.

'Oh, well, yes…' I reply. But I wonder why she is so incensed.

Did she have long hair when she was a teenager? Did she have her hair caressed by the young revolutionary who perhaps decided women must wear the hijab? Could love be limiting?

Ana starts again. 'I told him I would have none of that nonsense. For me it was the desperation of pseudo-intellectuals who wanted to prove they cannot live under a suppressive regime. Most of them were sleepwalking into a deceptive dream of the land of the free. For me, it was the fanaticism of the bazaar merchants, whose god was money, under the guise of reciting prayers. For me it was the ruthlessness of the mullahs who had nothing else in mind than domination of the poor illiterate mob who sat there, squatting in mosques with the mixed smell of rosewater and sweaty feet and armpits, with their open mouths as if breathing the air of the promised paradise. Oh, of course, anything above that for them was the noise of coins pouring into the religious shrines, going straight into their pockets, and the occupying of the oil ministry, where they could buy anything by its returns… paradise itself! Which they never believed in anyway. "Look what's happening, you're missing a great event in your life," he kept on telling me again and again. "Mullahs are nothing, we are using them to get rid of this dictator." Little he knew! Then the streets were calm, there was an eerie silence. Then the newspapers wrote in large fonts "Shah went". My grandmother had her rosary in her hand and shook her head slowly in despair, but said nothing, just sighed. I always wondered, still think, what happened to the collective unconscious of all the people, with a thousand years of monarchy. Did we just throw it away when the country was doing reasonably well? Or did we, despite all that we knew about the mullahs, hand our history, identity, future to them, in a state of stupor, to make a mockery of it, to ruin it… again, after what happened 1600 years ago.'

'But don't you think you're exaggerating? No one can steal your history, your identity,' I say.

'Yes, this is what I thought too. But when the children's history books are changed, the events are reported totally differently, in fact, when the events are wiped out, and some imaginary things introduced, it's a matter of time, only a couple of generations to have a different history, a carefully-crafted history.'

'I disagree. Even in your own history, Herodotus, with all his influence, could not sustain things he said about the Persians, as there were other entries too,' I say.

'I didn't know you know things about us, I'm impressed,' she says.

'Oh, I have been successful then. I have to confess, it was an innocent attempt on my side to impress you… it happened years ago! I read a bit, but there was no occasion to show off. Who knew that so many years later, I would impress you in a cold hotel lobby! Don't you feel cold? Perhaps we should go back,' I say.

As we stand up, Helen comes over.

'Don't you want your tea? It is getting cold.'

We sit back where we left. The floor is cleaned up and Ralph is talking with Colin.

'Look, Ana, I didn't mean to upset you. You know, I have seen destruction, when my home was destroyed, when my wife died. Devastation? *I* was devastated. But I see no point in talking about it. So, sorry for my behaviour. Really, there is nothing to trust in this life, no matter how much we philosophise, that's why I get angry, frustrated with Adam and Frank. I feel they are deceiving themselves. Perhaps they've chosen the easy way, they've convinced themselves. And now they talk, and talk, and I've had enough of listening. What I see is a life vulgar, aggressive, invasive, artificial,' says Roy. He has already finished his glass of beer.

'Hey, Ralph, can I have another one?' he says.

And I remember myself asking him, telling him, what's eating you.

Colin says, 'What happened? Can't I leave you people for a moment? Do you have to be so morose?'

No one says a thing for a while.

'I'll have another one, too,' Colin tells Ralph.

Ana has taken the lid off the teapot, looking inside it. Her face looks tired, and her eyelashes look heavy with bits of mascara. She looks ten years older in this moment compared to a couple of hours ago, in the room.

Your eyelids have come a long way; the teapot leaves the table, taking your glance... your glance has come a long way from the cold streets of Tehran years ago... all the way to precipitate here in this cold countryside. I see you with your long hair sitting across the table in front of your revolutionary boyfriend, with your cocktail glass in your hand, listening to him discussing the merits of regime change. These are the last days, for some time, that your hair will roam freely in the air. None of you knows this at the time, certainly your boyfriend doesn't know. He also doesn't know you will leave him. That you would've left him anyway, but those events would help you; you have a good reason, he's gone mad… revolution mad. He cannot see logic, cannot comprehend what's happening to the country. The country of poems and sleepwalkers. In any case, he faces a serious barrier, your father, who insists you have to leave the country as soon as possible. He gives you the ticket, passport is ready, money is no limitation. Your mother remains silent, and your grandmother? You see her reciting a poem, from that poet. Oh yes, Hafez, not a verse from the Quran. And you see her wiping very slowly a drop of tear from one of her eyes. Only you see that.

Ralph is back with glasses of beer.

'It is time to drink to something,' Colin says, and pauses. We are all waiting to see who he drinks to. But no word comes out of his mouth.

Frank says, 'Why don't you drink to Bacchus? You must have seen his sculpture in the garden. He seems to me to be a lonely bystander here going through the cold!'

'Why not? Indeed! I drink to Bacchus.' He looks at Roy with an enquiring glance.

'OK, OK, let's drink to Bacchus,' Roy says.

'We salute his spirit. I don't think he would appreciate us raising our teacups!' Helen says, laughing. She pours some sugar into her tea and stirs it.

'How can you have so much sugar?' Colin asks.

'Wait and see!' She drinks the tea. 'Like this,' she says.

'Whenever I had tea at home, I would wet a sugar cube, and give it to my budgie,' Maria says.

'Maybe that's what killed it,' Helen says. 'People say sugar is not good for budgies.'

'But I left her with my neighbour, *she* doesn't give her sugar,' Maria says.

'Well, perhaps that's the reason,' Colin says. 'You see, the poor bird was used to sugar, it was a sudden change in her habit!'

'Oh, that reassuring, calming effect of habit. How nice it is to get back home, sit on your sofa, in the corner you like, turn on the TV, watch the programme you like, have the dinner you have prepared, the one you are used to,' Maria says.

'You are making a statement on the benefits of not being married, you have all these freedoms when you are on your own, no one changes your routine, suggests her routine is better than yours, that you're better following her habits,' Frank says.

'But you settle in with your other half after a while,' Maria says, 'and you will have common delightful habits.'

'What a nightmare!' Frank says, 'a life of submission.'

'But to say you must follow my rules is not marriage, it is religion,' Ana says.

'Marriage is religion, darling, haven't you noticed? Oh, no, you haven't. I forgot you haven't had the blessing of being married!' Helen laughs.

'I agree with Frank, it can be a bind being married,' Colin says.

'Is it a bind for you, Colin?'

'Well, too much sacrifice,' Colin says.

'Mm, but being alone the way Maria says… I don't consider it freedom. If you are tied to habits, then what freedom?' I say.

'We are doomed! Married or unmarried,' Roy says.

'So, Roy, you see? You are talking philosophy yourself while always criticising us for philosophising!' says Ana.

'This is just a down-to-earth statement, that's all,' says Colin.

'My heart is bleeding for Colin, he is so low-key, subdued! What has happened? I think Maria's budgie has started a revolt in him,' Helen says.

'Leap of faith!' says Ana.

'You see? We are getting into philosophy again. Definitely our getting together has reignited our old time… university time… oh, how nice it was,' Maria says.

'Those were the days, my friend,' Helen starts singing.

'Talents are exposed,' Colin says.

'Were we settled in our ways then? Was it a comfortable time? Was it comfortable because we had the habit of being a student, with its structure?' Ana asks.

'But we suffered then too, we did suffer for all different reasons,' Roy says.

'Suffering is always there, even in the most routine life,' Frank says.

'You mean boring life!' Helen says.

'Yes, whatever you do, you are bound to suffer,' Frank says.

'Well, we'd better enjoy ourselves, do unexpected things. Now that suffering is inevitable, why stick to the routine?' Helen says.

'Yes, but who has the guts?' says Ana. 'I was talking about what happened in Iran. Before the revolution, people didn't have it better than that for decades, so they revolted! Perhaps boredom was the source of that national suicide. So much is said about it, so much is written about it, about why it all happened. But I doubt if anyone mentioned boredom!'

'Of course you say that, how much did you know about the pressure on people who had no food to eat…' asks Colin.

'Since when are you so knowledgeable about the social state of Iran? People were much, much better off than now. All you know is based on a couple of papers you read, and the media. We all know what it means – partial, and biased information,' Ana says.

'Do we need to get into this? So what, there was a revolution, and some people benefitted from it and some people didn't. There were, probably, many promises, and little or no delivery. What's new? Here, without revolution, politicians say things, and never deliver,' says Colin.

'People rise up for different reasons, many for personal reasons, but collectively, they shout for freedom, independence, equality,' Frank says.

'I don't think any of these can be achieved through revolution. Over the centuries, can you come up with a single example where social revolution has achieved any of these noble aims? These are all illusions. What does independence mean in this interconnected world? There are sources of power and there are subjects for submission! Freedom? Is it something to be taken or to be conferred upon you? Equality? Give us a chance!' I say.

'Now you are heated up, Adam! It's good we decided to get together in winter!' says Helen.

I suddenly stop.

I have tried, over the years, not to explode! Have gone through so much, and I thought I had the mastery of internal explosion, external calm! And in a second, all that is lost. Robbed of your most precious possession, not by a skilled robber, but by your own complacence. The eternal wise men have taught us not to erupt, to measure the words before they come out of your mouth. Now, they would add "measure the words before you jot them down." How things would be different if I was an obedient follower!

'It is not so much a matter of finding a meaning for freedom or independence. It's that so many people die for these,' I hear Frank saying.

'But you need to know what you are fighting for, surely,' says Helen.

'People have different things in their mind for a word, for a concept, they even see the same thing differently. They read a book, the same book, and they have totally different interpretations of it. Don't you agree?' Frank says.

'I say, when people talk about hunger, they mean the same thing, and they understand each other's language. Hunger talks, clearly, and without ambiguity. Revolutions are about hunger, that is the bottom line,' Helen says.

'What about justice? People get fed up with corruption, with their rights being ignored, simply ignored, their money being eaten up big time, and someone who steals a piece of bread is condemned,' Roy says.

'As I said, hunger!' Helen says.

'Did I hear right? Did you say justice, Roy?' Colin says.

'Yes, justice! Is it too abstract for you?'

'I think you are hallucinating! Justice! Are you still a first-year university kid? I thought you just wanted to show a primitive image of yourself, but no, you are!' says Colin.

'No need to be abusive, Colin,' says Frank. 'He has a point, people revolt for justice. Now, whether such a thing exists, is a different matter.'

'So, people are stupid,' Colin says.

'Well, that's what I say, when I talk about what happened in Iran,' says Ana.

"But it's not only Iran. People might not respond the way they did in Iran, but look at the state of other countries, those we consider "developed". Is there justice there? But the way people respond is to become more and more selfish, mentally recluse. We are a demoralised nation. And to console ourselves, we blame others for our own inefficiencies, problems. We are too fast to blame others. We are a nation of accusers!' Frank says.

'But in Iran, this is about a national catastrophe! People blame foreign powers for the misery.' Ana says.

'Not far from reality though. At least they are partly involved. This is a global village, interference is ripe! And those who get into power, always try to extend their domination, they benefit from chaos, benefit in different ways, mainly economic and political,' says Frank.

'It is not fair. You went and saw the town, but we haven't!' Helen tells me and Ana, totally ignoring what Frank says.

'There wasn't much to see, but who's stopping you? Go see for yourself,' Ana says.

'Isn't it a bit late?' Maria says.

'You don't have to come if you don't want to. We can go and grab something to eat, too,' Helen says.

'We shall go too, won't we?' Colin asks Roy.

'Yes, why not. Girls need protection!' Roy says.

'What about you, Frank?' Colin asks.

'I'm OK here.'

-35-

They walked together, all four of them, Helen and Colin talking. I imagined them each with a rucksack. I asked myself what were they carrying? Roy, a pack of stones, stones of different sizes. He was dragging himself. One day, he would fall to his knees, drunk, and heavy.

'Why are you doing this? Why are you doing this to yourself?' I ask him.
'What?'
'This, this... carrying all this?'
'Can't do without them, this is my life.'
'But this way, drinking so much, and carrying all these, you will die soon,' I tell him.
'So? You'll die too, you know. You think you are invincible?' he asks.
His face is red, and I tell myself, good that I don't need to shake hands with him... a wet and sweaty handshake.
And what about Helen, I asked myself. Is she imitating Helen of some forty years ago? In a sense I am closer to her now than that night, though I still remember the walnut tree,

her fingers, her thin dress, her arm... It was as if she was on a mission, mechanical, determined. OK, you achieved what you wanted, your goal. But were you really content with it? Did you even think about it? I blamed myself for being somewhere else all the time, not engaged with her... listening to the record player that was busy playing "Pictures in an Exhibition". Now, I pause. I look at her, think about her, her two children, am not sure if she has a husband. I didn't even ask her if such a person exists or existed in her life or not.

As they leave the hotel, Maria is laughing. How the passage of few hours can change the mood for some people. I feel cold remembering the coach, and her face.

Is there a truth in emotions when they can change so fast? Is there a truth in them or we want to believe in emotions under the unconscious pressure of morality? The budgie is not buried yet, and Maria is laughing away. What happened to all that sadness? What is so funny anyway?

Colin is laughing too, laughing loudly. Did he ever laugh while giving lectures in his classes? Or just shouted at the poor kids? He looks more like a primary school teacher than a university lecturer. Gone are those days when there was an exciting dialogue, things are more and more structured, instructive. Perhaps people like Colin are to be blamed for it, with their laziness, and the admin crept in, gradually, systematically. First in the guise of helping the lecturers to reduce admin load on them. Poor lazy Colin didn't know he would do the admin job for the admin! They prepared forms to be filled in, meetings to attend, and each time a lecturer, if any, started to voice an idea, the admin stopped them by saying "Oh, have you filled in the risks of such and such action? Have you done your due diligence?" Of course, no one would argue with that. Colin, actually, had chaired some of those meetings himself, feeling grand! Yes, laugh, Colin, laugh. Your students are encouraged by the support they get from the admin, they can now voice their views against you. After all, they pay! You have a duty to deliver – as if you wouldn't before all the new revolution in education – the "new gradual academic world order" that happened around you without a single one noticing it. And suddenly you found yourself being intimidated by what a student would allege. Gone are those times that you were innocent till found guilty, gone those times that there was a respect for the poor lecturer. Now, they pay, they are customers, and you are the shopkeeper. You sell them pre-packaged stuff, yes, stuff.

Colin left still laughing.

-36-

'So, we are alone,' Ana says, looking at us. Frank looks serious.

'What do you suggest doing?' Ana says.

'Just stay where we are, we can get some drinks later, then have dinner,' I say.

'Good idea, I am quite rested sitting here,' Frank says, looking at Ana. 'Helen didn't let me finish what I wanted to say. I understand the picture you give of the situation in Iran, but for someone who hasn't been there, it draws an ugly one. There are a lot of good things to talk about; the people, the way they treat you, the food, the countryside…'

'Yes, but the country is under occupation, it is occupied by groups of vultures who have no principles, they found the best way to cheat people from their assets; religion. And the simple-minded masses fell for what they claimed. If you listen to what they said in the beginning, what they promised when they invaded, and all is out there now, in videos, you'll be shocked to see what they are doing now. People simply believed them. They have stolen so much, they cannot trust each other. Each group is afraid another group might expose their crimes, so they have collected evidence against anyone they could. There is a very fragile balance, and the balance can be shattered any moment,' Ana says.

'And people?' I ask.

'You think anyone cares? When people are under pressure, they become selfish,' Ana says.

'Some say they get closer to each other, that's how the regime will fall,' Frank says.

'The mullahs are cunning, historically proven, recorded. Look how they behave against each other, yet, they have continued to do what they do,' Ana says. 'Take women's hijab, singing, sports,… whatever… they have made such issues out of them they've become symbols of freedom against suppression. Women think if they show a little bit of their hair, they have broken the back of the regime. So, all energies are channelled to avoid the hijab, go to music performances and sport activities. These are routes to freedom for women, for people. Little do they know that with these diversions, while their minds are occupied to achieve a little of so-called freedoms, the national wealth is given away, personal pockets of the few are filled in, and every day that passes, the quality of air that people breathe, the food that they eat, deteriorates further and further.'

We remain silent for a while. Frank has opened the book he's been reading.

'What are you reading?' asks Ana.

Frank shows her the book cover.

Ana reads, *Nineteenth Century Famous Stamp Collectors*. 'You're not serious!' she tells Frank.

Frank laughs. 'I know, rather corrupt reading, but it's fascinating, you'll be surprised to discover who were those interesting characters.'

'That's the last thing I want to know,' Ana says.

'I must say I have no interest either, but I understand Frank's passion,' I say.

'Nobody can understand someone else's passion. You might say that you respect his views,' Ana says.

'OK, are we now getting entangled in words?' I say.

'Oh, I love this, I love healthy arguments!' Ana says.

'It takes me back to—' Frank says.

Ana interrupts him, 'Don't tell me – university time.'

'No, not really, it takes me back to Iran, my passionate discussions with your friends, actually,' Frank tells Ana.

Ana goes silent.

'I wonder why we didn't keep in touch – properly, anyway – after university?' I say.

Ralph comes over. 'Can I bring you something?'

'Actually yes. Can you make me a cocktail?' Ana says.

'Of course, what would you like?'

'Surprise me, make me something you do best.'

'With pleasure, and gentlemen?'

'The same,' I say, and Frank says the same.

'I wonder how it would've been had we kept in touch,' I say.

'This moment wouldn't exist,' Frank says.

'Many other moments would exist, just imagine what we could do…' I say.

'Let's not speculate,' Ana says.

Ralph comes with the drinks in tall glasses with a tinge of pink.

'I've made you something you don't find in cocktail books, and perhaps you could not guess all the ingredients of it, but I warn you, it's strong. I can change it if you don't like it!'

'We will like it, Ralph,' says Ana.

She raises her glass. 'To our newly discovered old friendship!'

'To continued friendship,' I say.

'Cheers, folks, I can see we are going to be closer on our return,' Frank says.

'This is getting too corny, though I like it,' says Ana. 'Ralph, you are a star. Bring another round of whatever it was, it has already gone to my head. What about you two?'

Do I remember the first time I was drunk? I mean so drunk I couldn't stand on my feet? I wonder why the "first time" is so important. "When was the first time you went to cinema alone?" "When did you lose your virginity?" "How old were you when you had your first smoke?"

Now we are tipsy. Ana tries to tidy up Frank's jacket collar. I imagine her going back home from work. She must have difficult days as a social worker, always facing a dilemma. She goes back to her silent apartment, throws out her shoes, and pours herself a drink. The whole night is ahead of her, and before that, whatever is left from the day. And Frank?

He must have a very tidy place; it must be very practical, if not austere. As he arrives home, he turns the radio on, which is always on the same station, Classics. He pours a glass of whisky and starts reading a broadsheet. He continues reading till late. He might go out for a quick dinner. I'm afraid of going home early. I'm afraid of the walls, doors, glass of water forgotten on the table. They look at me with their cold glances; "Are you back? Do you want to eat the same thing you ate last night?" I am afraid of hearing their repetitious clichés. After closing the bookshop, I go to my local, or sometimes when I feel more adventurous, I go to the pub a couple of blocks away. I know all the bartenders in both pubs, and know their regulars.

Getting together with Frank and Ana will be good, come to think about it, it will be a good change in my life. I suppose it'll be the same for them too. I hope they'll feel the same as me. In any case, we shall be together, Ana and me... a big presumption! But in any case, I intend to see Frank more or less regularly; he is such a pleasant person, he speaks with authority, yet he's quite down to earth. I'm not sure how long he has, though. I know, I'm brutal. But we shall be ready for an unpleasant outcome of his cough. Do I have the courage to see him at least once a month, perhaps more often? Our shops are not far away from each other.

'Adam, do you think we are lonely?' Ana asks suddenly.

'What do you mean?'

'Lonely... lonely... you know what it means,' she says.

'Well, sometimes... sometimes I feel I'm lonely, well of course,' I say.

'I think Ana means in a cosmic way,' Frank says.

'What? You mean in the realm of science fiction?' I say.

'Oh, come on, Adam, you don't seem to be with it,' Ana says, and drinks the last drops of her drink. She calls Ralph. 'I don't know about these two, but bring me another, Ralph.'

'Sure.' He looks at us.

We say, 'Why not?'

'I mean, was Sisyphus lonely? Was Prometheus lonely? I know this is a cliché question, I know I'm not a teenager,' Ana says, 'but walking home sometimes, talking to these poor people I go and see, sometimes… and then thinking about all those back in Iran, who don't even have time to think about their life, they work, work, betray each other for a bit in their pocket, and die as slaves… I think they are lonely too.'

'We are doomed as a species! Dinosaurs were doomed, they say, because of meteorites, and we are doomed because of ourselves. Other animals are doomed because of us, trees, nature, the whole earth is doomed because of us,' says Frank, 'so let's not be so concerned, we, lonely, cruel species… this is a glorious moment, being drunk together.'

'We must repeat this when we go back, promise?' Ana has a sip from her drink and raises her glass. She asks, 'Promise?'

'Yes, sure, Frank says, 'but what is there in a promise?' He coughs.

I think he's coughed less and less since he's arrived.

'You see? We are lonely, and lonely people need each other,' Ana says.

'Now you're becoming French. We might be lonely, but we're not miserable!' I say. 'Perhaps in a way we like our loneliness. All those soothsayers of loneliness, prophets of doom, just enjoyed their moments of fame. The golden years of failed doomster writer-philosophers, black polo-neck jumper wearers, were fit for the last century. We are living in a post-loneliness age!' I laugh.

'I must say, though I don't agree with your argument, I liked it!' says Frank.

'This is the age of mobiles, reality TV, people don't know they are lonely, they say what's the fuss if you tell them they are lonely,' I say.

'Are we the corpses of what we were once? We have died in deep waters, have experienced the dark abyss, and now have surfaced. We float. Everything for us happens at the surface. Pretentious problems hide our deep injuries, and we continue with our "new reality" online!' Frank says.

Ana stands up with her glass in her hand and says, 'What happened to my Sisyphus? He and his stone look very much like mobile bearers of today.'

'You look like you are giving a TED talk!' Frank says.

While sitting down, Ana says, 'Seriously, is Sisyphus lonely today? Would he know he is lonely?'

'I wonder if he knew he was lonely. If he knew, he would've changed it,' I say.

'Easier said than done, he was condemned by God,' Ana says.

'He was condemned because he was full of himself, and he was deceitful. Anyone with these characteristics is lonely,' Frank says, 'but to answer your point, Ana, Prometheus, on the other hand, was not lonely, although he was also condemned. He was a hero, he remained committed to the mankind created from clay; he stole fire from the gods and gave it to man. He suffered. His liver, the source of all emotions, was eaten everyday by an eagle, but it grew back. Emotions never die! He was not lonely, because he had his emotions for his creation, he was not lonely, he had all humankind behind him.' Frank pauses. Then he says, 'But we cannot deny that he stole the fire of the gods, he betrayed them.'

'Did he? He was faithful to his people,' Ana says.

'You always betray someone if you want to remain faithful to someone else,' Frank says. 'Look at all relationships… the affairs… the heartaches… OK, here, there is no liver involved, only heart!' He laughs.

'But I disagree. Prometheus did not betray anyone. He knew what he wanted and went for it. He was truthful to himself. For me it is quite clear. The essence is to remain honest to yourself. The problem is that most people don't know what they really want! They just imitate, follow… that's the easiest way. They seek heroes,' I say.

'That's the story of my poor people,' says Ana. 'They carved a hero out of a figurehead, and once they did it, they could not accept they had deceived themselves, or they had been deceived; in fact, it was both!'

Frank says, 'When I was at school, we had a very suave maths teacher, tall, calm, soft-spoken. He was good, and when I say good, I mean someone admirable. He had excellent handwriting on the blackboard, and had a way of making maths attractive. Everyone knows this needs a special talent. He used to tell us things outside numbers and equations, three-dimensional shapes and imaginary numbers. But I remember a story he told us in his own calm passion. It was from Brecht's *Life of Galileo*. There is a scene where his pupil, Andrea, who admired Galileo, turns on him. Andrea considered Galileo as another Socrates who was ready to die for his principles. But Galileo recanted. As Andrea leaves Galileo in total disappointment, he tells Galileo, "Pity a land that has no hero", but Galileo responds, "No, Andrea, pity the land that needs a hero".'

'I always remember that day when our teacher told that story, and have thought about it many times. Was Socrates right to drink the poison or Galileo who recanted? I don't have an answer for it. Do you?' asks Frank.

'I don't know which was right, but in my mind, what Galileo says needs to be written in golden letters and people reminded of it. Pity the land that needs a hero,' Ana says.

'But people have heroes. They have role models in all aspects of life, from science to fashion, arts to the military,' I say.

'You call it *role model*. In Iran, it is called *source of emulation*. This is for the brain-dead, for the lazy people, the wishful thinkers who seek the easy way out, and this is the way a dictator is born!' Ana says.

'I never thought you were so passionate about Iran. You've lived here now for so many years, some people forget their country as they put foot in the country they emigrate to,' I say.

'Well, I am not one of those, but I do not shout my loyalty either. I love it here. In a way this is my country now, but the question of identity is discussed so much I get bored with it. What does it matter if Eliot was American or English, or Ezra Pound, for that matter. It's their poetry that counts. The Turks claim Maulana was Turkish, as his tomb is in Turkey. Iranians say he was born in Iran and has two huge volumes of poetry in Persian, so he is Iranian. But what would happen if he was cremated and his ashes were spread over the Scottish mountains? People want to stick themselves to famous characters as a matter of prestige. Maulana did not count himself as belonging to a particular country, he considered himself to be from nowhere… from everywhere,' Ana says.

'What about this sense of belonging then?' I ask.

'What about it? You may like… love… your country, but not belong to it. It is not a case of possession,' Ana says.

'No, but you speak with such commitment, you are loyal,' I say.

'For me, loyalty is not bound to a place and time. Loyalty is something internal. It relates to culture… it's derived from memories… unconscious. I could live in Iran, but be an alien. How could I be part of these imposters, modern-day fanatic invaders? Had I stayed there, I would have betrayed my country, my culture, my identity, because I would be ineffective. But here, the whole culture is in me, I carry it with me wherever I go, and I have enriched it by the culture of this country, and together with this fusion, I am enriched,' Ana says.

'This is big stuff,' I laugh. 'We should be glad Roy is not here.'

'You're right,' says Ana, 'I don't know what's wrong with me. I put it down to the drink… it's Ralph's fault!'

'We were together all those years, and we had no chat like this,' Frank says, 'Ana was never so open.'

'I told you, it's the drink,' Ana says.

'Oh, you can't fool me! I said. 'We used to drink much more than this.'

'OK then, it's Ralph,' Ana laughs.

'You might have a point here, though, things need to get to a critical state to create an event. I mean this hotel, this bar, Ralph, the drinks, us three, the statue of Bacchus out there in the garden… all have participated in this moment, in the eruption of these words, the way you expressed yourself,' I say.

'You mean this event is like a chemical reaction, you need to have the ingredients, the right temperature, pressure, to get a particular outcome,' Ana says.

'Yes, you see, this was corruption in Iran for so many years. I hope you don't mind me saying it, Ana, but it had to reach a particular point for the sudden eruption. Over the years, drop by drop, the internal and external elements worked, and then the moment arrived,' I say.

'Eternal order?' Frank says.

'To the contrary, utter chaos!' I say.

'Some call it historical determinism,' Ana says.

'Not if things are not pre-planned,' I say.

'So, you think those… those so-called elements happen to be in the right place, in the right time for a particular event to happen, just by chance,' Ana says.

'Call it what you want, the main thing is the process. Once it happens, the elements continue in a certain structure, until something else happens and the whole construction disintegrates for a different thing to assemble. There is perpetual change,' I say.

'Yet we crave for permanence,' Frank says.

'Well, that's an illusion, everyone knows it, but we ignore it, forget it, or try to keep things as they are. Safety in rigidity, in conserving things,' I say.

'But we witness it every day when we look in the mirror. Ah, there's a new line under my eyes – the change moves with us all the time.'

'It is not separate from us. Every moment, with each breath, each movement, change is embedded in our existence,' Ana says.

'Look, you mentioned mirror, it reminded me of something… something funny, you might consider it rather serious, actually!' Frank says.

'Do tell! I wonder what it is that makes you laugh,' Ana says.

'I assure you, it is not a laughing matter. It can be construed as funny, but it's not a laughing matter.'

'OK, OK, tell us what it is,' I say.

'Well, when looking in the mirror, some people tell the mirror, "Aren't you privileged to see me?" Now, some others, each time they look in the mirror, they tell themselves, "I should put a curtain in front of it." Or, "I must break this".'

'Is that all?' asks Ana.

'Yes, what did you expect? Can't you see? It's about people and the perception they have of themselves. Now extend this to the society, to the country.'

'And?' Ana asks.

'Some people are so proud of their country, they think they live in the land of opportunity! Land of opportunity – they do not see all the poverty, both physical and cultural poverty that surrounds them; and some other people are so ashamed of their nation... ashamed of themselves because of their poverty... or because of their corruption... something that they might not have any say in!' says Frank.

'I wonder what is our perception of ourselves? I'd say Roy asks the mirror to bow to him, Colin shouts at it so loudly, it cracks,' Ana says.

'For Helen, mirror is a time travel machine. Whenever she looks in it, she imagines herself with a long flower necklace... she hears Led Zeppelin too!' I say, 'and as for Maria, she sits in front of the mirror with a cat – I assume she has a cat, in spite of that budgie – she sees the mirror as a picture frame.'

'What about you, Frank?' Ana asks.

'I'm not terribly excited about this – so childish – but why don't we say what *we* do in front of the mirror?' he asks.

'Shall we ask for something? I feel a bit peckish,' I say.

'Good idea, shall we go to the restaurant, or ask Ralph to bring us something here, sandwiches or something?' Ana says.

'Let's go to the restaurant, good to have a change,' I say.

'Change? Indeed.' Frank smiles.

-37-

I stood facing the mirror. I thought some days the beard grows faster, like nails growing faster when you are on holiday! After dinner that night, I was so tired I could sleep on the lift going to my room. As we were having dinner, Colin and the others arrived, standing around us.

'You are eating *now*?' Helen asked. 'We had a great time in the town. You'd think it'd be a dead place, far from reality. We had early dinner in a nice bistro, then ended up in this pub, and met lovely people, didn't we, Colin?'

'One of them was a bagpipe player, a chubby lad with a designer moustache—' Colin said, but Roy interrupted him.

'And there was this guy, bigger than him, he was a weight lifter. He competes in the Olympics; would you believe it?'

'Well, we didn't go anywhere, but Socrates and Galileo came visiting us,' Ana laughed.

'Not to mention Homer himself,' I said.

'Nice to see you had a good time with your drinks. Seems you are still drunk,' said Roy.

'Not that much any longer, but you missed our philosophical intercourse,' Frank said.

'Athletics,' said Ana.

'Why don't you join us,' Frank asked, 'have something.'

Maria said, 'I'll be off, I'm too tired.'

'OK, let's have some tea,' said Helen, while Maria left.

'I think we should do more of this, getting together I mean. We've had a good time chatting away,' Helen said.

'Yeah, but we haven't seen each other for years. Do this more often, and the novelty wears off,' Roy said.

'It's not the time for this sort of discussion. It's late at night, we are tired, all of us, and anyway, Maria is not here. We will talk about it later,' Colin said.

The waiter brought the food.

'This steak is cold,' Ana said.

I was hungry, but somehow didn't have an appetite. Frank had asked for a salad.

'Well, I'm OK with this salad, perhaps you might want to try this,' Frank told Ana.

'Thanks Frank, I'm not hungry anymore.'

We asked for coffee, there was little to say. We were as tired as if we had walked for miles. We went back to our rooms.

What is there in a mirror? What is there when it faces a wall, a white wall with nothing hanging from it? Then I stand in front of it. Does it perceive me as a two-dimensional creature? I touch it, it's cold when it feels my finger. And what about a car's mirror? Oh, it experiences so many scenes, yet, what happens when it goes into the garage? A fixed image. Do mirrors have memories? Where do they keep them? They are invisible; so are my memories. They are invisible, but whisper in my ears. Perhaps mirrors have invisible ears, like their invisible memories, whispering...

And what do mirrors do at night? Do they go to sleep? I should say, I have to appreciate their readiness. The moment I look at them, they are ready to respond. They respond, they tell me all sorts of things in their own language, which must be obvious and clear to me, but I do not pay attention. I look but do not notice, I do not listen to all those hints the mirror gives. Mirrors are such calm, non-interfering, non-imposing creatures. They do not take offence when I shout at them, when I ignore them. And when, after a long time, I decide to dust them, clean them, they immediately respond, shining on me.

I touch my face. Oh, I have gone old. And the mirror must say, "Yes, I kept on telling you each time you came to me, but you chose to ignore me. Not that you could do anything about it, but it's good to know your own skin, see its changes as it happens." If mirrors have a memory, they must think, too, don't they? They must have some feelings at least. But when I break a mirror, all it does is it shows me to myself... many times more, depending on how badly I have broken it. An injured mirror talks to you more than ever. It only hurts you if you try to forcefully invade its boundaries. Funny... one mirror shows me to myself once; the same mirror broken, repeats me at once, many times. It doesn't die. We think it's dead as we don't like to see it having changed its shape, so we throw away the pieces, while those pieces are all talking to us. Is it the story of dying?

There is a drop of blood on the sink. I've been too harsh again… against myself. What is skin, after all, that I want it to be so smooth? And in trying too hard, I damage it. An injury that soon will be forgotten, tissue paper is at hand. But what about those injuries inside me? How do I forget internal haemorrhages? I have so many mirrors inside me, all broken to small pieces. As they go through the sudden whirlwinds of memories, old wounds rupture, silently as I blink, as I shave. I leave the razor next to the tap. My fingers are covered with foam. I go back to the room, I drop my body on the soft chair next to the bed. I try to recall that memory… the one that has thrown me. I try to pick it out of all my memories, but this mirror is hidden, too silent to be heard. The mirror standing there above the tap must be calling me. "We have unfinished business." It is so easy for it, everything happens instantly for it. But I need to dig deep… I cannot grab the elusive particles of the mirrors in me, and I cannot find the sources of my bleeding. The invisible droplet from my unlocatable wounds diffuse in my mind, colonise all events that are happening in me. I am good in cutting, my skin is recovering under the tissue paper, but my internal wound…

The chair is comfortable, but my back is hurting. And I must finish shaving. I do not move, let the back hurt, let this unknown corrosive blood dissolve all my invisible mind. I will not move. What would happen? An hour would pass, Ana and perhaps Frank would ask where Adam is. Maria would say she is wondering too. Nobody would move, they would continue with their second cups of coffee after breakfast. Two hours would pass, they are then all in the lobby. Ana would look at her watch, and this would be the time that even Roy starts asking questions. Helen would say,

"He drank too much last night." Colin would say, *"OK, OK, I'll go have a look."*

This must not happen. I'd better get up. As I stand up, I suddenly tell myself, you don't deserve to be in a relationship, what's wrong with you? You are a madman. Living with all those books, day and night, has taken away from you any passion to understand relationships. You prefer to live in stories than to make stories. You are afraid of people. You make love with pages of books as you devour them reading. You… you are devoid of character, you have lost your personality in characters of the books you've read. Each time, you see yourself differently. You even walk differently, unconsciously, I know, imitating characters of the books. In short, you are a mess! But perhaps this is easier for you. You have relinquished your personality. You think this is easier, living as a recluse, but you are bleeding, in a continuous state of stupor. Have you asked yourself why you came here? And… and, what is this thing with Ana? Are you serious or do you think you are reading a novel? You cannot deny there is something between you, can you? There has always been, and you know it.

It was the way she looked at you, the way she looked at others. What is there in a glance? I know the physics, I know something about lenses, and light. But what is there in a glance? Is it of the same nature as the mirror? The light, the reflection… what is there that makes me reflect? Ah, what about the memories? My mirror and its memory, my hidden memories and the small, quantum memories they carry – perhaps they don't carry them, they are the same. In her glance, all my past emotions, future, and this moment, were asleep. Like her sleepy eyes, her mystic movements, her history… subdued yet in flames.

I continue shaving. Now it's time for the water. A splash and memories are gone. The mirror looks at me, factual and determined; time to go, better be faster, Adam. You are right, I must hurry up. But I like the feel of water on my face, let me just wait to see that drop falling from my chin. Ah, as I bring the towel close to my face, there is a short breeze from the movement, such a good feeling after the night sleep, after those drinks. We are getting close to the end of our get-together. Now I've seen Maria and know about her dead budgie, Helen and her love for comic books, Roy and his temper. Colin has kept his loud voice, but I'm so happy I've seen Ana and Frank. Do we keep in touch? I'd better go. They must be waiting.

-38-

Everyone is sitting around the breakfast table but Roy. As I say hello, he arrives with a big plate of English breakfast, the whole gamut of it. The plate is full and bulging!

'You must be kidding!' Helen tells Roy, laughing.

'Haven't you seen anyone with a healthy appetite?' Roy says. 'Clearly not, judging by your puny body.' He looks at Maria. 'And you, don't you start saying anything, young lady, otherwise I'll say something about your pale face with spots!'

Maria says nothing, but Ana says, 'You cannot utter a good word, Roy, can you? You spread repulsion as you move!'

'Actually not! It is pure hypocrisy to see something and pretend you haven't seen it. No, actually, if I do, it's self-censorship.'

'One sees so many things, but there is no necessity to write an essay about them,' says Ana.

'Yes, but Helen started it all,' Roy said, with his mouth full of egg and hash browns, and his fork loaded with baked beans.

'What about Maria?'

'What about her? Are you her lawyer? She has a mouth, you know.'

'Yes, but she doesn't talk with her mouth full!'

'Friends, let's compliment each other for a change. We are too much at each other's throats,' Frank says.

'Compliment for what?' I say.

'For taking the time off, making the effort to come all the way here, in this cold. Surely something was interesting for us.'

'Yes, before coming over!' Roy says.

'It seems to me something is eating us from the inside, has been eating us, perhaps for a long time. That's why we came over to attack each other, we'd had enough of flogging ourselves from the inside, internal bleeding,' I say.

'Melodramatic again, Adam,' says Helen. 'I am happy I've come. Even meeting Roy with his comments is jolly for me. I like challenges!'

'I'm grateful to Colin for organising this. I hope we keep meeting when we go back,' Maria says.

'Are you going to get another budgie?' asks Colin.

'No.' Maria looks sad.

'You are allowed to change your mind, you know,' Roy says.

'Now, this is a grand statement, Roy!' says Frank.

'Yes, Roy, it is,' I say.

'I don't know what you are talking about,' Roy says.

'Change!' Ana says.

'You people make such a big thing out of nothing! You want to go see a movie. You have a couple of drinks on your sofa, and then think it's best not to go. I am cosy here, and it's cold outside. So, you change your mind. Simple!' Roy says.

'Ah, but you think so! What happens when you see someone, you fall in love, you tell each other love forever. Then... then you know what happens.'

'Yes, it happens all the time, people change their minds and go their own way,' Roy says. 'It's change.'

'I agree with you! I cannot believe myself saying it! But what happens to politicians? Can they promise something, and then change their mind? They will be massacred. Look what happened in Iran, masses went out to kiss the hands of that fake holy man. Then they changed their minds. They are considered as conspirators and traitors now,' Ana says.

'To me, they are courageous people. One who can face himself and see the change, accept it, and announce it, is a bold person,' I say.

'But things are not that simple,' Frank says, 'look at your habits. Can you change them that easily? It's just that we seem to settle down on the surface... it's gravity... life on earth... we settle for stability, no change. Always following the same route.'

'But, that's boring... boring like hell,' Helen says.

'Boring, yes, but not like hell! Hell, I've heard them saying it's a very volatile place!' Colin says.

'It is a dilemma for me. We seek excitement, new things, fresh air... yet, we stick to the status quo, as if there is safety in banality!' I say.

'Yes, it is a deception,' Ana says.

'All this is so sad... so sad,' says Maria.

Has there been a happy time for her? Have I ever seen her with a smiling face? A really smiling face? Rarely! Did she ever marry? Get into fights? There was no one at university, and here, she came up with no stories, but the budgie; and we got to know that only because the poor bird died. Perhaps some people are born that way, lonely. Perhaps they like it that way. She is kind, always kind and calm. The picture of a quiet sufferer. But no one knows what there is to suffer for. Perhaps, as a nurse she found what she really wanted. What she had always wanted to be, perhaps that's what makes her happy inside. She is serene, composed, considerate. But I doubt if she ever openly demands anything. Is it her pride? Or has she no confidence in being loved. Perhaps this is her suffering, and she offers her kindness, on a daily basis, to the patients she cares for as a sympathy for herself. Her skin on her face will remain soft, and her face calm and reassuring. She will not get another budgie, I doubt she does, but she will pick up and revive her interest in embroidery. She will need two pairs of glasses, far-sighted and short-sighted. Varifocal? No, never. She will remember, always, to have the right pair with her. She does have a good relationship with her neighbours, will look after their dogs while they are away, will check their houses to make sure everything is in order. And her outfit will always be ironed. Tidiness of lonely people!

'Adam, pass me the salt, please,' Helen says. She looks refreshed today. Her long, curled hair, with grey bits showing, is wet. She has taken a shower, but didn't bother to dry it well.

She is a puzzle to me. If one person would not marry, it would've been her. But she has two grown-up daughters. A hippy mother listening to Led Zeppelin, and talking about dismantling Trident. Yet, there is something unique about her. She doesn't bother speaking her mind, unlike Roy, who appears to be radical, but it's all a façade.

'You owe me something, Adam, do you remember?' Helen says.

'Me? What?'

'You are a cruel man, to forget so soon what you promised,' Helen says.

All look at me.

'What did I promise you, Helen?'

'A walk… to walk with me before we return. Do you remember?'

'Ah… I remember that. I thought I had committed myself to a—'

'What? Life-long promise? Nothing exists like that; whoever says it either lies intentionally, or deludes himself,' Helen says. 'Would you accompany me while I have my after-breakfast cigarette?'

'Well of course, my pleasure.'

'Pleasure will be all mine. What a polite man, I like etiquette,' Helen says.

'I thought you didn't care for this sort of crap!' Roy says.

'Watch your mouth, young man,' Helen laughs. 'I like to choose moments of vulgarity and seconds of politeness!' Helen says.

'Roy and I have decided to buy Maria a budgie. We

want to convince her to let us do so. So, we will have a small after-breakfast meeting, a real threesome!' Colin says.

'I see you are using colourful language too, Colin,' says Ana.

'He is using his one-minute vulgarity allowance,' Roy laughs.

'So, it leaves me and Frank for after-breakfast activity, that is, if Frank is happy to,' says Ana.

'Well of course. I can give you a short tour on the history of stamps,' Frank says.

'Yes, you will treat me to an exciting lecture,' Ana says.

'Exciting? Maybe marginally after Colin's usual boring lectures.' Roy laughs again.

'You are jolly today!' Colin looks at Roy.

'It's all thanks to you people,' Roy says.

We continued with our breakfast, silently. A ray of sun penetrated into the room. I thought it would be sunny at least when I go walking with Helen. I went to the coffee machine and poured myself a long hot coffee. When I returned, Maria, Roy and Colin had gone, and Ana and Frank were standing up.

'Oh. I thought people would have another coffee,' I said.

'Yet another? Frank asked.

I sat with my mug, looking at Helen as Ana and Frank left.

-39-

'So, we are alone at last; how many years did it take? I cannot count, and exceptionally, I'm not drunk!' Helen swirls the coffee cup, looking at the remaining coffee at the bottom of the cup.

'It has been a long time,' I say.

'Has it? Has it been for you? Let's face it, if Colin hadn't organised this event, you wouldn't remember us… me.'

'Nonsense! You think you are the only one with memories, you should give a bit more credit to people.'

'I used to, believe me, I used to. It was years ago, but then I found people get what they want, and then – the next day – they pass you by, don't recognise you as if you didn't exist. So, I told myself let's go to this reunion, let's see what was in these people's minds, in him, that I was so keen to appreciate, then to be part of. And then I found I was so lucky – boy, it was a close escape! Mind you, I suffered at the time, I suffered. But it was all for the best, this trip showed me. Don't get me wrong, I am happy I've seen you, seen you all, but now I have no regrets for not following you, not trying to convince you for us to be together. But I don't regret coming over either.'

'Don't you think you have taken things too seriously? I always thought you were easy-going,' I say.

'No, you thought I was easy... you know what I mean. But I wanted to be open, free, a no-frills sort of person. The fault was not mine, it was yours; you people didn't have the capacity to see, to feel.'

'Perhaps you're right, perhaps I would have behaved differently if I was grown-up; I had come from home to uni. From the house of everything ready for you with all its limitations, to a place of total chaos where nobody would ask me, where are you are going, when are you coming home? So, I had to create some internal rules based on my new home.'

'You know, it's funny! An innocent boy should've seen the innocence, but no, he had to assume the open society was the environment for corruption, and I was the symbol of decadence!'

'You are too hard on yourself. Let's go for that walk,' I say.

'Yes, good idea, a change of atmosphere. You are good at it, escaping.'

'Come on, Helen, be nice to me.'

'Nice? Nice? Was I ever anything but that? Who was quick to forget everything, the insignificant night of a university student?'

'You have such a memory...'

'Unlike some others!'

We came out of the lobby, and stood outside the building. There was hazy sunshine. I started to walk to the garden.

'You cannot find the walnut tree here! They don't have it; even if they had, it is too late now. Too little, too late! I'm not interested in the garden. Let's go out, walk in that field,' Helen said.

'It's too wet and muddy,' I said.

'I had forgotten how squeamish you are! It's only a bit of mud. You can always wash your shoes,' Helen said.

'And you? I cannot see you cleaning your shoes,' I said.

'You'll see… it's not a big issue for me.'

'OK then, let's walk in the fields.'

We walked towards the field. There was a cold breeze, cows were walking slowly in the far end of the field, and the mountain range in the background was filled with snow. As we were about to enter the field, she took off her shoes.

'It's mud! Your feet are naked, naked, naked!' I said.

'So?'

'You're mad, you'll catch cold, you're not used to this.'

'What's wrong with experiencing something new? You are too institutionalised in your bookshop. What do you do? Get up, go to the shop. Sit there, talk to a couple of customers, take stock, do some accounts, I don't know, perhaps turning some pages of a new book, or an old book perhaps. But you never turn a page in your life. Where is the excitement?'

'You assume I'm looking for excitement. The time has passed for looking for thrills. We call it maturity,' I said.

'*You* call it maturity! I call it stagnation! And with this thinking, you are quite successful. But why did you agree to walk with me? I wonder! You know how I am. You should've escaped, like in the old times.'

'Don't you believe in change?'

'I do, but I also know where to look for it.'

'Then why did you ask me to go for a walk with you?'

'Curiosity. Perhaps there is still a touch of romanticism in me!' Helen said.

'So, that's why you cannot accept me the way I am. Romantics have a warped vision of people around them, particularly their friends! They create different characters in their mind, and they get disappointed. That's why they are always in agony,' I said.

'I'm not!'

'So, in your case, it is deeper than that! You have a different vision of yourself!'

'You are entitled to your views.'

'Thanks! You are very generous.' I said.

'I know. This is what, those who were polite, would tell their friends about me in the old times; she is generous, you should know her better!' Helen said.

'Do you know? I wonder why you are so concerned about your past, what people said about you, the images of those times, what I did,' I said.

'I am not! This is what you think. But in your case, if I want to be honest, I am.'

'But why?'

'Is it not obvious? Some events in your life stay with you. I wanted to see you, to see how you are now, I cannot explain it… as if to go back and, when you pass me by, I grab your hand and say hey, this is me, look at me, do not ignore what there was. Perhaps I want, desperately, to convince myself after so many years that there was something more than a trivial event under the walnut tree!' Helen said.

I only have myself to blame. Why did I agree to go for a walk with her? Was I wiser years ago not to get involved with her? Why is it that I put myself in situations to feel guilty? All those who had engaged with her, in one way or another, didn't care, just had fun. Perhaps she was more at ease with them too, rather than with me. I get too concerned; why? I do not know. Simply, don't know. The outcome is that the other side responds proportionally. Am I treating this as a mechanistic relationship? Far from it. So, what is this action-reaction, proportionality equation I bring in?

'Sorry Adam, I really didn't mean to appear incensed, I'm not angry, just a bit emotional, that's all. Let's talk about something else, now that we have this short time to be together,' Helen said.

'I am all for it. What do you do these days?'

'Apart from mothering two daughters?' She laughed. 'I try to live my life.'

'And the husband?'

'Got rid of him after the second one. To be fair, neither of us could tolerate the other. He wanted a routine, calm and quiet life.' Helen said.

'Ideal husband.'

'Yes, not for me though. I should've known better, I wasn't the marrying type. I guess I wanted to prove to myself that I was not loose when it came to men!'

'What a funny way to describe yourself! I hadn't heard that word for years.'

'And you are the reading type!'

'Should be difficult for you with two kids.' I said.

'It was difficult in the beginning, but now they have grown, just about, and I am beginning to be myself.'

'Do you know, it is really difficult to imagine you as a mother; as a married woman perhaps, but a mother…'

'I cannot imagine it myself!' Helen said.

'So what happened?'

'The same thing that I told you, I wanted to prove to myself I could be like any other woman, have a family, do normal things…' Helen said.

'But what is normal? I'm not married, so many people live differently nowadays.' I said.

'I guess we all want to prove things, one way or another. We don't live, we struggle to prove… that's not living, is it?' Helen said.

'I agree with you, unfortunately.'

'Why unfortunately?' Helen said.

'I'd love to claim otherwise. Funny thing is that we either *think* we are free, while we are proving something, or we are not happy and yet continue to prove that we are strong, that we can tolerate difficult times.' I said.

'Yes, and if we don't, then we are tagged as timid, weak,' Helen said.

'It is much more than that, living based on people's expectations, and very often it is unconscious… but enough of this, aren't you feeling cold? Walking barefoot?' I asked.

'I feel cold inside, Adam, I enjoy walking on the mud.'

'You are taking revenge on yourself!' I said.

'For what?'

'For betraying yourself, having married!'

'Oh, that… but I resolved the problem, I divorced. But you may have a point. I take revenge on myself for some other reason. I wish I had been stronger at university, stopping them talking about me like that.'

'You see? Now you are regretting that you did not prove something!'

'True…'

'Tell me, don't you think a married life can be successful?' I asked.

'Successful? What is it? You are asking the wrong person! Most marriages continue because of certain considerations rather than love. Most divorces happen because of intolerance.'

'But when you get to this stage? Tolerance? Better stop it. What is tolerance after all? Isn't it suppression of one's desires… opinions?' Helen said.

'I agree. But if there is no tolerance… forget about marriage, look at the bigger picture, the relationships between people at large, the relations among countries. There will be bloodshed!' I said.

'As if it is not the case now! There is intolerance and bloodshed!'

'So, we are damned anyway! But look at it this way, whatever we do is subject to interpretation. There are always different opinions, but from time to time some of them become dominant and others suppressed. There are some issues that people prefer not to think about.'

'Oh, which ones are you talking about? There are many things people prefer not to talk about!' Helen said.

'OK, the obvious one is the intricacies of human relationships. Imagine two people are in love, one of them sleeps with someone else…'

'Wait! If they are in love, why does he go with someone else?' Helen asked.

'Firstly, who said it was a man? You automatically assumed it! Secondly, you are assuming that love is limiting! You are the last one who should say this, I mean, judging by how you like to be, how you have been,' I said.

'Perhaps I was never in love!' Helen said.

'In any case, why is it not accepted? If, in a moment, one of the two sides is attracted to someone else, why should they suppress their feelings? We assume that the other side must confront, threaten, leave, or tolerate! Now, what if the guy, let's say the guy, does not go with the other person, but only fancies her. Is this acceptable? Is this betrayal of love?'

Helen remained silent.

'You know? We get attracted to so many different things; is it that, just because we desire or imagine something else, we have betrayed our partner? Why is it that if we go out with someone else, and are open about it, then the relationship with our partner is damaged, but if we keep it secret – if at all possible to do so – it is OK? Do I sense a smell of possession here? Do we possess each other once we say we are in love?' I asked.

'You are too intense. You haven't changed a bit! You were intense then, and you are severe now!' Helen said.

'Why do you say this? Just because I delve into things?'

'Just let things be, OK? Why are you so determined to question everything? People live, lie, and get on with their lives,' Helen said.

'Yes, but for me that is not life. Of course they can do whatever they wish to do, but for me, I do love to question everything. I suppose, in your mind, I haven't grown up. It is a child that always asks questions. And children are suppressed by their parents who get tired of their incessant questions, embarrassed by being unable to answer at least some of the questions, and the children are suppressed in school because of the rigid structure. "Follow this or else", "follow that or you will be…" and this is the way the damage is done. Imagine if people kept on questioning their own actions and reactions, what sort of society we would have. I think a mature one in a world that humanity deserves to have,' I said.

'Oh, come on; you've gone too far. You are too big for your boots! Better walk like me! You think you are the know-it-all! If children are so suppressed, how is it that *you* can say these things? How did you escape your suppressed childhood? Did you have extraordinary parents, or are you a genius?' Helen asked.

'Not at all. I have all these problems. But all I'm saying is that there are so many things that we accept and pass them by, while, if we analysed them, we would live a different life,' I said.

'You are full of words. You know? I think that you have grown up in a bubble. During the university time, you lived under illusions, images of people and things around you, not the way things were; and now? Now you cannot see things the way they are. You just talk, and while talking, you love your own image. You are a good example of a self-admiring critic, an "intellectual", lots of words, no action,' Helen said.

'What do you do, madam go-getter? You are walking barefoot in the mud and consider this as the ultimate liberation! You are a show-off!'

'At least I do this, what do you do? You cannot be challenged about anything. You are a ghost… walk in the bookstore, probably at 8.30 sharp in the morning, walk out of it at 7 pm, your autobiography is one page… oh, sorry, one paragraph… if that,' Helen said.

'So, who is free here? You? You are obsessed by having a legacy! And that's why you loathe your life, having married, having children. These are too normal for you. So, what do you do? You decide to walk in mud! But you *do* walk in mud, every day!' I said.

'Adam, you are full of stories. Keep at it, maybe one day you will have your own book in your bookstore window.'

How did it happen? I am walking with Helen – Helen! In this farmland, in winter, in mud? Her naked feet, red with cold. She struggles now walking, the mud has got stickier. I try to avoid it where I can, by walking over the straw remaining in the soil. Why did I agree to walk with her? Redemption! I felt guilty the moment I saw her here. I don't like the sight of a walnut tree, the sound of heavy rock guitar, the look of shabby-clothed, cigarette-smoker women with frizzy hair. All this because they remind me of that night, and worse, the day after when I passed her by. I shiver inside me. Why was I so weak?

It clouded over and it was getting cold, with wind starting up.

'I think we should go back,' I said.

'Don't panic, we will.'

We turned around and started walking back to the hotel. In the hotel, there was a group of people gathering around reception. Colin and Maria came over, looking at Helen.

'What's this?' he said, looking at Helen's feet, laughing, 'we let you two alone for one minute and see what happens; complete chaos!'

'Let me bring something for you to clean up with,' Maria said.

'What a fuss! It's just some dirt!' said Helen.

'But this is a hotel lobby. And there's going to be a wedding reception,' Maria said.

'So?' Helen said. 'Where did you dump Roy?'

'He's around; they tried to change my mind,' Maria said.

'That shouldn't be difficult!' said Helen.

'You think so? Then you don't know her at all,' Colin said. 'She is a bastion of resistance. She looks calm and innocent, but in reality, she doesn't budge.'

'Are you talking about the budgie?' Helen started laughing.

'Yes, you can be playful with this appearance, but yes, we tried to show her the benefits of having a budgie,' Colin said.

'And?' I said.

'No way, she said, what is gone, is gone. Nothing replaces it.'

'But you didn't suggest to her to replace it, did you?'

'Well…'

Roy came over.

'There is a wedding. We are in for fun tonight,' he said.

'What has it got to do with us? I asked.

'Oh, people in the north are so hospitable. I was talking to the best man. He was such fun, he insisted we must join their party; what's wrong with you?' he asked Helen, looking at her feet.

'Oh, for God's sake. This is none of your business,' Helen said. 'I'm off to change, otherwise I will be cross-examined all day.'

'Someone's in a bad mood,' said Colin.

'I need to refresh, too,' I said, and left to go to my room.

I'm still shaken inside. I blame myself for getting involved in discussion with Helen. There was no need for it, was there? We have met here after some thirty-five years, and might not meet again. There was no need for the discussion, no need. I repeat this in my mind, no need, no need. I guess I've had so many quiet lonely days, I jump into conversation. Is this a sign of loneliness? Being alone? The latter, definitely. I was trapped in the discussion with Helen, but internally... a court of justice. Did I do the right thing years ago? Do I deserve to be punished? Was the discussion my punishment? What is right anyway? Am I not trying to get rid of all this? Oh... Nirvana!

Roy is so excited being invited to the wedding. I suppose he is tired of our chats. Do I go to this wedding party? Oh come on, why not? Am I waiting to see if Ana goes? Why's that? What's wrong with waiting for her decision? Oh! You don't know? I'll tell you. You have met her here after so many years, you seem to have struck a chord. But beware! This must not be the end of your freedom! You seem to have the tendency of losing it fast! Waiting to see what she says? This is bad, very bad. Pull yourself together.

It is clear, going back from here, I won't be the same person. Nothing drastic has happened here, yet I feel I will live differently on my return. I will give more time to myself, I mean going places, perhaps a concert, a film or two, theatre? Particularly if I continue to meet up with Ana, and with Frank. It seems to me we are very much in tune with each other's way of living. I am pleased that I have met them... an underestimation! But what if I get disappointed? What if I regret all this? Don't I regret having walked with Helen? In this case, it would be even worse, simply because I didn't expect anything from Helen; but with Ana and Frank, there is this good feeling, I expect happy times together on my return. What if all this shatters? Is it better not to start, or continue something that might end up in disappointment?

I know, I know, I'm too protective, too scared of failure. Failure in relationships. But so what, yes, I am scared, and I know it. Knowing it means I can act in a certain way. And it's not only me... they will be protected against disappointment, too. But here I assume they have the same attitude as I have towards friendship. Oh... I can go on and on about this. I read and read and read again about living in the moment, enjoy the events while they last, ignore the future. It is easier said than done!

A glass of water, when at correct temperature, can change your mood. I feel much better already. The glass is sitting in front of me. The room is hot, I have taken off my jumper. I hear noises, excited hums from outside. I suppose it's about the wedding. I suppose the best man is rehearsing his talk, reading from a piece of paper in his sweaty hands, the bride and her friend are chatting away incessantly in her room laughing, the parents are arguing, the groom is watching football! You see? My mind is full of speculations. I assume all is cliché... not that it's not, but I don't give it a chance. I have decided!

There is a knock at the door.
'Can I come in?' asks Ana.
'Well of course, are you OK?'
'Yes, I'm fine, just needed to talk.'
'Where is Frank? Weren't you together?'

'Yes, but he felt tired and went to his room. I couldn't tolerate my room. I needed to see someone.' She sat on the chair behind the small desk.

'I hate these tables; good for nothing, waste of space.'

'I thought you were talking about *me* being a waste of space,' I laughed.

'I'm sure you are… at least sometimes!' She was serious.

'Drink?' I asked.

'No, but I could do with a cup of tea.'

I put the kettle on to boil.

'I'm not sure how you can drink this tea. The bag has been sitting here, I guess, for five years. The bags of dust!'

'I don't care, I need something hot, some comforting drink.'

I poured the tea for her.

'I had an interesting talk with Helen walking up the fields,' I said.

'Not interested,' she said.

'What's wrong? You don't seem to be yourself. Did anything happen? I doubt if Frank said something.'

'No, not at all, poor Frank. He is a lovely man. If anything, I'm angry with myself.'

'Why? Did you say something to him?'

'Now, come on, would I?' She started drinking the tea.

'Someone told me everything is possible. I have made sure to remember it. Whether I believe in it or not, that's a different matter,' I said.

'It's simple, a tree does not fly, it's obvious, it's *not* possible. So, don't bother your mind with all this mumbo jumbo.'

'Things that appear to be simple, are often not so! In what you said, the moment it passed through your mind that a tree cannot fly, you imagined a tree flying, then you compared it with what you consider "reality" and decided a tree cannot fly. But it did, in your mind!' I said.

'I don't know why I always get into discussions with you. I came over to feel better, to release my frustration,' she said.

'But what happened? You don't tell me.'

'It's got nothing to do with Frank. It's me, it's me. All the time I was careful not to say anything about my views on what happens in Iran, what has happened there. After all, there's enough in the papers, the media, but I couldn't keep quiet. That Roy just infuriates me, he's so crass.'

'You take it too seriously.'

'Well, it *is* serious. Just look what happens in Iran and how the media reports it. Cleverly, any negative report has a deeper subliminal support. Look at the attitudes, the indifference to a massive injustice.'

'Do you expect justice? Do you really? This is a word used for self-deception. This is the terminology of the weak, the incompetent majority!' I said.

'I cannot understand. If the Iranian atrocities had happened anywhere else…' Ana said.

'Oh, get real! So, *you* have kept your eyes closed to what happens in the world. You are only concerned about Iran. I can understand it, though.'

'You see? Iran is the forgotten country. Secretly, someone's pockets are filled in with oil and mineral reserves, as for the rest, who cares?' Ana said.

'Look, you are, for obvious reasons, emotional about Iran, but if you look at other countries, all have problems; perhaps different problems, but problems. I think we are doomed. Human beings are doomed. Animals are killed by us, trees are cut by us, environment is polluted by us. So something must be out there to contain us, should be something to get rid of us. For this, it seems we have taken the task in our own hands. I know this is a cliché, but needs to be said,' I said.

'We can talk philosophy *ad infinitum*, but for me, it's simple. I cannot go back, for obvious reasons, but more than that because I cannot face the changes in Iran, the changes to the cities, to people's faces. People are angry, sad, defeated, disillusioned. You see this in their eyes, their lips, the way they walk… and then I think of the time I was in Iran. There was an air of achievement, of being able to achieve what you want. The economy was doing well… you know? We had huge cash reserves, now we are, in effect, bankrupt. Yes, I wasn't grown-up enough to understand many things, but I could feel the atmosphere, could see what was happening, the festivals, the art, the restaurants, all those things we know as freedom. I know you have your own views of freedom, but there are certain things which are basics. None of it now. No one dared increase prices of essentials then; now the price of bread, fuel, food goes up overnight, nobody says anything because people are afraid.'

She is sitting on that chair talking about things I can only try to understand. I compare what she says with what I have read on revolutions. I try to understand her, but her image as a child of a wealthy family makes it difficult. It is a judgement, of course, but I cannot free myself from it; as if a wealthy person has no right to talk about people and what they feel. As if the voice of a wealthy person does not fit with the purity of revolution. Something that people assume. People assume revolutions are innocent revolts against injustice. But if I don't believe that justice can exist, then revolution will be a folly, a useless exercise, an out of order emotion destined for destruction… very much welcomed by powers who will benefit from it! Yes, there will be changes, some of them perhaps for the better, but in the main, no revolution has fulfilled its aims.

'I'm sorry I bothered you with my invasion of your space. You were resting,' Ana says.

'Don't be silly. I'm happy you're here. Would you like another tea?'

'I don't mind actually.'

'I'm going to accompany you this time.'

I made tea for both of us. We drank in silence.

Her eyes are tired, and her skin looks older, just in a short time. Is it possible that our body, as it grows old, experiences transitory moments of youth and oldness? It is easy to feel this, but what about the appearance? I like the shine in her eyes, that sign of naughtiness, vitality, protest. But at this moment, as she drinks her tea, she seems resigned, disappointed. Why does she put herself in a situation to suffer? Why all that outrage about what happens in Iran? I know she can't help it. This is not something that time will resolve for her. People say that time is the best healer. But I doubt it works, at least not in this case. I suppose time is a healer when we want to be healed. Ana wants to keep this pain. She thinks if there is no pain, she has betrayed her country, has forgotten it. What would she do if she went back? Back to the routine, to the usual petty annoyances, regulations, instructions, revelations, people with their own problems… and hers, with her internal suffering; a lonely life! But is she lonely? Lonely is a person who has no emotions. Ana cannot put her emotions aside.

And what about me? Have I changed as an emotional man? Remembering myself, when I first saw Ana in that queue for enrolment at university, to merely an observer now sitting in front of her in a hotel in the middle of nowhere? Why do I want to deny my emotions? Changing face of love! Love, a magician, stretching a moment into an eternity and melting the eternity into drops evaporating to a sigh. I put down the cup.

'Please don't hurt yourself so much. Please,' I said.

'You are a nice man, Adam. I wish we had had this moment at university,' Ana says.

'It is an enigma; to have this moment, we must have had all those moments without each other!' I said.

'Turning a huge regret to a calm, fulfilled moment!' Ana said.

'And why not?' I watched her having tea.

Your eyes blink and the night draws me into labyrinths of condensed memories stretching to the leaves growing in the sunrise. I vacillate between moments of living and minutes of death. My mind flows in currents of madness and flies into spaces without walls where your hair blows smallest blossoms of mystical origin that sweep me calmly into the back of your eyelids where I see myself wandering with no aim, free from endings and trimmings.

'I think we should get a move on, let's go down and see what the gang are planning to do with this wedding thing,' Ana said.

'What about Frank?'

'Perhaps you could ask after him? He should feel better by now.'

'Sure, see you in the lobby.'

-40-

'What's this, young man?' I ask, standing at his door.

'Come in, Adam, don't stand there.' Frank was sitting on a comfortable chair in his elaborate dressing gown.

'Are you feeling better?'

'Oh, yes, thank you, it was just a passing headache.'

'Don't you want to come down? People are considering going to the wedding,' I said.

'Yes, I know. Do take a seat, there is time.'

I sat on the chair by the desk. Frank had the book of stamps open on his lap.

'You don't give yourself a holiday,' I said.

'I do what I like. Here's not the place to get a tan!' he laughed. He showed me the picture of a stamp.

'Look, isn't it fascinating?'

'It looks to me like a very repetitive theme. Jesus on the cross.'

'You need to look much more carefully. Isn't something odd here?' he asked.

'I can't think of anything particular,' I said.

'Look at his right-hand side.'
'OK, and?'
'Still haven't got it?'
'Oh, come on, tell me.'
'What do you expect to see on his right hand-side?'
'You lost me,' I said.
'Wound! Blood!'
'Oh, yes.'
'There is none! The wound is on the left-hand side in this picture.'
'I see!'
'This is intriguing for me. You go to galleries, museums, you look at endless pictures and sculptures of Christ. But none shows Christ's wound on his left-hand side.'
'I wonder if anyone realises this. I don't know what people look at in museums? Go to the Uffizi, you'll see row after row of Christ on the cross. What makes a piece stand out? These are boring for me. I know you will talk to me about the lighting, the colours, the perspective. But these are all techniques. And those we call artists, are craftsmen! They have done excellently, they have produced exquisite paintings, sculptures. But those pieces, in my mind, are artefacts. Where is their imagination? Christ after Christ on the cross, a baby in Mary's arms, being baptised, giving sermons in the countryside… where is the creativity? They choose a fixed image, and play with colours, light, thickness of the brush. This, to me, is not art. I insist, where has their imagination gone? There are so many topics to choose from, to let your ideas fly… has

the church killed their imagination? Repeat paintings of those rigid themes? Well, to be fair, some craftsmen used some other theme – apples, horses. I put this down to the stifling nature of Christianity. Mind you, it is worse in some other religions. Ana should've been here to elaborate!' Frank said.

'Don't you think you are a bit unkind? So many pieces of art are based on religion. Have you listened to exquisite pieces of music?' I asked.

'It is different! It is different to have an internal faith than to follow instructive religion. When you believe in an idea, you live with it, your mind flourishes with it, you fly with it. You come up with new initiatives, new images; you create. It is liberating. It limits your potential, it is a barrier to free thinking. Religion is suffocating. It instructs you in what you must do to end up in heaven. Heaven! Can you believe it? The catastrophe is that many people believe in it, no matter how educated they are. Perhaps they confuse faith with religion. An artist's mind goes all over the place, goes beyond the stars. A religious mind stops at an imposed image comfortably and repeats it,' Frank said.

'Is it possible to define art? It is more difficult now, in our time. Is a pile of dirt a piece of art? Apparently it is if you convince a gallery to devote a huge room to it, but in the open air on the street, it is not! I try to keep away from this debate. But I believe that a painter can create many varieties of the same event… image… look at Munch's works, and that is just one example,' I said.

'For me, in that picture of the stamp, there was a difference in outlook, a sort of – if you like –

rebellion. You have seen the same repetitious image for centuries. But then, you see Christ wounded on his left side. A fresh stance on a perceived image,' Frank said.

'That is, hopefully it wasn't a printing error when copying it on paper!' I said.

'I hope so too. You are a cynic!'

'Perhaps I am.'

'So, you have condemned yourself to a life of fear, doubting everything, following the ongoing belief in the "what if" agenda. Constant fear, anxiety and extreme conservatism,' Frank said.

'This is the essence of current civility. Perhaps we are lucky with our shops… we are lucky we are not part of education, health, big organisations,' I said.

'But you, with your scepticism, are behaving as an employee. Is the damage done already? Is my friend Adam a lost soul?'

'Frank, perhaps I am, but you cannot imagine how happy I am I have met you – and Ana – in this gathering. I hope we will remain close on our return. I'm not sure if you like this.'

Frank laughed. 'You should at least trust your feelings more than you do; give more credit to them. Now, I thought people were down there in the lobby? We've talked too much.'

'Yes, let's get a move on.' I stood up to leave.

'You don't need to leave. I can change rapidly. Take a drink from the fridge if you like.'

'I'm OK.'

I imagine him with his woollen striped scarf, and a book under his arm during the university time. I hear water running in the bathroom. The past and the present fuse. As he comes back to the room, I expect to see him as he was over thirty years ago!

'I'm ready, let's go.'

We walked through the hotel corridors. It was quiet.

-41-

I could never have imagined myself in that big hall with an elaborate outfit sitting at a table in a corner at a wedding party miles away in the north. In a wedding party where I did not know a single person! But, there we were, all of us sitting around the table; even Roy had made an effort. Maria was trying to tidy up his tie. We were all absorbed in the ongoing shenanigans of the people at the wedding.

The bride was laughing away, standing next to a table of some twelve people. She was plump, attractive, with a rosy smiling face. She leaned towards another young woman at the table to listen to what she was saying. She continued laughing, louder.

The bridegroom looked younger than her, was puny and tall, and was standing at the other side of the hall, talking with two other boys.

All the guests were divided at round tables with the name of a flower on the table. Only our table did not have a name. There was a long rectangular table for the family of the bride and bridegroom. Men and women from both sides were drinking incessantly.

'I'd love to know what she told the bride,' said Helen.

'So what? One said something funny, the other laughed,' said Roy.

'Do you always look at things like that?' Helen said.

'Like what?'

'Shallowly!' Helen said.

'Now, wait a minute. *You* get a kick out of tittle tattle, *I* am shallow?' asked Roy.

'Folks, let's sit here and enjoy! Don't forget it was Roy with Colin's initiative that we are here,' said Maria.

'By the way, you didn't tell us how we got this invite,' asked Ana.

'Well, pure animal magnetism!' Roy said, laughing.

'Actually, it was the best man who invited us! So I'm not sure how Roy's animal magnetism has worked here!' Colin laughed.

'How did this happen, then?' asked Ana.

'Well, there is so much good that bars do. People underestimate them. We met the best man, Bruce, in the bar. I ordered a whisky for him,' Colin said.

'And one thing led to another… your honour!' Roy laughed, looking at Ana.

'We can laugh about it, but something serious is happening over there!' said Helen.

'What serious thing? Since when you are concerned with things serious?' said Roy.

'Have you forgotten you are talking to a married woman with two children? I know how serious it is,' Helen said.

'Don't forget I was married, and lost my wife. So if anyone should defend your view, it must be me. But no! I still think marriage is a bad joke. What's the necessity? The idea, I suppose, is to live with someone you love or are attracted to. OK, you can do that anyway. And when there is no attraction, you leave without the fuss,' said Roy.

'Surely, it is not that simple. You reduce this issue to a mere transaction. While there are a lot of emotions involved, no matter whether you love the other side or not,' Ana said.

'Is that why you haven't married?' asked Roy.

'People have all sorts of reasons,' Ana said.

'Ana doesn't want to answer; what about you, Adam?' asked Roy.

'Simple, I didn't come across anyone I could marry,' I said.

'What does that mean?' Maria asked.

'I must say, I agree that marrying someone is a serious matter. I tried to separate two things… marrying my wife, and her leaving me. I told myself these are two different issues. But each time that all those images came back to me, I felt… I felt a rush of emotions all sorts,' Frank said.

'I suppose everything could be serious, as serious as you want it to be. And everything is a joke… it depends on how you look at things,' I said.

'You look at it only from the perspective of two people, and their relationship. But there is much more than that to it. It is a unit. The kids arrive at the unit and you have a mini-society,' Colin said.

'Now you are lecturing us!' said Helen.

'But it's true. Isn't it?'

'Red or white?' Roy said, with two bottles in his hands.

How can a happy occasion make me sad? There is too much quibbling between us. I am tired, I wish I was on that train going back right now. I am a child who wants its toy here and now! Ana is talking to Frank while Frank is sipping his red thoughtfully. Maria is absorbed in what people are doing at the top table. What is she looking at? She cannot hear a word, they are so far away. She is using her imagination, I suppose. How come she never married? This is interesting. The fact that I didn't marry, or even Ana didn't marry, is not a question for me. In my mind, Maria is the most marrying type among us. Looking at her, I feel sad. But I was sad before looking at Maria. One moment I am so happy, energised... happy that I came here, that I met Frank, and particularly Ana... I tell this to myself repeatedly. And I am happy for this. I keep on telling myself we must continue meeting when we go back. But then, there is a deep sadness in me. It's like particles of ash settling on me after a sudden and uncontrollable fire that abruptly dies off with so much ash in the air that I can't see around me properly. Suddenly the whole surrounding is an abstract entity. I think I can wrap it up and throw it away... away... somewhere I cannot reach it. Create a new life, a new life, but not at the age I am; much younger. Is it melancholy of things not done, or days past? Why don't I celebrate the days to come? Why don't I look at the happy people in this wedding party? Clearly, there is something wrong with me. Am I doomed to suffer? It seems I like to suffer. It seems that once you start looking into details, once you question things, suffering starts. Perhaps that's why people love to live a shallow life. Look at all those people over there. They are drinking themselves into a stupor. Perhaps we should search for a permanent state of stupor. This is the faith of humanity. Now, in our current state, we fluctuate between turmoil, exhaustion, and stupor. But the robots are at hand, and we can surrender our responsibilities to them, and resign to blissful stupor.

Maria's face is glowing, and it is not because of the nice, cosy temperature of this hall. It is as if the wedding is hers.

'You seem to be enjoying yourself,' I told Maria.

'Isn't it nice? It's good to be a bystander of happiness,' she said.

'It is better to be part of it,' Colin said.

'I am happy. Look at the bride's father.'

'He seems to me to be a bit on the serious side!' Helen said.

'But happy!' Maria said.

Ana was going to say something, but she noticed the orchestra coming in; a plump singer with ginger curly hair touching her bare shoulders, a short guitarist with generously-oiled thick black hair, a fat saxophonist, and a tall puny drummer. The whole party applauded, clapping. So did Maria.

The singer started with "Strangers in the night". Helen murmured, reciting with her. The bride and bridegroom walked to the top table and sat next to each other.

'Was it like this for you?' Colin asked Helen.

'You must be kidding!' Helen said.

'No party?'

'Of course not. The agony of going to the registry office was enough. I cannot understand why people do this,' Helen said.

'It's a happy occasion, they want to share it with people they love,' Maria said.

'Oh yes of course, I forgot,' Helen laughed.

'When you announce the start of life together, and share the celebrations with your family and friends, it makes it ever so difficult to separate,' Maria said.

'Do you really think so?' asked Colin.

'She can't be that stupid,' Roy said. Maria went red in the face.

'You'd be surprised, but many people think this way,' Frank said.

'Did you have a wedding ceremony, Frank?' asked Maria.

'Well, we decided to go on a long holiday instead,' Frank said.

'Oh,' said Maria.

'And look what happened,' Roy laughed.

'I can assure you, with or without a party, we wouldn't have continued together,' Frank said.

'We had a party, but I will never know if we would've continued. Jessika died; mind you, my wife was very organised, determined. I don't know how I could've survived in that environment,' Roy said.

The music was in full swing, a couple of small children were dancing on the dance floor. The bride leaned towards the groom and said something in his ear. The groom turned and started kissing her.

'How nice,' Maria said. 'I wonder what is going on in her mind.'

'It's pretty obvious if you ask me,' Roy said.

'You are a cynic. I don't ask you, you always see the bad things in people,' Maria said.

'Far from it, I think she is very happy for herself!' Roy said.

'But she is not the only one who's happy, look at the groom, their parents,' Maria said.

'How can you say this? All pretence. People can laugh, and really cry at the same time. They are experts in pretending,' Roy said.

'Why do I think you are talking about yourself?' Helen said.

'Because you cannot tolerate what I say. Were you really happy to be married? Perhaps you were because you felt that for once you were like other people.'

'Do you remember this song?' Frank asked me.

'Of course, how could I not remember it?' I said.

'But Willie Nelson sang it too,' Frank said.

'What about Cave and MacGowen?' Helen said, excited.

Colin shook hands with Roy, singing. Both were drunk.

'But Armstrong is something else,' Ana said and joined them – 'They really say I love you…'

Her eyes carry memories of years tired of carrying themselves. Her lips live in a world of forgotten languages. The shape of her smile reminds me of the curves of young, skinny, Egyptian dancers of Akhenaten's mesmerising movements in praise of sunlight. Her hair absorbs desires of those who know by heart the secrets of papyri. I am from the world of the mad and the lost, living with the scent of books written by laments of unknown authors. In my refuge my dialogue is with creatures out of touch! What am I doing in this rational world of assessments, judgements, gossip, incessant manipulation of emotions?

Two waiters came to our table with food. Other waiters were serving other tables at the same time.

'The manager must be happy!' said Roy. 'I wonder how many weddings they do in here. It must be a one-off, this time of year.'

'The bride's father is a friend of the hotel owner,' Colin said.

'You are a bank of knowledge,' teased Helen.

'I have my ways!' He winked.

'But the groom's father is a jazz buff. He paid for the band,' Roy said.

'You two have done a great job drinking with the family,' Ana said.

A child runs to the dance floor and takes a stem of rose fallen on the floor. She runs to the top table.

'How sweet,' Maria said.

Remember the leaves... the leaves in the small courtyard. Remember your childhood fingers, the stony wall, the tall plane tree shading the veranda. Remember the leaves with the smell of food coming from the kitchen, and the quiet voices from the big room. You're not going to see your father again. There's going to be a remembrance, and the smell of his skin will fly to the courtyard where you are collecting the leaves. And the autumn wind will scatter the leaves you have collected so carefully one over the other. And they take your father away. The box is shiny in maroon colour with refined lines and curves. You sit down and collect another leaf. It's yellow, red and green.

'It *is* a good party. They are lovely family, they are going to have a happy life. A happy party, a happy life!' Maria continued.

'Maria, you have received a new lease of life with this wedding, it seems! If I didn't know, I would say you are the bride!' Colin said.

'Thank you, Colin; I miss a big family, the warmth of Sunday lunches together, the children looking forward to Christmas,' Maria said.

'Well, that's because you haven't married! Otherwise I doubt if you missed carrying two small kids with you to the airport for that summer holiday in the Algarve! You cannot imagine – think about the luggage, the fight with the husband in the car getting to the airport, children crying. And that's the start!' Helen said.

'But when you love someone, all these are nothing,' Maria said.

Frank coughed and wiped his forehead. 'I wonder if we are missing an important question here. These tittle-tattles are just appearances. The main issue is… are we social? Is man a social animal, as they say?'

'I don't think this is a smart topic for a wedding dinner,' Colin said, biting into his Atlantic salmon.

'Don't worry, you enjoy the party. I'm sure some people here are interested in my question,' said Frank.

'But how can you deny the fact that man is a social animal? Just look! Hello! Anywhere you look, you see a society; from tribes in the depth of the Amazon to the crowds in London, from families to university societies!' Helen said.

'A group of people who live or work together does not necessarily give us a proof of man being social!'

'So pray tell, what does!' Roy mocked.

'Being social has got nothing to do with lives together under the same roof,' Frank said. 'Primitive man lived very differently until fire was discovered.'

'So?' asked Helen.

'Well, with fire, came protection, possession, religion!'

'Oh, come on, not one of those mumbo jumbo arguments of yours!' Roy said.

'What we call society is the coming together of people through religious encouragement, and greed. People have found that being together, they can rob, exploit each other, and accumulate what they call wealth! And, strangely, all this can be done under the emblem of ethics; there is justification for each and every action, what you *must* follow to end up in heaven. And heaven is basically something so ridiculous I cannot fathom how people, even intelligent people, believe in it,' Frank said.

'Simple; greed! A place you don't need to do anything, but you receive all sorts of services,' Ana said.

'With this mentality humankind will lose its abilities, faculties!' I said. 'Greed is obsession. And by being obsessive, we lose so much. We are rich when we can see wider opportunities, rather than focusing only on narrow goals. So greed effectively works against being rich.'

'Look, can we change the topic, please? Let's enjoy the party,' Maria said.

The waiters were collecting the plates.

'What is the pudding?' asked Helen.

'We have a dessert called Ice in Paradise!' Ana laughed.

'I bet chocolate cake,' said Roy.

'Some sort of tart,' Colin said.

'Zabaglione,' Ana said.

'Tiramisu,' I said, 'but don't forget the wedding cake!'

'I could do with a good cup of coffee,' Frank said.

There was a sound of spoon on wine glass. The bride's father stood up. He was serious but chirpy, and his gestures were slow, trying to measure any word he said.

'I am a man of few words, had preferred not to say anything, but this is Emma's wedding, and I cannot sit here and drink myself to oblivion. Emma is a gem. I know this sort of thing must not be said, but I say it – said it. I would be very uncomfortable if I had given her away to anyone but Mike. I can see them both having a happy life together, with one, two, *five* children playing in their garden, no matter summer or winter, because their house will always be warm with their love. So, please raise your glasses to Emma and Mike. I would like to thank you all for accepting the invitation to join this happy occasion, and I would like to welcome our guests from London, who brightened our party tonight by agreeing to join us. I know they are leaving us tomorrow. I hope they have had an enjoyable time in our neck of the woods and have a good trip back with good memories.'

Emma turned to her father and kissed him. Mike said something to Bruce before he stood up. He took a piece of paper from his pocket and smiled. Ana looked at me. 'I really cannot sit here listening to the clichés,' she said. 'I need silence, somewhere far away.'

As I look at Mike and Emma kissing, I think of Frank and what he said about the non-social man. I wonder if he has any theories about kissing. Is it a primordial event, a discovery, or perhaps mothers have learnt it from birds giving food to their newly-hatched babies? Are there any landmark stamps on kissing? I must ask Frank! Is it something to do with self-satisfaction through sensory perception, or fulfilment by witnessing someone else's satisfaction? Whatever it is, it is a means of communication; isn't communication a proof of us being social? Frank will say no! For him, society has a sacred meaning, I think. But I agree with him that there is a clear distinction between faith and religion, internal belief and external imposition of dogma. If religion is the cohesive glue to keep us together in a society, shouldn't we be happy about it? Perhaps this is why in this wedding party – any wedding party – the couples are happy; there is a sense of security, safety in numbers, danger in being alone. And this takes us to the primordial search for safety. When fire kept our ancestors warm and cosy for the first time, away from the danger of wild animals attacking them, they realised the benefits of keeping together; around fire, following set instructions, how to keep fire going, how to keep children close to fire. And we call this society. This is being together as a result of externally imposing, yet beneficial, factors. Frank is seeking a society where its people are driven together by their internal fire, without fear that one day the fire might die out. For him, animals are social, humans are not! Animals are social because they are not bound by promises, oaths, definitions of how to behave. They are together when they want to be, they are alone when they want to be. They look after their offspring in a natural manner. Their love does not need to be officiated by a third person, by words dictated to keep them together. For Frank, animals are civilised.

The waiters roll in, carefully, a large table carrying a big, tall, multi-storey cake. The orchestra plays a familiar tune. The bride and groom stand up and move to the cake. Mobiles start flickering in hands.

'Nice way to end up our trip, don't you think?' Maria says.

'What do you mean? Night is young. We haven't danced yet,' Helen says.

'We have the whole night. Ralph at the bar will be fed-up with us,' Roy says.

The party is in full swing on the dance floor. The waiters bring in pieces of wedding cake. Roy and Helen stand up to dance. A couple of children are dancing the tango.

'I was a good dancer,' says Ana.

'You were? Not any longer?' I ask.

'Do you know, I'm not sure. Perhaps it's related to age. Comes a time when you don't feel like going for it.'

'It could be that something has happened that has put you off dancing,' Frank says.

'Perhaps, I had such passion for it. I like watching people dancing, though,' Ana says.

'But even if you don't dance, it doesn't mean you are not a good dancer,' Maria says.

'It's irrelevant; it's like a relationship finished. No matter how good I might be, when I don't dance, when I don't have the passion for it, it doesn't matter,' Ana says.

'I tend to agree with Ana,' Frank says.

'It's sad, what about you? Do you dance, Adam?' asks Maria.

'Oh, I think I haven't danced for twenty… thirty years,' I say.

'So, this is a test for you to see if you can still dance,' Maria says.

'OK, I take on the challenge,' I say.

We stand up. Maria's fingers are cold.

Her fingers were cold. They were always cold. Now she was lying on her bed facing the wall.

'Are you feeling better?'

'Better? When would I feel better? This back is killing me, and you don't care, don't pretend you do. If you did, you would've been here with me, with your poor mother. But it's not the pain that's killing me, it's being alone, all day, with

people I don't know. They sit there playing cards, Thursday nights we have dancing – dancing session! It's a joke, you know, it's pretentious shit! Creating a happy environment! Play cards, have afternoon tea, and dance!'

'Do you always have cold fingers?' I ask Maria.

'Yes, since I was a child. My father used to tell me that I should play more. My mother wasn't keen. She preferred me going to the flower-making classes, they were fashionable. I ended up going to some dancing classes when I was fifteen; after a couple of sessions, I quit.'

We are dancing the tango with children next to us dancing.

'You dance very well for someone who quit dancing classes,' I say.

'You dance well for someone who hasn't danced for many years,' Maria says.

'It's good we compliment each other. I'm sure others won't be so complimentary,' I say.

Helen and Roy dance towards us.

'We are putting fire to the dance floor,' Roy says, laughing. 'Helen is aflame!'

'Fred and Ginger eat your hearts out,' Helen says. We dance away.

'What're your plans on return?' Maria says.

'Life goes on, getting back to the routine,' I say.

'Have you enjoyed this trip?'

'Yes.'

Now it is a waltz.

Her face has changed, but has kept the young look. You can't recognise some people when they've grown old. I must say I wouldn't recognise her had I seen her on the street, although she hasn't changed much. She asks me what my plans are on return. But I do not ask her. I don't imagine I will see her again. I don't have any interest in the life of an older than middle-aged woman living alone with or without a budgie. That's fine, but why do I judge her life? As I dance with her, I think of the make-up she uses, her toothpaste, her choice of underwear. I have no interest in her life, her physique, yet, I ask myself all these questions and in front of each question, I have a tick rejecting my answer. These must be the remainders of my university time, under the emblem of intellectualism, mocking everyone, touching the surface, pretending we are deep in thought. And this would go down very nicely. We found in our group those who were praised, those who agreed, those who opposed and some observers. Now, after so many years, have we changed at all? Changed, we have, but in what way? Have we moved on or moved in? Are we stratified in our old life or have events blown us away? I didn't know about the depth of Ana's feelings about Iran then, maybe she didn't know it either. What about myself? Maria's question is a simple one; what my plans are on my return. I always judge her being bland, having a dreary life with no questions. A typically ideal wife for a religious man seeking a family with four kids. I have never let myself see people's lives the way they really are, rather than the way I see them. I have, unintentionally, forced them to behave in a certain way, I have convinced myself with preconceived images. Oh, what a limited life! Yet I read so many books, so many stories. Has all this had any effect on my viewpoints? Do I still live the university life? I guess this is a lonely person's syndrome. Stick to that set, comfortable, safe lifestyle of yours.

Maria's fingers are still cold as we go back to our seats. I look at Ana, who is sitting silently. I smile at her and she doesn't see.

Do you know, Ana? You and I will sink under the weight of our memories. You are sad sitting there, looking at people dancing, the singer with her mechanical gestures, reminding you of the singer you loved when she came to London to sing those Persian songs. The old, old singer threw packets of memories at you to add to your bag, the bag you have been carrying with you. Your eyes were wet, yet you did not move to wipe a single drop. You let them fall, fall to burn your skin to remember you were a child, you were a child once, and you were a young girl once, and you were in love with petunias and geraniums and your grandmother's small garden. You smelt the whiff of jasmine sitting in that hall listening to her leaning against her stick. And you saw how your memories evaded you with those events – killings, people shouting for elusive freedom, shouting death to him and death to her, and you witnessed trees being cut, flowers drooping, and you walked and walked in this cloudy, grey land seeking your memories in unfamiliar coffee shops, unfamiliar faces. And then a single note, and there was no escape anymore. Do you know, Ana? We are creatures of the past, ghosts of daily life… walking to work, coming to this reunion. I see your eyes fixated on that singer… I see your ghost.

The waiter brought the espresso. It was cold and weak. He puts down cups for Roy and Helen, who are still dancing.

'I never thought those two would talk again after we leave. If you didn't know, you would think they are an item!' Colin said.

'We are too hard on each other,' Frank said.

'We are too hard on ourselves,' I said.

'Why do you think that is?' Ana said, in a low voice.

'Religion!' Frank said. 'We are hard on ourselves because religion has taught us to behave in a certain way, and has put boundaries; do this, and paradise is yours… do that, and you are in the depths of hell. So, we are constantly monitoring ourselves – judging – and once we judge ourselves, it is, obviously, much easier to judge others.'

'You cannot put all problems down to religion,' I said.

Frank laughed. 'Not *all* problems, but pretty much close!'

'Don't we need all these limitations, though? Imagine what would happen if we didn't have laws to keep us in our place, to guard our freedom,' Colin said.

'Don't let Frank start,' Ana said, laughing, 'I know where this will take us!'

'Yes, they say we are born with sin. First of all, what is the basis of that sin? Two people enjoying themselves? If that's the case, then religion is against enjoyment, against happiness. Who wants to follow a discipline that is against their joy in life? Religion says you must be controlled otherwise you will harm others. Animals don't have religion, and they live in harmony, alone or in groups. They only attack each other under very extreme circumstances. But humans? No! Our greed is unlimited! And what is the origin of greed?' Frank asked.

'I have a calculated guess, you'd say religion!' Colin said.

'You guessed well! I don't think I need to give examples, you are intelligent enough to look around yourself. And as for freedom – do you really think religion is concerned about our freedom? Ha ha ha!' Frank took a bite from the cake left on his plate.

Helen and Roy came over. Roy was sweating; as he sat, he cleaned his face with the napkin.

'Roy is full of untapped talent, it's official!' Helen said.

'Happy to hear that from you,' Colin said.

'The woman is right, she has sharp eyes, is quick-witted, and outspoken.' Roy laughed and took a big bite from his cake, followed by a single gulp of coffee.

'We must develop our talent, Helen,' he said.

'Always ready for challenges!' Helen said.

'Don't we thank the bride's father?' Frank asked.

'Don't worry, we shall do the necessary,' Colin said, looking at Roy.

-42-

'We have the bar to ourselves,' says Helen, dancing between the chairs and the bar.

We sit around the table where we sat previously. We wait, and nobody comes.

'I'll go and find Ralph.' She disappears behind the bar.

'So, that's it. Tomorrow… and we'll be off,' Maria says.

Colin looks at his watch. 'It's already tomorrow!'

'So, when do we meet again?' Maria asks.

'Who knows! Perhaps Colin can organise another get-together,' Maria asks herself, looking at Colin.

'Missing me already?' Roy laughs. 'Why not, if everyone is game. I am sure Colin is game too, aren't you, Colin?'

Helen comes back, together with Ralph.

'Guess where I found him, in a small room at the back of the bar, sleeping!'

'You are cruel, Helen,' Roy says.

'Look who's talking,' says Helen.

'Let's lighten up our final night,' says Helen. 'Who wants what? I'm buying.'

Ralph looks tired and uninterested.

'What do people want?' he asks.

We order in silence, with the background sound of a famous old song and people laughing.

'Now, that's what I call a good wedding party,' Colin says.

'They appear to be a happy family, on both sides,' Ana says.

'The bridegroom was fun. I liked his naughtiness,' Maria says.

'How untypical of you. You liked the bridegroom? You liked Gavin?' Roy says.

'What's wrong with her liking Gavin? Woman shouldn't fancy younger men?' Helen says.

'I didn't say that. It was just strange to me, that's all. Anyway, in your case, we know you don't discriminate!' laughs Roy.

'Tomorrow night, we will be miles away from here, back at home. So let's enjoy these last hours, folks,' Frank says.

'Let's see what we liked best about here,' Helen says.

'Here or our meeting up?' Colin asks.

'Whatever,' says Helen.

'Then for me it's seeing you after all these years, I was so curious… I'm glad I arranged this reunion,' Colin says.

Ralph comes back with the drinks.

'I am really grateful to Colin for organising this gathering. It was out of the blue, but it worked,' Maria says.

'I think we all agree this was a good idea, but specifically, it's been good seeing what we look like after so many years, what we do, what we feel,' I say.

'All that, and remembering the past,' Ana says.

'And not thinking about the future! This getting together is an emblematic event telling us – I mean me – how important it is to be with people, and enjoy their presence,' Frank says.

Roy stands up and smiles, going towards Gavin, who is coming over to us.

'I asked Gavin to join us if he could, albeit for a short time,' Roy says.

'How nice,' Helen says. 'Gavin, you were a star in that party.'

'Before Gavin says anything, I must thank him on behalf of all of us for inviting us to the party,' Colin says.

'You are a happy family,' Ana says.

'Here, we are a small community, that makes the difference,' Gavin says.

'True, but that could make things worse,' Helen says.

'Cheers to you and the lucky couple.' Colin raised his glass, and called Ralph. 'Ralph, see what our friend drinks.'

'I'm OK, really, I've been drinking all night. I'm going back drinking,' Gavin says.

'Emma – the bride – do you know her well?' asks Maria.

'Know her well?' Gavin laughs. 'We were in the same class in school, then high school, then she did nursing.'

'Oh, I am a nurse,' Maria says.

'I see that you are a very close group of friends. I feel that,' Gavin says, 'I knew it when I met Colin and Roy. You must be having fun together,' Gavin says.

'You are psychic!' Helen laughs.

'You have a point there, though. I'm famous for it,' Gavin says. 'I knew Emma and Mike would marry, I'd seen the day, I'd seen her in the dress.'

'Come on! Anyone would have predicted that, you've been with them for a long time,' Roy says.

'No, but really, I can see what people feel.'

'OK then, Mr. Feel-it-all, what can you say about our friend here?' Helen looked at Maria. 'Tell us what you sense about Maria.'

Gavin looks at Maria, who's gone red in the face, takes his hands close to her face and then moves them up and down slowly.

'You are a very sensitive soul. I sense a feeling of grief – yes, you have lost a loved one very recently, or someone is ill.'

Maria looks at Gavin with the eyes of a believer who is convinced about her faith yet again!

'But not to worry, this sad period will pass. You should wait for good news… something good will happen.'

Gavin stands up abruptly. 'On that note, I must go back to the party, they will miss me… are missing me already… he laughs.

Maria looks in a daze at Gavin leaving. 'How did he know? It's fascinating,' she says.

'Oh, don't be ridiculous, they all say the same sort of thing. Of course people have sad events and look for happy events all the time. He didn't say anything special. You are so naïve,' Helen says.

'He was specific, he said I've lost someone very recently… very recently. If he hadn't sensed it, how could he say recently?' Maria says.

'But he said someone, not something,' Helen says.

'It might be a "thing" for you, but for me, the budgie was a close friend.' Maria's eyes are wet.

'Folks, I must say something. When we met Gavin in the bar earlier today, we told him we had been to the distillery, and… told him that on our return, one of us heard that she had lost her budgie. So he had prior knowledge,' Colin says.

'What a devious man, how could he play like that with Maria's emotions?' Ana asked.

'Easily, people want to show off. It is a disease. They want to be loved,' Frank says.

'Rubbish! This is all a case of showing power. "I know things that others don't. I know things about the other world." Spooky!' Helen says.

'I don't take this seriously. So what? Whether he seeks love and attention, or he's a power junkie, he's gone now,' Frank says.

'He thought he was funny. Some people are so selfish, they can't think of other people. I thought he was fun, but not anymore; he is so ruthless,' Maria says.

'How are you getting back, Frank?' I ask.

'Like Ana, by train, what about you?' Frank asks.

'Train,' I say.

'Oh good, we can go back together, anyone else for the train?' Ana asks.

'I can take three people in my car,' says Roy.

'I'm in,' says Helen.

'Count me in, Roy,' says Colin.

'If it's OK with you, can I join too?' says Maria.

'We've reached capacity!' laughs Roy.

'Now that is all arranged, let's have another round of drinks,' says Colin.

I see a shade of sadness in him. I can imagine him enjoying himself giving lectures to those students. A sense of power over disenchanted youth. Perhaps there was a time he cared. Then came a time all his ambitions for professorship were dashed. Bring in money for the university or forget it! So, he thought it was enough for him to speak loudly in lecture rooms for two hundred first-year students to hear him without the need for a microphone. Gradually he saw himself more and more as an army colonel. The transformation was fascinating. His ambitions for discoveries had turned to strategies to overcome the cheating students. Who had plagiarised in their coursework! He would go through hours of investigation looking into all those essays, welcoming new technologies to sieve the unruly from the obedient. This would keep him clean, away from his forceful wife, who had become increasingly dictatorial with her age, with those individual thick persistent short strings of hair growing on her blatantly white stony face. In the old days, men in his situation would resort to their shed to read the Times. He didn't have a garden, let alone a shed. So exam scripts were his best friends. He would moan and groan, but was happy for another exam to come, more coursework to be set.

So why this sadness? Am I correct in my sensing a sadness in him? It is a particular sadness, not that obvious, a silent sadness stifled under repetitious mundane sentences. Oh, perhaps I should organise a reunion! Yes, and for him, we are a reminder of the time he could desire, aspire for a future anywhere but where he has ended up.

The smoky aroma of the whisky stays as the warm feeling moves through my body. Would I see Colin when we go back? I don't see it. I don't seem to have a thing to share with a married man with a couple of kids and a wife who is, probably, far from friendly. Seeing Roy on return? Obviously not! He is too much! His presence is announced, wherever you are, with an attack. It seems to me he has to disagree with whatever you say. Basically, I won't make an effort to meet Maria or Helen either; both boring in their own way.

'I'm going to see Hopper's exhibition on Thursday, it's the last day,' Ana says.

I have seen it already; a rare event having his works on show here in London, I'm not sure why. How does he make a total sense of isolation through an ordinary scene? Is it those colours? The brush? How does he transfer that alienation from a woman sitting on a chair to me walking in the gallery?

'He is the master of colour,' Frank says.

'I cannot tolerate him,' Helen says, 'his works suffocate me.'

'That's the idea, to feel the weight of his alienation on your chest,' I say.

'Then he's successful. What a sad successful man!' Helen says.

It's not only the taste of the whisky, nor is it the aroma or the colour. As I keep the thick short glass in both my hands, I feel a degree of closeness. I feel closer to this glass of whisky than to Colin! What a comparison. There is something to say about whisky… it invites you to ponder, pause and ponder. It never invites you to a jolly moment, rather takes your hand, your whole body, and walks with you through the labyrinths of your mind. You walk through with it and watch your images – past, present – hung on the walls of your mind. It takes you to visit your own gallery, a gallery open only for you to visit.

'So, there will be plenty of time to chat while you drive,' Colin tells Roy.

'We should be careful, our lives are in danger with Roy driving. God forbid if he gets angry,' says Helen.

'If or when?' Colin laughs.

'You are an ungrateful bunch. You must thank me for taking you,' Roy says.

'Oh, so you'd like to drive all the way alone? Really? You should be thankful to us for giving you the pleasure of our company!' says Helen.

'I can see that I will enjoy the trip. Roy, do you have any petrol in the car?' Colin says.

'Do we need petrol? I thought we would be thankful for Helen pushing it all the way!' Roy laughs.

'Joking aside, it's good to be together the whole way back; pity all of us can't be returning together,' Colin says.

'Perhaps we should repeat this,' Maria says.

'What? Coming here? No way!' Roy says.

'It doesn't need to be here, somewhere else,' Maria says.

'Somewhere hot,' Helen says.

'In ten years!' says Ana.

'And Colin must promise to arrange it again,' Frank says.

'I'm game,' Colin says. He takes a large sip of his beer, and stands up. 'That's me, off to bed. When do we set off tomorrow?'

'As you wish, we have some seven… eight hours non-stop! Stopping makes it some eleven, twelve hours,' Roy says.

'Better start early then,' says Maria.

'Let's play it by ear,' Colin says. 'If we don't see you tomorrow, we shall see you in ten years' time!' Colin laughs, looking at us.

'Don't laugh,' Roy says, standing up, 'it might happen, you know!'

'Are you off too?' Ana asks Roy.

'Me too,' says Maria.

We look at them walking to the lift. Maria looks back and waves her hand. Helen is talking to Roy.

'We don't want to go to bed now, do we?' asks Ana.

'I'm fine,' I say.

'Our train is early,' says Frank.

'We can sleep on the train,' Ana says.

'Oh, not before I tell you some stories about stamps,' Frank smiles.

'You must be kidding,' says Ana.

'Not at all. We must have special respect for stamps, stamps are symbols of our past images. The dearest possessions we have. How could you say you don't want to hear about them?' says Frank.

'My dearest possessions are somewhere inside me, deep inside… no one can access them,' Ana says.

'Yes, and exactly because they are so deeply hidden, we forget them, it's easy to lose them in our inner labyrinths. A stamp brings them all back to life from their hidden abodes, stamps collect all those scattered images,' Frank says.

'Oh, come on, you give your stamps powers of the Messiah!' Ana says.

'You see, this is a topic for our train conversation,' Frank coughs, laughing.

'I can't win, talking with you,' Ana says.

'I am on your side, you just need to listen to what I say.' Frank laughs.

They argue about something dear to us, but the argument itself takes them away from the essence. The images… scattered images? Yes, but those images have the habit of stunning us. Out of the blue, comes a sharp spark, it's a spike piercing, flowing through our nerves. They never disappear. We move in our seats looking at people around us, we smile while an image links to another image and flows through our nerves. What's the meaning of these possessions if they are hidden in a corner? They become a disease! They might as well be dead if hidden stagnant in a hole somewhere. They come to life when they are expressed, when they flow. Those images relating to each other are meaningful because they form our memories.

I look at Ana. Her pearl necklace and her maroon polo-neck jumper take me back to university time. She always wore some sort of necklace, but she had a black polo-neck then. All these years I have remembered her in that jumper. What she wore, always, invited me to say something. But what could I say then? What a nice jumper? The intention losing its essence when expressed! But this has been my problem all the time, all my life. I look at Ana; seeing her is seeing my failure. Failure to relate, failure to tell her what I felt all those years ago. And how my life would've been a different one! The moments, the activities, the friends... hah, friends that I have never had, sitting in the bookshop, walking between the short narrow corridors, between the parallel bookshelves when I get tired. Oh, I talk like any other man recounting his failures. Why don't I look at this event as an opportunity for a new start? Now I must be able to talk to Ana as she is sitting there looking at her empty whisky glass. There is no relationship between two people better expressed than through looking at each other talking and talking. Skins talk, movements of bodies in moments of short utterances count, but nothing matches the power of words when they are cooked with the heat of your blood, when they come out from the heat of memories as if an inferno talks, sharing all the earth's emotions kept inside for years.

I see Frank sipping his whisky slowly. He is another one driving me to admit my failure. I should've been in touch with him, should have been friends with him. I like his mind, the way he carries himself. Yet I deemed him arrogant, presumptuous, self-important. Perhaps I was insecure getting close to him, perhaps I was protecting my ignorance.

Frank coughs, but quickly composes himself and finishing his whisky, stands up. 'I'm off, too. I see you two have some fuel left in you, but that's me, exhausted. See you tomorrow.'

'Anytime?' Ana says.

'Anytime! All train drivers are at our disposal, as long as we don't worry about getting to London late.'

Frank walks away, and I tell myself it is good to be on the train with him, and with Ana.

'Another round?' Ana asks.

'Of course,' I answer joyfully. I ask Ralph to make them doubles.

'I hope it's OK with you, Ralph, I feel we are keeping you late. It's nearly two in the morning.'

'Normally I'm in bed for three hours! But tonight, we are all staying late for the wedding,' Ralph says.

'Even you?'

'Yes, I'm both here and there.'

'So, it's been our luck,' Ana says.

'It's my pleasure, ma'am. I have enjoyed serving your group. We don't get such lively groups from the south here. It's sort of lonely, most of the time, particularly in the winter.'

'Is it not a boring place for a young person? With your experience, you could easily find jobs up in London,' Ana says.

'It's mother, she needs help, and I sort of like it here. I went for a holiday to London a couple of years ago. I wouldn't survive there, too noisy, too crowded for my liking,' Ralph says.

The whisky is large, in its real meaning. The liquid has filled nearly to the rim of the glass.

'If I drink all this, I will sleep here,' Ana says.

'If I drink this, I'll pass away here,' I say. Ralph laughs. 'I'm sure you can deal with it, I've seen you, all of you can compete nicely with the locals.' Ralph says this and leaves us alone.

'I'm glad I came over, I had a different view about everyone before coming,' I say.

'I found them odd,' Ana says.

'Odd?'

'Not Frank, and of course not you, but look at Roy, he looks like a thug most of the time.'

'He's a troubled soul! All those responses are only gesturing machismo,' I say.

'He loves to confront, as if he's in a battle all the time. He confronts just for the sake of confronting,' Ana says, 'and poor Maria – at least Helen didn't take the nonsense, good for her! But she's sort of weird too.'

'I thought she'd stayed frozen at the university stage, but perhaps not,' I say. 'We should accept people the way they are.'

'Yes, but in a squeezed few days' party, things can get muddled,' Ana says. 'I have treated the past like the present for a long time, ignoring that things change, people change. Meeting Helen, I thought I was right in thinking nothing changes in people. But then I've seen also this continuous change, albeit too small to detect; I have seen it. Now it's time to avoid seeing the past as present, it's time to file it as it is, the past. I should leave all my Persian saga where it is, where it belongs.'

'It's impossible. We are our memories, and we continue as memories. Memories breathe and change too. Even our recent past is not the same as it happened. Frank's stamps of historical events are different creatures, having a life of their own, while those events have assumed different lives in people's minds. Your images of the revolution, or whatever you call it, is different from another Iranian's. Your memories of the same incidents are different as you are different. And as you have changed with time, those memories have changed too,' I say.

'You think we are modern-day Sisyphus carrying our memories, and each time we try to leave them, it's impossible,' Ana says.

'Sisyphus was condemned, the stone was imposed on him, he was tired… but we are not separate from our memories. I say it again all the time, we are our memories, and if we are tired of them, it is perhaps because of guilt about what we have done, or because we measure our past, balance them out against good experiences and bad experiences while it really doesn't matter. We are our experiences, and once we stop measuring them, we will be free,' I say.

'Are you free, Adam? Are you?' Ana asks.

'No, but I'm trying,' I say.

We continue drinking. I tell myself I've arrived at the next stage of my life.

-43-

Frank is standing by the hotel counter, his scarf carefully wrapped around his neck, and his luggage, a very neat dark brown leather suitcase, is standing next to his feet. Ana is walking towards him. I'm sitting on the armchair in the lobby. I stand up and go towards them.

'Morning, folks,' I say.

'Morning,' Frank says with a husky voice.

'Are you OK?' asks Ana.

'Yes, perfectly, it is just in the morning,' Frank says. 'Let's order a taxi.'

'They are bringing down my suitcase,' Ana says.

'Perfect,' I say.

'Have you seen the gang of four?' asks Ana.

'They've gone already. I saw them briefly. Helen was sleepwalking, Roy was in his normal state!' I say.

I look at the revolving door of the hotel. There is a white layer of snow.

'I thought we'd seen the last of the snow,' Ana says.

'It's not finished. They will have more of it, I'm sure,' Frank says.

In the taxi, as the taxi turns around the hotel, I see the Bacchus sculpture under snow. Small flakes are falling.

-44-

I've come here again to reunite!

I told myself, Frank, you want it… you want to go to that hotel again, and in winter intentionally; where you and the gang went. So what if no one else wants to go, you go. And so, here I am.

It was some ten years ago when we gathered here. Then, I had no idea why I had decided to go to that reunion. But it happened, and it was good that I went. I say it now though, at the time, I had a feeling of… well, let's do it, why not. Yes, there was a degree of curiosity, but with the condition I was in then, everyone must have thought it was the last time they would see me. I had thought the same, and perhaps that's why I had gone, to see them… as a farewell.

Now, a thin layer of snow has covered the garden; fresh, not like that time when some snow was left with quite a bit of ice. I remember it started snowing when we left. Now, there is no ice, and no more coughs, no sweating! I am ten years older, feeling good.

There is little change in the façade of the hotel, the exterior is the same, the garden looks the same after all these years. The gravel looks the same, the gate, the Cyprus trees… all look the same. But I felt an emptiness as I walked around the grounds. Then I noticed that Bacchus has gone. Its base is left, though. I stand next to the base. This is where Bacchus used to watch hotel guests coming, going around it, some noticing it, talking about it. Now that the statue is gone, there is a feel of loneliness in the garden, the garden is colder. Yes, the Bacchus statue is gone; perhaps thrown into a rubbish dump, undamaged but toppled, perhaps someone has taken it to his own garden. The point is, it is not here anymore.

I think there is a sickness, a sickness in people, the urge for destruction. What was wrong with that statue? I remember when I walked, coughing, with Adam in the cold, talking, passing by Bacchus several times. I did not particularly pay too much attention to it, but it has had its imprint, it was part of the scenery of my past. Now, I miss him! I remember Ana when she was talking about the revolution in Iran, that the Shah's statue was taken down, had gone. I remember her face changing as she talked. There was a mixture of nostalgia, sadness, resignation, and anger. I feel her.

No, there was no call from Colin. We didn't hear from him after we returned last time; surprising after all the interest everyone showed to get together. We were even keen to have a yearly get-together. One of those things, I suppose. I learnt, soon after we returned, that

Roy had committed suicide. He had thrown himself under a high-speed train during the rush hour. I suppose he took his revenge, though I'm not sure on whom. If he wanted to annoy people, he was very successful. I used to get frustrated by his behaviour, but then, after I listened to him that afternoon, my views about him changed. He wasn't that tough, he loved to pretend. He was a victim of his pretence. Showing off, I suppose. He was ready to die for his pretence.

In our monthly get-together, something that the three of us have taken care of like a ritual since we came back from that reunion, I asked Adam and Ana to come with me to have a mini-reunion, but they rejected the idea outright, and I didn't bother either. In fact, it would be odd to go there for a reunion again, while we have been together pretty routinely. It was a whim of the moment I think; perhaps I wanted to remind myself of that gathering, perhaps to celebrate now that I am healthy, and remind myself how lucky I've been. Perhaps these are all true, but something else must've driven me. The fact that I am here, and didn't bother when Ana or Adam didn't take my suggestion on board, suggests that something inside me, something different, has pushed me to come all the way here.

On the train, for some odd reason, I started thinking about her… the woman I met in Iran. I went scene by scene over the moments we were together. I was surprised how much I remembered. I guess remembering Adam when we were walking here…

remembering talking with Adam about her, ignited it all again. Perhaps that's why I am here again; talking with Adam about her then created a space, a presence for her. So, I'm here with a peculiar hope to see her, to have a reunion with her, not with the old gang. I know… I know this is bizarre, it's like a lonely child creating and reading a story for himself, and telling it to himself, only in my case, I don't talk to myself. Perhaps I wanted Ana and Adam here to talk to them about it, to hide my sadness about facing the fact that she wouldn't be here.

I wonder where she could be now. Does she still have her travel agency? Perhaps married again… a case of hiding fantasy under a layer of reality to keep the fantasy alive! Oh, I always told Adam *he* was the romantic one. Why should I avoid being a romantic? Interesting. As I have grown older, I mean old, the boundaries of reality and imagination have become thinner and thinner for me. The moments with the skin that I hadn't touched, the lips… the hair I hadn't caressed for a very long time… I have lived all those moments again, and again, each time differently; and all the time truthful to myself. As I talk, I feel the words are Adam's too. Getting old has somehow fused my emotions with those of Adam, or at least this is what I feel, and I do not care if someone, someone like Roy, says that these are all claptrap. He is dead anyway!

I met Helen by chance a couple of years ago in the street, going to my shop. She was walking with a young girl, talking passionately, when she saw me.

'Hello Frank! Fancy seeing you! You look tip-top.'

'I guess I am. You look very well, too; you must've thought I was dead by now,' I said.

She turned red. This was the first time I had seen her blush in all the years I had known her.

'I'm so happy to see you in good shape, Frank,' she said.

It was so untypical of her mannerism.

'But I have some sad news, I doubt if you have heard about it. Colin is dead,' she said.

'What do you mean, dead? Was there an accident? What happened?'

'Just a year ago. There were some changes, you know all universities went through a tough time. He was dropped; shortly after that he had a heart attack, and that was that.'

'I didn't hear from him after we came back,' I said.

'I know, he meant to arrange another get-together, but I suppose it was his wife,' Helen said. 'Anyway, this is my daughter, would you believe it? I never thought I would be introducing my daughter to one of the gang members from pre-history, time immemorial!'

'You don't look pre-history at all, Helen. In fact, I thought you haven't changed much, and it's what... some ten years or so?' I asked.

'Well, you are very kind, Frank, better say you are very polite! Like the old times, once polite always polite. Listen, I am in sort of a rush. It's so good to see you even like this. I won't say we must meet up, we never do. Anyway, must dash, have fun, don't let it get to you!'

And that was it. She'd gone. As she was walking away, I watched her and her daughter who had grabbed her arm. I thought it so unusual of her not to want to know about me, say something about herself, her daughter even. She didn't ask about Adam, or Ana, or anyone else. And I didn't ask how she heard about Colin's death.

I often wonder what Maria's doing. She was so calm, so unassuming all the time when we had that reunion. I suppose she is one of those people who are irrelevant, no matter if they existed or not. Probably she is a matron by now, although I cannot see her being able to instruct people. She would wear a pair of glasses though. As for a budgie… I really can't say!

I go to the bar and sit at the counter. I wonder if Ralph has left the place, if both Ralph and Bacchus are memories of the past. But then, and unexpectedly, Ralph comes over from the lobby side. He is wearing a stylish beard, and has put on weight. He recognises me.

'Mr. Frank, how nice to see you.'

I know he is genuine. I am happy to see him too.

'How are your friends? You are alone, I gather.'

'Yes Ralph, I am here alone this time, and staying just for the night.'

'But why? Would've been good to see you more… and your friends?' He looks around.

'They couldn't make it this time,' I say.

Oh, what a pity, I would have loved to see them,' Ralph says.

'Perhaps in the future, who knows,' I say, 'but what are you up to these days, Ralph?'

'Well, I am the manager of food and beverages now.'

'Oh, congratulations, should be exciting.'

'It's different. I enjoy it for now, tomorrow? Who knows.'

'Indeed. I shall tell my friends when I see them,' I say. But I don't tell him about Roy or Colin. I ask for a glass of whisky. There is an old song playing in the background. It's Nat King Cole. I drink the whisky slowly. The hotel is quiet.

Coming over, I asked Ana and Adam what they would like me to take them.

'Apart from a good bottle of whisky?' Ana asked.

'That's granted, of course,' I said.

'You don't need to go that far for what I want,' said Adam.

'And what's that?' I asked.

'A stamp showing three friends drinking together,' he said.